The Decision

A Novel

Mastin,
Thanks for your example!

Brad Du—

By

Brad Duncan

Acknowledgements

Thank you to my Mom and Dad, family, friends, Pastors, Sunday-School teachers, and all who shared the gospel of Jesus Christ with me through words and in action. God used a variety of people to draw me to Himself. While I'm still a work in progress, I know Jesus is my Savior and for that I'm eternally grateful.

Foreword

Decisions. Our lives are full of them. Some hold very little consequence. "What should I wear today? What's for breakfast?" Others may determine something as important as your job status. "Should I turn the alarm off and just go back to sleep?" Major decisions, minor decisions and decisions that we make without even realizing it fill our days. Others shape our future. "Should I try out for the team? Where should I attend college? Is she the ONE? Do I really want to move across the country for that job?" All of them in their own way direct our paths.

What we may not realize is how one decision in particular influences every other conclusion that we come to for the rest of our lives. In Matthew chapter 16, Jesus asks Peter, *"Who do you say I am?"* Yours, mine or anyone's answer to that question affects the outcome of each and every decision we are faced with from that point on. Peter answered, *"You are the Christ, the Son of the living God."* No matter how you answer, the decision you come to reaches into every area of your life. Where you go, what you say, why you do anything is all weighed according to your decision to reject or accept Jesus as *"the Christ, the Son of the living God."* If Jesus truly is who the Bible says He is and you believe that, your direction in life will no doubt reflect that decision.

In this book, Brad Duncan gives an eye opening account of one young man's life after being confronted with the Gospel. He powerfully describes the lead character's life in light of this all-important decision. The pages paint a beautiful picture of the impact that a relationship with Christ can have when dealing with the inevitable ups and downs of life. We follow this young man through a lifetime of choices, but perhaps the most intriguing aspect of this story is the realization that one decision reaches far beyond himself. Not only does our resolve to follow or deny Jesus factor into our decision making but as you'll discover in these pages, it also creates a ripple effect into all of our relationships. Every person that you interact with in this life has the potential to be influenced by your answer to Jesus' question. I pray that Brad's gift of writing causes you, as it has me, to consider the impact that our decision to bring Christ into our lives has on those He places among us.

Pastor Nick Calaway, Holland Chapel

Prologue

May 8, 2018

"We make decisions every day, but in the end our decisions make us." Senior pitcher Chase Barkley had no idea why his English teacher's "quote of the day" was running through his mind right now. Maybe it was because his team's biggest game of the year was resting on his next pitch. They were one strike away from beating their rivals and advancing to the state playoffs. Chase was facing the other team's best batter and decided he was throwing a fastball and striking this kid out.

He shook off his best friend Andrew's pitch sign for the second time. With the bases loaded and only a one-run lead, a hit could cost them the game. Realizing the pitch Chase wanted, Andrew reluctantly called for a fastball and set up for the throw.

The capacity crowd was on the edge of their seats. Chase's mom and dad, who were always at his games, waited anxiously in the midst of the frenzied crowd.

Chase dug his spikes into the dirt and adjusted the laces of the ball in his left hand. He went into his wind-up and hurled the baseball as hard as he could throw it. The powerful batter swung with all his might. It sounded like a rifle blast as the ball popped into the catcher's mitt. The umpire roared, "Strike three! You're out!"

The Silver Springs stadium erupted into cheers for the winning team. Chase's dad pumped his fists in the air celebrating. His mom clapped and cheered as tears ran down her face. Chase was dogpiled by his teammates.

The following night Chase and Andrew entered Grace Fellowship Church. Loud music and kids' laughter filled the lobby of the auditorium, which was packed with high school students. Although Chase had only been to church a few times, usually around Christmas, his friends had talked him into coming tonight. A lot of his classmates were excited about a popular band who was playing. The youth minister, Nick Cunningham, walked up, happy to see them. Chase had met him several times at school events and ball games. While he had never accepted any offers to attend the youth group, he liked Nick.

"Congratulations on making state! Great to see both of you guys!"

Chase replied, "Thanks for inviting us."

"You're both seniors, right? Andrew, have you decided what you're doing after graduation in a few weeks?"

"I'm going to play baseball over at Crossland. Chase has his choice of schools. He's hoping to play Division 1 ball."

"I heard you have several offers, Chase. Have you got a favorite?"

"I like the idea of rooming with Andrew at Crossland. They said I could play football there too. My dad really wants me hold out for D-1 and concentrate on pitching."

Nick exclaimed, "Man, you guys have a lot going for you! I hope you enjoy the band tonight. I have to get around here. Have fun. I'll catch up with you later."

As Chase and Andrew got some pizza, they ran into a group of girls they knew from school.

Misty Dobbins exclaimed, "Wow! They're letting anyone in here tonight!"

All the girls giggled.

Andrew shot back, "If they let you in, Misty, then I guess you're right!"

She replied sharply, "I'll have you know I've gone to this church my whole life!"

Chase answered, "Judging from your Instagram page, I'm more than a little surprised."

Misty huffed, "Come on girls. I don't think we need to be hanging around these misfits."

The guys laughed as the girls paraded away. Chase turned to see Heather Hopkins. Time seemed to stand still when she smiled at him. Everything inside of Chase's mind froze. He thought Heather was not only the prettiest girl in their school, but perfect in every imaginable way. There was something much more to her than just her good looks. Chase could sense a beauty that went deep within her soul.

Heather smiled, "Hey guys. It's good to see you."

Andrew replied, "Great to be seen! How you doing, Heather?"

"I'm blessed. I'm so glad you're here tonight. Chase, you pitched a really good game yesterday. I hear we're going to the state playoffs."

"Uh, yeah. Uh ...thanks."

Heather giggled, and Chase felt like an idiot.

Heather put her hand on Chase's arm, "You two have fun tonight. The band is awesome. And Nick always has something great to share. See you later."

As Heather walked away, Andrew said, "Come on, Rainman. Let's grab a seat."

Chase punched his friend as they headed into the auditorium. They saw some of their baseball teammates and sat towards the back with them.

A few minutes later, the background music suddenly went silent as the lights went out. The crowd of kids were engulfed in darkness and began cheering wildly. A spotlight hit the band as they began playing. Having never listened to Christian music, Chase didn't recognize the song, but decided quickly he liked their sound. A few songs later the band transitioned from playing loud upbeat music to a slower, more reverent song. Chase experienced a weird feeling. It was like every nerve in his body was on sensory overload. It felt as if he was sensing something all around him, yet deep within himself as well. He noticed several kids in front of him to begin raising their hands up into the air. After finishing their song and saying a soft-spoken prayer, the band left the stage. A feeling of tranquility filled the room as Nick made his way up to the front.

He announced he was thankful for God showing up. Chase thought, *I wonder if God had something to do with what I was feeling? It sure was weird.* Nick asked if everyone could give him 15 minutes to share something that could change their life. Several students yelled out their approval.

Nick then read a story from the book of John in the Bible about a guy named Nicodemus who was coming to visit Jesus at night. As he told the story, Chase felt something inside him stirring again. He had heard about God before, but this was different. Everything Nick was saying made perfect sense. Nick shared the Bible verse John 3:16: "For God so loved the world that he gave his only begotten Son, that whoever believes in Him shall not perish, but have eternal life." For the first time in his entire life, Chase completely understood that he was a sinner and Jesus was offering him salvation. Nick was explaining how to put his faith in Jesus in an easy-to-understand way. He explained how God points out sin to you. How He makes you aware of it. How He calls you to repent. Nick explained that repenting means to turn from the way you're going, and to follow the way Jesus leads. To stop doing what you want, and to start doing what Jesus wants. He went on to explain that if you confess with your mouth Jesus is Lord, and believe in your heart God raised Him from the dead, you will be saved. That was it!

With authority in his voice Nick shared, "In the Bible, Joshua tells the people of his country, 'Choose this day whom you will serve.' Then Joshua boldly proclaims, 'As for me and my house we will serve the Lord!' Tonight I'm asking each one of you, who will you serve?"

The band began to softly play. Chase heard Nick explain that right now was an exciting time. He said God was inviting anyone who wanted to accept his forgiveness the opportunity to do so in this very moment. If they wanted to come up to pray with him they could, or if they wanted to do it right there where they were standing, that was fine too. All they had to do was repent of their sin, acknowledge Jesus as their Lord and follow Him. Chase felt an overwhelming desire to know more about Jesus. He wanted the forgiveness Nick had described. Even though Nick had said he could pray right where he was standing, Chase knew in his heart if he was really going to make this decision, he needed to go up front.

Chase felt compelled to move toward the front of the church. He knew if he made one motion to move, it would be like sliding down a hill. But would he regret it? Would he be laughed at by his friends?

If he only knew the huge ramifications of this decision, it would be an easy choice. But like all of the students around him, he didn't.

Chase's mind was racing as Nick gave the invitation to come forward. He wanted to move. With his heart pounding and sweat beading up on his brow, he tightly gripped the chair in front of him. A war was raging in his soul! Chase knew now was the time. He had to make the decision.

Chapter 1

May 9, 2018

Chase looked up. No one was moving. Two guys were between him and the aisle that led to the front of the auditorium where Nick was standing. Chase made his decision:

No. He wouldn't go forward right now.

Nobody else was moving and it would be embarrassing. Also, there were graduation parties coming up he didn't want to miss. The way Nick explained it, following Jesus was a complete life-change. Why miss out on all of the fun coming up when he could get saved later? Maybe when he was older and ready to settle down. He didn't act any worse than his friends who went to church anyway- even better than some of them.

Still, this was a strong feeling he couldn't just ignore. He would try to catch Nick after the event and talk to him about what he was experiencing. Although he still had an enormous desire to go up front, putting it off until later seemed easier.

Nick interrupted his train of thought, "I really feel like there are several of you who want to come forward. Don't be embarrassed or intimidated. It's been said that following God starts out hard and ends up easy, but not following God starts out easy and ends up hard. It may seem hard for you to move right now, but I promise, ultimately, you won't ever regret following Jesus. I'm not going to draw this out. Please move now if you want to come forward."

Once again, Chase wanted to go! He wanted to scoot past those two guys and run to the front and tell Nick he wanted to follow Jesus. He wanted this heavy feeling of sin to be gone. But he didn't move. He decided to stick with his plan to talk to Nick after the service. It would be less uncomfortable.

Nick began speaking again. "Thank you for listening so attentively tonight. We're going to have one more song by the band and then be dismissed. Remember, if you would like to talk more about knowing and following Jesus, please talk to me or another adult leader after our service. I love you, and I'm always available if you ever need me."

As the band played its last song, Chase felt the regret of having not gone forward. He promised himself he would talk to Nick as soon as possible. The weight of the decision he had made lifted as the band finished playing and the noise from the crowd of kids began filling the room.

The group of guys Chase was with all began talking about the upcoming state playoffs. He still felt regret about not going forward, but as the guys were laughing and talking, it slowly faded. Nick walked back to their group.

"I'm glad all of you fellas were here tonight."

As Nick continued to talk to the guys, Chase wanted to interrupt and ask him to tell him more about Jesus. But that would be embarrassing in front of his friends. Nick eventually wandered over to another group of students. Chase decided he would wait a few minutes and catch him alone.

Misty walked up, interrupting Chase's thoughts. "What did you think about the band, Chase?"

"They were good. I've never heard them before, but I liked them."

Misty replied, "I thought they were okay. We've had more popular bands here before though. Are you going to the party Saturday night? It's out at David's farm. He's having a bonfire."

"I don't know. State playoffs begin Monday. But it sounds like fun."

"You should go. I think it will be a blast. Gotta run. Talk to ya later, cutie-pie."

Misty walked away and Andrew turned to Chase. "What's Little Miss Priss up to now?"

Chase answered, "I don't know. Something about a bonfire out at David's farm this weekend. She wants to know if we're going."

"What does she care? That girl has issues."

"I don't know, Andrew. She can be okay sometimes. And you have to admit she is pretty."

"I agree she's pretty - Pretty crazy!"

Chase laughed.

Andrew looked at his phone and exclaimed, "Man, we've got to go! I forgot I have to study for that history test tomorrow."

Chase said, "Can we wait just a few more minutes? I want to shout at Nick real quick."

"No dude. It's already late. My mom will kill me if I don't do good on that test."

Chase surveyed the room for Nick as they walked out. He didn't see him anywhere. His spirit fell as they left the church.

◀ ◆ ◆ ◆ ▶

Chase looked up. No one was moving. He thought about the graduation parties coming up. Nick had made it sound like following Jesus would be a complete life change. He wondered if he would miss out on a lot of fun.

Chase had two guys between him and the aisle that led to the front of the auditorium, where Nick was standing. Chase made his decision. He stepped passed the guys beside him and into the aisle. His mind raced as he walked towards Nick at the front of the auditorium. Nick was smiling as Chase reached him.

Nick asked, "What is it you want, Chase?"

Chase blurted out, "I want the forgiveness you said Jesus offers me. I want to know more about Him and what he wants me to do with my life." Chase was surprised to feel tears running down his face.

"Chase, do you understand that everyone has sinned in some way? That we have all messed up?"

"Yes, sir."

Nick continued, "God sent his son Jesus to live a perfect life and die on a cross for our sins. He knew we couldn't be good enough, no matter how hard we try, so Jesus offers to trade our sin for His perfection. Forgiveness is available when we acknowledge what he did for us in our hearts and with our mouths. We can't earn it, but He offers it freely. Is that what you are saying you want tonight?"

"I want Jesus more than anything I have ever wanted in my entire life. I can't explain it exactly, but there's something going on inside of me, and I know it's God wanting me. Does that make any sense?"

Nick smiled, "It makes perfect sense. God wants to take away your sin and replace it with his love. You can only have this salvation by faith in Jesus. You can't earn it. The Bible also teaches that if you receive that forgiveness you will change how you live and begin to follow Jesus. We do this by being obedient to Jesus and His Word. Are you willing to give up your own hopes and desires and follow Jesus, no matter what He calls you to do? It's not an easy journey. Jesus even says the world will hate you for following Him. Don't take this decision lightly, Chase."

Chase answered, "I want Jesus. I don't care what it costs me."

Nick spent some time praying with Chase about his decision to follow Jesus. When they finished praying, Chase hugged Nick. He felt more alive and free than he ever had before.

Chase looked up and was surprised to see students kneeling down, crying, praying, laughing and hugging all around the room. He saw Andrew talking to one of the adult youth workers. Heather was praying with a group of girls. With the love flowing all around the room, Misty stood out in stark contrast. She was staring at Chase with a mean, judgmental look on her face. Chase was too happy to worry about her right now.

As the kids made their way back to their seats, the band played a song of celebration. Nick came back up on stage to dismiss everyone.

"Isn't God good?! I appreciate all of you being here tonight. If anyone needs to talk, please grab me when we're dismissed, or call me anytime."

After a short prayer, the students began talking and moving around. One of Chase's friends told him he was relieved when Chase went forward, because he was too scared to be the first one to move.

Heather came up to Chase, "I'm so glad you and Andrew were here tonight! Wasn't it great?!"

"It was amazing. I never knew anything could be so good. I loved it!"

This was the first time Chase hadn't frozen up around Heather. His mind wasn't focused on her as much as it was on his new relationship with God.

Nick walked up to them, "Awesome night! Thank you for being here."

Chase proclaimed, "I plan on being here from now on!"

Nick laughed, "Great! Heather, thank you for praying with those younger girls. They really look up to you."

"Oh, they're wonderful! It was my pleasure."

Nick asked, "Chase, can I call you tomorrow night and talk to you more about your decision to follow Jesus?"

Heather exclaimed, "You got saved tonight, Chase? How awesome!"

She threw her arms around him giving him a big hug.

While hugging Heather, Chase answered, "Uh, yeah...I did."

His nervousness around Heather wasn't completely gone.

Nick laughed, "Great! We'll talk more tomorrow."

Andrew came bounding up, "Man, we've got to go! I forgot I have to study for that history test tomorrow. My mom will kill me if I do bad on it."

"We better go then. See you later, Heather. Talk to you tomorrow, Nick!"

Chase couldn't remember ever being this happy in his entire life. His spirit was soaring as he left the church.

Chapter 2

May 10, 2018

The buzzing from his cell phone alarm woke Chase from his deep sleep. The night before felt like a dream. A twinge of regret washed over him for not talking to Nick about Jesus. The urgency had subsided this morning though. He reasoned with himself, *"Nobody else went up front, so maybe it's a good thing I didn't. I would be embarrassed at school today. I'll still talk to Nick before too long."*

Chase was eating breakfast and talking to his mom.

"How was the church event last night?"

"It was okay. The band was good. Mom, why don't we go to church?"

"Chase, you know how hard your dad works. And with you playing tournament baseball almost year-round it's just hard to go. I used to go regularly growing up. I do miss it sometimes."

Chase's dad bolted into the kitchen.

"I just checked my e-mail and a coach from Shelton University is flying in to see you at practice today! They're D-1 and very competitive in their league. They made the College World Series twice in the past four years. This could be a great opportunity!"

Chase high-fived his dad, "Shelton University! That's where Devon Hightower played. He's in the starting rotation for the Cardinals."

"That's right! And that could be you, Chase, if you keep working hard."

Chase said, "Who knows, if I keep developing, maybe I can get there. I don't guess they would be interested in me playing football though."

Chase's mom interjected, "Football is too rough anyway."

His dad admonished him, "Chase, your future is in baseball. You're a good quarterback, but you'll need to focus on pitching at the next level. It's a year-round grind if you want to be the best."

"You're probably right, Dad. I enjoy football, but I guess if have a chance to play for a college like Shelton, I need to jump on it."

When Chase got to school everyone was talking about the upcoming state tournament. Excitement for the upcoming game flooded the halls of the high school.

Misty caught up with Chase between classes, "Hey, Mr. Popular! Everyone is talking about how you're going to win us state this year!"

"Baseball is a team game. We'll all have to play great to win."

"Yeah, but you're the star and everybody knows it! Have you decided if you're coming to David's party Saturday night? It's going to be a blast! It's kind of a pep rally for the baseball team, so you have to be there!"

"A pep rally? I think it's more like a beer-bash. David Baker doesn't even play baseball. He's a football defensive lineman. But I'll think about it. Hey, what did you think about the church thing last night? Did you notice anything special?"

Misty scoffed, "I noticed that your friend Andrew was being a jerk as usual. You were too a little bit, but I'll forgive you."

Chase dug a little deeper, "Right, but did you notice anything special about the night as a whole. Like did you feel anything...different?"

Misty answered, "No. But I've gone to church my whole life and you hardly ever go, so it was probably weird for you."

Chase said, "I don't know. I guess so. I'll see you later."

Misty smiled, "See you soon, Mr. Superstar!"

Chase was heading to the fieldhouse for baseball practice when he saw Heather. Her beauty, once again, intimidated him.

"Uh, hey, Heather. How's it going?"

"It's going good, Chase. Are you headed to practice?"

"Yeah. We, uh, have to get ready for state."

"I know! How exciting! Hey Chase, I don't know if you're interested, but we're having some pizza and hanging out at the church gym Saturday night if you want to come by."

"That sounds like fun. I'll try to make it."

Heather smiled, "Great! I hope to see you there. Have fun at practice!"

A few minutes later, Chase nodded at his dad in the bleachers as he walked onto the field. Later, during practice, he noticed a man arrive wearing Shelton University gear. Sitting down behind home plate, he pulled out a radar gun from one of his bags.

Chase had been playing first base, but when the scout arrived, Coach Sanders moved him to pitcher. Chase knew this was his opportunity. He stepped up to the mound and focused on Andrew's glove. Chase had never felt better. He was in the zone and pitching fantastic.

After practice, Coach Sanders asked Chase to step into his office. Chase's dad and the coach from Shelton were already in there talking.

Coach Sanders introduced them, "Ricardo Garcia, this is Chase Barkley. Chase, Coach Garcia is the recruiting coordinator and pitching coach for Shelton University."

"Chase, it's very nice to meet you. Please call me Coach Ric like the rest of my players do."

"Thanks for coming to see me pitch, Coach Ric."

"I'm very happy I came to Silver Springs to see you in person, Chase. I've watched the scouting videos your dad sent us, but your poise on the mound is much more impressive in person."

"Thank you!"

"Chase, I understand you haven't signed with any school yet?"

"No sir. My dad wanted me to wait and see if I get any D-1 offers."

"Well your Dad is a very smart man. Chase, one of our pitching recruits is not going to qualify academically and is going to accept wherever he is chosen in the MLB draft next month. I can't blame him. He will receive a lucrative offer, and we want our athletes to make it to the majors if that is their dream. But, that leaves us with one partial scholarship. Along with your academic scholarships you would have a full ride to Shelton. We always prepare for this situation, because our recruits are top-notch. We have had our eye on you and another young man. He's a lefty as well. I'll be honest with you, Chase, he's good. But I believe you might have more potential.

'You wouldn't start right away. You would be considered a project and hopefully work your way into the starting rotation in a year or two. But if you work hard, we will develop you into the best pitcher you can be. We're going to be watching both of you perform in your state tournaments. Don't be surprised if you receive an offer from us next week. If that happens, I hope you will consider Shelton University."

Chase's dad exclaimed, "Of course he'll accept your offer! His mom and I love the thought of him playing for you."

"We like everything we've seen so far from Chase. Good grades, solid pitching and no off-the-field issues. I know it's late in the process, but hopefully we can extend an offer soon! Thank you gentlemen for your time."

Chase, his dad and Coach Sanders stayed a long time afterward excitedly talking about the visit and his future.

The thought of contacting Nick completely slipped from Chase's mind.

◀ ◆ ◆ ◆ ▶

The next morning, Chase woke up with the previous night feeling like a dream. His spirit was filled with overwhelming joy and excitement about the decision he had made at church. He thought to himself, *"Now that I'm a Christian, I need to figure out what I need to do. I'm glad Nick is going to help me."*

Chase said a quick prayer, thanking God for saving him and asking for wisdom. The first thing he felt like he needed to do was to tell his parents. His mom was in the kitchen.

"Good morning, Chase!"

"Good morning, Mom. I have something to tell you. I don't really know how to say this, but I want you to know I got saved last night."

"That's great, Chase! It must have been a really good event."

"It was mom, but that's not what I'm saying. It was more than just good event. Jesus saved me. I'm different now."

"I think that's wonderful, Chase."

24

His dad sprang into the kitchen, "I just checked my e-mail and a coach from Shelton University is flying in to see you today! They're D-1 and very competitive in their league. You probably remember that they made the College World Series twice in the past four years. This could be a great opportunity!"

Chase high-fived his dad!

"Shelton University. That's where Devon Hightower played! He starts for the Cards! How cool!"

"That's right, Chase! That could be you."

His mom said, "I'm so proud of you Chase!"

Chase looked at his dad, "Dad, I have some more good news for you. Last night I got saved. Jesus is the Lord of my life now!"

"Well that's great son. Religion is a very important part of your life. I'm proud of you. Shelton University, Chase! This could be life changing."

Chase knew his dad didn't understand. He didn't know how to make him, so he moved on.

"Are you going to be there this afternoon, Dad?"

"Wouldn't miss it for the world!"

When Chase got to school, many of the students who had been at the church service were talking about it. It stirred his spirit to talk to his friends about Jesus. Other students were excitedly talking about the upcoming state baseball tournament.

Misty caught up with him between classes, "Hey, Mr. Christian. You really started a revolution at church last night. Do you think God will help you win state now?"

"What? Last night has nothing to do with state. I think God has more important things to worry about than baseball games."

Misty laughed, "Don't be so sensitive. I know that silly. But you're a superstar! Are you going to David's bonfire out at his parent's farm Saturday night? It's kind of a pep rally for the baseball team, so you need to be there!"

"Pep rally? It's more like a beer-bash. David just wants an excuse to smoke some dope. I don't think it's what Jesus would want me to do."

Misty huffed, "Now you're going to get all judgmental. Trust me, I've gone to church my whole life, and Jesus doesn't care if you go have some fun with your friends."

"Misty, I don't care if you go. And I'm not judging anyone. But I'm not going. I have to get to class. See you later."

Chase went to class frustrated about how some people didn't understand his new faith. His mom and dad didn't. Misty didn't either. He was glad Andrew was there and got saved too. He wondered if there was a better way he could explain it.

Heading to the field house, he saw Heather. It was weird how he didn't feel as nervous around her, even though she was still the most beautiful girl he had ever met. He figured it had something to do with the fact they had their faith in common, and he wasn't only concerned with wanting to date her.

"Hey, Chase!"

"Hey. It's good to see you."

"How are you feeling today? Any regrets about last night?"

"Not at all! I'm so excited about following Jesus. But I think I'm doing a bad job of explaining it. A lot of people don't understand what I'm saying."

"That's okay, Chase. You don't have to know everything right away. I talked to Nick and Saturday night we're going to have some pizza and talk about the basics of our Christian faith. He's going to invite everyone who got saved last night. I hope you can be there."

"That sounds great! Count me in. I bet Andrew will want to come too. I'm supposed to talk to Nick tonight, so I'll let him know I'm coming. I better get to practice."

"I've got to get to choir practice, too. See you later, Chase!"

Chase got to baseball practice and waved to his dad, who was about halfway up the bleachers, as he ran out onto the field. Later on during practice, he noticed the Shelton University coach arrive. Chase's coach told him to warm up to pitch. He felt fantastic and his pitching showed it.

After practice, he met the Shelton pitching recruiter. Coach Ric explained they would be watching Chase pitch next week, and would possibly be making him an offer. Chase's dad was ecstatic. Chase was happy, but was ready to talk to Nick. Everything, including his college decision, seemed secondary to understanding more about Jesus.

After Coach Ric left, Chase talked with his dad and coach for a few more minutes, but excused himself to get home.

He ran into the house, "Hey Mom. I'll grab something to eat in a little while."

"How did your practice go?"

"It went great! They might offer me. We'll see."

Chase went to his room and dialed Nick's number.

Nick answered, "Hello?"

"Hey, Nick. It's Chase Barkley."

"Hey, Chase! Great to hear from you. Did you have a good day?"

"Yeah, it was great! Several of the kids from last night were talking about the service and how God was there. Heather told me there's something going on Saturday night."

"Yes. We're going to meet in the gym and go over some of the basics of the Christian faith. Are you interested in coming?"

"Definitely! I'll tell Andrew too. I'm not really sure about a lot of things. I don't think I'm doing a good job of explaining what happened last night."

"Chase, that's totally normal. It will take some time and effort to understand your faith, but God will teach you. Just relax and enjoy God. We'll talk more soon."

"That sounds great, Nick. Thank you for taking the time to talk. Oh, guess what? I met with the recruiter from Shelton University and they might make me an offer to play baseball. Isn't that cool?"

"I'd say so! Wait, so you're telling me you got to meet with a coach from Shelton University, and you start off talking to me about your relationship with Jesus? Chase, I think you're way ahead of where you think you are with this whole Christianity thing!"

"Thanks, Nick! I really feel like a new person! See you Saturday!"

Chapter 3

May 12, 2018

Saturday morning, Chase laid in bed thinking about the past week. He had pitched his team into the high school state playoffs, was praised by a great college pitching coach and became the most popular guy on campus. His phone buzzed interrupting his thoughts.

"Hello?"

"Hey, this is Nick from Grace Fellowship Church. Is this Chase?"

"Yes, sir. It is. How are you?"

"I'm doing great! I was really glad to see you Wednesday night. Did you have fun?"

"Yeah, I had a good time. I thought the band was good and everything you said made a lot of sense. I kinda wanted to talk to you after it, but there was a lot going on."

"Chase, anytime you want to talk, I'll be happy to. What did you want to talk to me about?"

Chase paused. He wasn't sure if he wanted to discuss the questions he had about his faith right now. It felt awkward.

"Just about some things you said, I guess."

"Actually we're having a youth get-together tonight at the church if you want to come by. We can talk there. If you're busy tonight, we can meet whenever you want. Just let me know when a good time is for you!"

Chase thought about Heather's invitation. "I think I'll try to come tonight. It sounds like fun."

"Okay! Great! See you tonight then."

Chase hung up, hopeful that tonight he could finally talk to Nick about all these things he was feeling.

That afternoon, Andrew stopped by Chase's house. "Hey, dude! We are totally going out to David's bonfire tonight! It's going to be epic!"

"I heard there are going to be a lot of people out there. But I kind of agreed to go to this church event over at Grace."

"Chase, we did the church thing Wednesday night. It was fine, but this is going to be an incredible party! They're celebrating our baseball team. And there will be lots of girls hoping to see the star of our team!"

"Andrew, without your bat we wouldn't have made it to state."

"I know that! I was talking about me being the star. Not you!

Chase laughed. Andrew was a great friend. They had been best friends since they met in kindergarten when Chase helped Andrew learn to tie his shoes.

Chase gave in, "Okay, okay. I'll go to the bonfire. But you're driving. Let's grab some Taco Bell before we go."

"Great! I'll pick you up at 6:30."

Later that evening, Andrew had the music blaring as they drove the three miles out of town to David's parents' farm. Chase's mind was wandering. He thought about Heather. A big part of him wished he was on his way to the church event right now to see her. He also would like to talk to Nick about what he had felt Wednesday night. For some reason, he couldn't get that weird feeling out of his mind.

The other part of Chase reasoned that he wasn't as bad as some of his friends, even some who went to church. He could have his fun now and deal with the spiritual stuff later when he got a little older.

Normally Chase was a man of his word. He felt guilty for committing to go to the church event tonight and then not going. He promised himself he would go to church in the morning to make up for it. And even talk to Nick about his faith.

As Andrew topped a hill on the dirt road, Chase was snapped back into the moment by a gigantic towering inferno lighting up the night sky.

"I've never seen a fire that big, Andrew!"

"That is one humongous blaze! This is going to be a night we'll never forget."

Andrew slowly pulled off the dirt road onto a dirt road leading toward the bonfire. There were several trucks and cars parked all around the open field. Kids were sitting on the tailgates of pick-ups, standing around the fire and wandering around from group to group, laughing and having a good time.

Andrew parked and the guys walked up to the gathering.

Kids kept pulling up and joining in the festivities. Beer and alcohol were flowing freely. One truck had a couple of beer kegs in the back. Chase noticed a group of kids gathered in a circle, smoking weed.

The guys talked to some of their friends as they walked up to the gathering. Chase took a beer that was offered and sipped on it while they talked and laughed. At one point, someone snuck up to the fire and threw some firecrackers into it. Everyone jumped in surprise, and then laughed and cussed at him when they realized what had happened.

Around 10:30 p.m., David moved to a spot in front of the fire. He called the baseball players up to the front of the group. The crowd gathered around to hear what he was saying.

He announced, "Listen up! We're here tonight to celebrate winning the district title!"

The crowd roared its youthful drunken praise.

"These guys are going to win us a state title next week! Then we'll have another party to celebrate our state championship! All of our players are great. I think we need to hear from the team captain, Chase Barkley!"

The crowd cheered.

Chase smiled, but shook his head no.

The rowdy crowd began to chant, "Chase! Chase! Chase!"

He reluctantly stepped forward, a little wobbly from the booze he had been drinking. He smiled and held up his hand for silence.

He proclaimed, "These are the best guys I've ever played with. I have no doubt we will bring home the state championship! We won't be denied!"

The crowd cheered once again. David waved his hand in the air and several girls brought out red Solo cups filled with large shots of alcohol for each player.

David raised his cup and through slurred speech said, "I want to make a toast! We've practiced hard to get here. We deserve to win it all. Not even God and his angels, or Satan and his demons could defeat our team! Silver Springs destiny is that of champions!"

The crowd cheered as the players drank. The bitter drink burned Chase's throat like nothing he had ever tasted. He thought he would throw up. A couple of the guys did, unable to keep the stout liquor down.

Around midnight, Misty came up to Chase, who was now completely wasted, with a fresh drink.

"You look handsome, Mr. Superstar. Great speech."

Chase smiled back at her, thinking about how incredibly sexy Misty looked with the fire blazing behind her. He took another drink as she collapsed beside him, leaving her hand on his knee. He looked lustfully into her dark eyes. She leaned in and they threw themselves together, sharing a hard, drunken, animalistic kiss. Chase wasn't sure what he was doing, but in that moment he didn't care.

In his drunken state, it took some time for the screaming around him to register. He tore himself away from Misty and saw flashing blue lights surrounding the field. A man's voice filled the cool night air over a loudspeaker. "Stay where you are. You are under arrest!"

Pandemonium set in as kids frantically ran in all directions. Police stormed the field, throwing fleeing kids to the ground and handcuffing them. Chase sprang to his feet disoriented from the alcohol. Andrew was running toward him when a policeman tackled him. Chase rushed over and threw the cop off of Andrew. Someone forcefully grabbed Chase's right arm. Instinctively he spun and swung his powerful left fist toward his attacker. His punch connected with the young man's face, crushing the officer's nose. Another policeman tackled Chase. He felt something strike his head, and everything went black.

◄ ♦ ♦ ♦ ►

Saturday morning Chase laid in bed thinking about the past week. He pitched his team into the high school state playoffs, was praised by a great college pitching coach and became a follower of Jesus. Everything felt secondary to his relationship with Jesus.

His phone buzzed. "Hello?"

"Hi Chase! This is Misty. I didn't wake you up, did I?"

"No. I'm awake. What's up?"

"I was just wondering if you're coming out to David's party tonight. It's going to be a lot of fun. It's supposed to be a celebration for the baseball team, but some of the guys are going to a church event."

"Yeah. I called several guys last night and invited them. Nick is supposed to be putting something together tonight to help us understand our faith better."

"Chase, couldn't you tell the guys to come out to David's and just go to church on Sunday like you're supposed to?"

"Misty, I'm actually very excited about going to the youth event tonight. I hope you have fun at the party."

"Oh, I will! Too bad you're going to miss a great time. You'll regret not being at the bonfire tonight. Bye!"

Chase looked down at his phone and laughed, "Andrew might be right about that girl being trouble."

Later that afternoon, Andrew stopped by Chase's house.

"Chase, what are we doing tonight? Several guys are headed out to David's farm. Are we still going to the church thing?"

"Yeah man. You know what David's parties are like. If we're going to follow the commitment we made, we can't be doing all that nonsense."

"I guess you're right. It does sound like fun though."

"Well, Misty called me this morning wanting a date for the party. If you want, I can set you two up."

"What time should I pick you up for church?"

Both guys laughed. They agreed to ride together.

At 6:30, Chase hopped into Andrew's car to ride the three miles to church.

"What are you listening to, Andrew?"

"It's some band called Crowder. I like it! I had to listen to it a few times, but it grows on you quickly!"

Chase listened for a minute. "It actually sounds pretty good. But he's singing about God. I guess this is a Christian band? I've never heard you listen to Christian music."

"Well Chase, I've never been a Christian before. I figure if we're going to do this, we might as well be all in! I downloaded another dude named Toby Mac. He's a little more hip-hop."

The guys listened to their new Christian music on the ride through Silver Springs to church.

As they pulled into the church parking lot, they were surprised by how many cars and students were there. They were excited to see some of their teammates had made it.

Grace Fellowship Church had a gym with a game room on one end. It was filled with several pool tables, foosball games, ping-pong tables and a snack bar. Andrew jumped in a game of foosball with some other guys. Chase was watching them play when the center from his football team, Matt Tyler, came up to him.

"Hey Chase!"

"What's up, Matt. Good to see you."

"I wasn't sure about coming tonight. Thanks for calling me and telling me you were going to be here."

"No problem. I think it's going to be fun. This is a cool place, isn't it?"

"Yeah man. Hey, can I tell you something?"

"Of course, Matt. What's up?"

"You know last Wednesday night? Well, I really wanted to go down front during the service, but I was scared. Now you know me. I'm not scared of much, but my heart was pounding and I had decided I was just going to ignore it and just stay put. But when I saw you walk up front, I knew I could do it. I just wanted you to know."

"Matt, that's awesome! Thanks for telling me. It means a lot. I was scared too. But I'm so glad I met Jesus. Hopefully we'll learn more tonight, because I've tried to read some of my Bible, and it was confusing."

They both laughed.

The pizza was delivered and everyone lined up to eat. Chase and Andrew were sitting with some friends when Heather arrived with Tonya, a friend of hers.

They laughed and ate together until it was time to gather in the youth room. This area was off to the side of the basketball court. There was a stage at one end. About fifty people were in there, filling up about half the room.

A college-aged guy and Heather sat on stools up on the stage. He began to play his guitar. Chase thought Heather sounded like an angel. He enjoyed the music and began to feel that weird feeling inside him once again. He decided it had to be something to do with God. After a few songs, Nick stepped up onto the stage.

"It's fantastic to see everyone here tonight! I'm so excited about what God is doing in your lives. We had already planned a game night for tonight, but with so many of you asking me for a chance to discuss your faith, I felt like we needed to use this time for that instead. I know some of you are totally new to the church, so I want to break all of this down in really easy-to-understand terms. Everyone good with that?"

The kids yelled out their approval.

Nick continued, "I love talking to you about what's going on at school and how your teams are doing, but I get super excited to get to talk about Jesus with you!

"I'm going to use a very simple example to describe our relationship with God. It's sometimes called the Colors of Salvation. I'm going to use these six colors to explain how our existence with God should proceed. The colors are black, red, white, blue, green and gold.

"The color black represents our sin. This isn't talking about the color of our skin. It's talking about the color of our spirit. Jesus loves people of every skin color. The Bible teaches that every person, no matter their skin color, is separated from God because of something called sin. Basically, sin is doing or not doing something God wants us to do. But even before that, because of Adam and Eve sinning way, way, way back in the day, we are all born with a sinful nature. Romans 3:23 says, 'For all have sinned and fall short of the glory of God.'

"So we're all sinful. All separated from God. Because God is perfect, he requires us to be perfect to be with Him. Romans 6:23 says this about people's sinful condition: 'For the wages of sin is death, but the gift of God is eternal life through Jesus Christ our Lord.'

"God knows we have sinned and can't be perfect. So what does He do? He makes a way for us to be with Him. Romans 5:8 says, 'While we were still sinners, Christ died for us.'

"The color red represents the blood of Jesus. By shedding His sinless blood, he allows those who believe in Him to be saved. Even when we were his enemy and didn't want anything to do with Him, Jesus loved us and gave up His life for us.

"Let's review what we have talked about so far. Number one: The color black represents the sin that has separated all people from God. Number two: Red represents Jesus' blood shed on the cross to allow us to be saved. God loves us so much He sent His only son Jesus to die for us. Jesus took all of our sins on the cross and died in our place.

"If you are tracking with me so far, say 'got it!'"

The crowd shouted, "Got it!"

Nick continued, "The color white symbolizes being clean from sin. The Bible says in the Book of Psalms God can take our sin-filled dirty soul and make us whiter than snow. Okay, this next verse should sound familiar, because a lot of you recently did this. Romans 10:9 says that, 'if you confess with your mouth Jesus as Lord, and believe in your heart that God raised Him from the dead, you will be saved.' How many of you in here have confessed Jesus with your mouth and believed God raised Him from the dead for the very first time in the past week?"

One by one, hands went up around the room until there were seventeen hands raised.

Nick began clapping and shouted, "Praise the Lord! This is amazing. Don't miss this: each of you has moved from death to life. From a future without hope to a relationship with the King of kings and Lord of lords!"

The crowd continued to celebrate for a few more minutes. They finally settled down and Nick continued.

"The next color is blue. The first thing God tells us to do once we're saved is to be baptized. Blue represents the water. I'll be meeting with you individually to discuss getting baptized soon.

"This is just the very beginning of your relationship with Jesus. There's a lot more to learn, and you will discover that you actually want to spend more and more time with Him. You'll find yourself excited to search the scriptures and talk to Him through prayer."

"The color green represents growing in godliness. Wanting to be more like Jesus.

"It's like when I first met my wife, Robin. I talked to her as much as I could, because I was attracted to her. I didn't read the notes she wrote me because I felt like I had too. I was excited to read them. God's love letter to you is the Bible. As you read the Bible you'll get to know Jesus better and become more like Him.

"Finally, gold is the color we use to represent heaven, although heaven will be much better than any earthly gold. It will be a place with no sorrow, pain, sickness or death. Sounds pretty good, doesn't it?"

The kids nodded in agreement.

"We're going to begin meeting on Sunday nights to cover the things we've talked about in more detail. Now we're going to break up into some small groups. I've asked some of our leaders to meet with you and answer any questions you might have about what I've shared tonight.

"As a believer in Jesus, we are called to know, grow and show the truth. We're all going to learn how to do those things better! Let's pray and then break up into small groups."

Chase's mind, body and soul felt more alive than ever. He desired even more of Jesus. Deep down he knew the course of his life was changing.

Chapter 4

May 13, 2018

Chase awoke with a pounding headache. Raising his left hand up to rub his head, he felt something heavy on it. He opened his eyes and saw a cast covering his left hand and forearm. Switching to his right hand, it moved only a few inches before catching in place. Looking down he saw a shiny silver handcuff wrapped around his wrist. The other end was locked to his bed rail. Chase had no idea where he was.

Confused he looked around the room. His vision wasn't clear yet, and he couldn't reach his eyes to wipe the sleep from them. He heard some monitors beeping and could make out some squiggly lines running across them.

Chase rested his head back and closed his eyes again. A man's voice startled him. "Finally decide to wake-up? You caused quite a stir last night."

Everything was a blur. It was hard to think with his throbbing headache. He remembered being at the bonfire and everyone partying. The last thing he could recall was giving some sort of speech about winning state.

"Can I get something for this headache? Why do I have on handcuffs? Who are you?"

A man in a police uniform leaned over Chase. He had a bandage across his nose. His voice became stern, "Hi, Chase. Before we talk, let's get this out of the way. Chase Barkley, you are under arrest. You have the right to remain silent. Anything you say can and will be used against you in a court of law. You have the right to an attorney. If you cannot afford an attorney, one will be provided for you. Chase, do you understand your rights?"

What was happening? Arrested? My rights?

"Chase, do you understand your rights?"

"Yes sir."

"Now, what was it you were asking?"

Chase didn't know what to do. Why was he under arrest? Something about the party. It was slowly coming back to him. Blue lights. The party got busted. Kissing Misty. Had he really kissed Misty? Andrew was attacked. He had tried to protect him. Was Andrew okay? It still wasn't clear, but it was slowly coming back to him.

"CHASE!"

The sudden outburst hammered Chase's already pounding head. It was painful. He couldn't clearly remember anything about last night.

"Why am I handcuffed? Can you please take these things off?"

"Chase, you are handcuffed because you decided to resist arrest and attacked me. My name is Officer Harrison Majors. You broke my nose last night. I assure you, Chase, I will do everything in my power to make sure you are punished as severely as possible. To answer your second question, no, I will not be removing your handcuffs, or doing anything else to relieve your pain in any way whatsoever."

Attacking a police officer? How could he have been so stupid? Along with the several beers he had drank, the shot David had given him made him oblivious to his actions.

"I'm sorry I hurt you. I honestly didn't know what I was doing."

"Here's what's going to happen, Chase. The minute your doctor releases you, we will be moving you to the Silver Springs city jail. I will do everything in my power to make sure you serve as much hard time as possible. I don't care if you say you don't remember hitting me. You chose to be at that party, and you chose to get wasted. My main concern now is seeing you prosecuted to the fullest extent of the law."

The hospital room's door swung open and a lady's voice asked sternly,

"Why are you speaking to my client without my consent?"

"Oh, we're just taking care of some business. I'm making sure he understands his Miranda rights. Do you understand what I'm saying, Chase?"

Chase answered despondently, "Yeah."

His attorney said, "Thank you. I would like to speak with my client now. Alone."

The officer left the room and the attorney introduced herself.

"I'm Gabriella Cortez. I've been appointed to handle your case. Chase, can you tell me what happened last night?"

Chase was glad to have someone here who seemed to care about him, someone who was on his side.

"I'll tell you what I can remember. I went out to this party with my best friend Andrew. It was at David Baker's parents' farm. He played football with us. It was kind of crazy. I had a couple of beers, but then David made a big production of giving all of the baseball team a shot. I'm not sure what was in it, but it burned all the way down and the rest of the night is a blur. I do remember trying to protect Andrew from someone. I guess it was that cop, I had no idea. How much trouble am I in, Ms. Cortez?"

"It's pretty bad, Chase. You're charged with underage drinking, public intoxication, resisting arrest, assaulting an officer in the line of duty and inciting a riot. They're also testing your blood for drugs. Do you use illegal or prescription drugs, Chase?"

"Drugs? No! Not at all. I hardly even drink. It was a party."

"So they shouldn't find any drugs in your system, that's good. I'm sure they will move you to jail as soon as your doctor releases you. It will probably be tomorrow. Chase, they're going to give you a hard time, because you hurt an officer. Don't take the bait and fight them. It will only be worse on you in court."

"I can't believe this is happening to me. It's like a bad dream. Can you get me anything for this headache?"

"I'll make sure your nurse gets you something. I'll see you in court for your bail hearing. Hopefully we can get you out of jail soon. Your parents are in the waiting room. Would you like to see them?"

Chase hadn't thought about the disappointment his parents were going to have to endure. He wanted to see them so bad right now, but dreaded it all at the same time.

"Yes. Send them in, please."

A few minutes later, his parents came into the room. His mom rushed over and leaned down to hug him. He could only raise up a little and kiss her on the cheek. He hated being handcuffed in front of her.

She exclaimed, "Oh, Chase. What in the world happened? Are you okay?"

"Yes, Ma'am. I don't really know what happened. It's all a blur."

"Chase, you know better than to be out drinking. And hitting that poor policeman."

"I know, Mom. I didn't intend for any of that to happen. I thought he was beating up Andrew. It was a mistake."

Chase's dad yelled, "A MISTAKE? Yeah, I'd say it's a mistake! A HUGE one, Chase!"

"Honey, lower your voice. We're in a hospital."

"I don't care where we are! Chase, do you realize you've probably blown your chance to play D-1 ball? You'll be lucky if any of the lower division schools want you now. All of our hard work, and you have just thrown it all away!"

A nurse opened the door. "Sir, I'm going to have to ask you to lower your voice."

"No problem. I'm leaving."

As he stormed past the nurse, his mom began crying.

"Mom, I'm sorry. Please don't cry."

Through her tears she said, "Chase, don't worry about me. You be strong and do what Gabriella tells you to do. We'll get past all this and figure out what to do next. I love you."

"I love you too, Mom."

His mom leaned down and kissed her son. Then she turned and rushed out of the room.

Chase's head was still pounding, but he didn't care about it anymore.

◄ ♦ ♦ ♦ ►

Chase woke up before his alarm went off. He normally slept in on Sunday mornings, but he was excited to go to church today. He had never been to Sunday school. The excitement from the night before was still fresh on his mind. Nick's explanation about Jesus taking the punishment we deserve overwhelmed Chase once again this morning. How much God must love us to offer to take our sin and give us life in its place, Chase smiled. After he cleaned up and ate breakfast, he stuck his head in his parents' room, "I'm headed to church. See you for lunch."

His mom sleepily mumbled to her husband, "He's really into this church thing."

His dad replied, "I guess there are worse places he could be, but I can't think of any. Sitting through a judgmental sermon is about as bad as it gets."

Heather and her friend Tonya were talking to Andrew in front of the church when Chase arrived. Sunday school went well. They had a lesson, taught by a sweet lady named Mrs. Lowe, about Deborah from a book in the Bible called Judges. It was action-packed and surprisingly exciting. Chase had never heard anything about this story. He had always assumed the Bible was just a boring old book with stuff in it that really didn't matter anymore. He was finding out he was wrong.

After Sunday school they moved over to the sanctuary, where the youth event had taken place the previous Wednesday night. Chase felt his spirit soar when he thought back to that night. His life had changed here. Looking at the very place where he and so many of his friends had acknowledged Jesus as their savior made him happy.

The pastor, Tad Allen, came onto the stage and welcomed everyone. He said some funny things that made everyone laugh and then he prayed. Chase thought Pastor Tad was really good at praying. He wondered if he would ever be able to pray out loud in front of people someday. He definitely wasn't ready for that yet. Another guy came up with a guitar and began playing. The worship music was wonderful. Chase and Andrew looked at each other and smiled when they played a song by Crowder they had been listening to the day before.

A video about how they could help a child in another country through something called Compassion International began playing. Chase had never heard of it, but it looked like it helped a lot of kids around the world. It really didn't cost a lot of money each month to help. He made a mental note to talk to Nick about the Compassion kids when he got a chance. They passed around a bucket while the video played and people were putting money into it. Chase had heard his dad complain about how churches were only focused on money, but everyone here seemed pretty happy to give. Chase didn't get the feeling this church was only about taking people's money.

Pastor Tad stood up to preach. Chase really enjoyed the message. The scripture he used was from the same Bible story they had read in Sunday school. Chase figured this was planned. Although it was the same story, Pastor Tad emphasized different points from the story. It was amazing to Chase how much Mrs. Lowe and Pastor Tad could get from this short story in the Bible. He wondered how much more he could learn about God if he was ever able to read the whole Bible.

After church, Chase, Andrew, Heather and Tonya gathered outside in front of the building. People were moving all around them, leaving church while they talked.

Heather asked, "Well, what did you guys think about your first Sunday at church as believers?"

Andrew answered, "It was great! I really had a good time."

Chase added, "I'm surprised at how much I learned. But I've got a long way to go."

Tonya said, "It takes time. I'm really proud of you guys. It's not easy to just start going to church. Especially when your parents don't make you!"

Andrew asked, "So what's it like being homeschooled, Tonya? I'm not sure me or my parents could handle it."

Tonya replied, "It's not for everyone. It works for our family, but it's nice to come to church and see people who don't have the same last name as me!"

The group all laughed. After talking for a few more minutes and saying their goodbyes, Chase headed home.

He was driving through his neighborhood, thinking about the incredible morning he had at church, when the car behind him made its blue lights flash. Surprised by the sudden light show and siren, Chase pulled over to the side of the road.

He got out his license and registration, and rolled down his window. The officer walked up to the driver's side of his car. "Can I see your driver's license, please?"

"Yes, officer. Was I speeding?"

He took Chase's license and replied, "No, Mr. Barkley, you rolled through the stop sign back there."

"I'm sorry. I guess I was just thinking about this morning and not paying attention."

"Interesting morning?"

"Yes, sir. It's the first time I've gone to church. The first time as a believer, I mean."

"Chase Barkley. Are you the young man who pitches for the Silver Springs high school team?"

"Yes sir."

"Well it's a good thing you weren't out at the party we busted last night. Unfortunately, I arrested some of your teammates. I guess you've heard all about it."

"No sir. I haven't checked my phone all day. What happened?"

"Step out of your vehicle, please."

Chase got out of his truck. The policeman shook Chase's hand and said, "I'm Officer Harrison Majors."

"I'm Chase. Nice to meet you. So there was trouble with some guys on my team?"

"Yeah they had a big party out at the Baker farm. Lots of underage drinking and some drugs. Hate to see them making such bad decisions at such a young age. And right here before the state playoffs begin."

"Oh man! I can't believe this."

"The only real trouble we had was with David Baker. He was higher than a kite and tried to flee. We tracked him down in the woods and he put up a fight. He'll probably get some jail time. The rest of the group will most likely get probation.

"I played for Coach Sanders five years ago. Those players won't get to play in state this week."

"Yeah, Coach is going to be mad."

"We won region in football my senior year. I still wear my ring!" Harrison held out his right hand.

"Man! That's a nice ring. I heard the football team was really good that season. As you know, Coach Sanders teaches his current players about the players and teams in various sports who played before them."

"Yep. He's famous for that!"

"I hope we can win a state title in baseball. We came up short in football, even though it was a pretty good season."

"I was at that game. You got some pretty rotten calls against you that night."

"I thought so, but no one remembers the bad calls. Only who wins. This week I have to overcome anything in our way."

"Tell you what, Chase. I'll just give you a warning and you can be on your way. Be sure to come to a complete stop from now on."

"Thank you, Officer Majors."

"No problem, kid. You can call me Harrison. Good luck in state this week. I think you'll need it."

"Thanks! Hey, can I ask you something before you go?"

"Sure."

"Do you go to church anywhere?"

"Not regularly."

"Well if you ever have a chance you should check out Grace Fellowship. I just started going there, and I love it!"

"Thanks for the offer. Maybe I'll take you up on that sometime. Be careful out there. You seem like a good kid, and this world can be tough."

Chase smiled and answered, "Yes sir!"

Chapter 5

May 14, 2018

On Monday, morning Chase woke up still very sore. After struggling to eat breakfast with only his right hand, his doctor came by.

"Hello, Chase. How are you feeling this morning?"

"Better, but I still have a slight headache."

"That's normal with a concussion. It may hang around a few days, but should eventually clear up. Your hand will take longer. The X-rays showed a boxer's fracture. Officially, it's a break in the head of your fifth metacarpal, the knuckle on your pinky finger. It will heal up in a few weeks."

"Will I be able to pitch again?"

"You should be able to, but I don't think you're going to be pitching anytime soon, Chase."

"I know. I guess I'm just hoping someday, when all this is behind me, I might be able to play ball again."

"I'm going to sign your release, and from what I understand, they'll be moving you to the jailhouse right away. You'll be seeing their doctors from now on. Normally, since you're only seventeen, I would explain all of this to you with your parents here, but I understand they are limiting your visitations. I'll call your parents and inform them of everything we've talked about. Good luck, Chase."

"Thank you."

A few minutes later a nurse and policeman entered the hospital room. The nurse unhooked all of Chase's monitors and IVs. After she left the room the police officer unlocked his handcuffs, and told him to get dressed. The guard escorted him to the front of the hospital. As he swung the tinted hospital door open, he said, "Smile for the cameras."

The sudden burst of bright sunlight bit into Chase's eyes, making him squint. Simultaneously, he heard a barrage of questions being yelled at him.

"Chase, why did you attack an innocent police officer?"

"Mr. Barkley, what's it like to go from a high school hero to zero?"

"Chase, Chase! Can you explain what it's like to let down your team and your school?"

Chase didn't say anything. He hung his head down in shame. Obviously, this wasn't going away quietly like he had hoped.

On the ride over to the jail, Chase asked the officer, "Why was the press out there?"

"You seem to have become an overnight sensation. One of your little party friends captured you hitting Officer Majors. The video went viral yesterday. Seems like a lot of people are interested in knowing the star of the video sensation, 'Pop a Cop.'"

"What?"

"Yeah. They titled the video 'Pop a Cop.' You're a Star."

"Oh no. Honestly, I had no idea what I was doing. You have to believe me!"

"Settle down, Chase. Everything's going to be okay. We're going to take good care of you."

The policeman's ominous tone made Chase realize he was in big trouble. He decided not to say anything else the rest of the trip.

He noticed they took the long way around town to the city jail. Once they arrived, he realized why - The same reporters were waiting here to video him entering the jail and pepper him with more questions. Chase hung his head down as he was led past them through the front door.

"We normally bring in our transfers through the back door, but I know how much you enjoy being the star. Football quarterback. Baseball starting pitcher. Now, jailhouse red carpet. Step through the door to your right. Photo and fingerprints time. I might have to get your autograph for myself."

After being processed in, he was led down a hallway and was buzzed through a locked metal door. A fluorescent light flickered as they walked down another dimly-lit hallway. They entered a door on their left. This room was cooler with a distinct musty smell. Chase noticed a water hose hanging on the wall and a drain in the floor.

The guard told him to strip. He obeyed. Then he was told to put his hands against the far wall. As he did, he heard the water come on. Moments later, the sting of the high-pressure hose and cold water took his breath away. After being sprayed down thoroughly, the guard ordered him to put on his orange prison coveralls. As Chase put them on, he looked at the cast on his hand. He wondered if it was going to be of any use after getting soaked.

Chase was passed off to a different guard and led down to his cell. The jail cell wasn't anything like what he had imagined. This room didn't have iron bars like he had seen in the movies. It was just a plain, dingy white room. The heavy door had a rectangular slot below a small clear window. The guard radioed someone, and Chase heard the door make a buzzing noise and open. Chase entered the room. Without saying a word, the guard closed the door, leaving him all alone.

He looked around the small room. It was six-by-eight foot and didn't have any windows other than the one in the door. The only furniture in there was a bunk bed and a silver chair with armrests on it. A dirty metal commode and sink were in the corner. Chase stepped over to the bed and sat down on the bottom bunk. He was glad to be alone.

Chase didn't know how long he had been laying there when he heard the door buzz open. He sat up.

To his surprise, Officer Majors and another officer stepped into his cell. "Sit in the chair."

Chase stood up and moved to the chair.

Officer Majors handcuffed Chase's right wrist to the armrest. He then used a zip tie to restrain his left hand with the cast on it.

"What are you doing?!"

"I'm making sure we can have a conversation without you attacking me!"

"Why would I attack you? I'm in jail."

Officer Majors said, "I'll need some privacy now, Jeff."

Chase pleaded with the other policeman, "No! Don't leave me alone with him."

"Jeff, I said I need to talk with this inmate alone."

The other officer replied quietly, "Okay Harrison. Remember what we talked about. No rough stuff."

"It's fine, we just need to talk."

Jeff left the room. Harrison turned to Chase. "Do you have any idea how big of an idiot I look like because of you?"

"I didn't mean to...."

"SHUT UP!"

"There's a viral video out there of you smashing my face! I'm the joke of the department. Who will respect me after this?"

"It was an accident. I had no idea what I was doing."

"Chase, I don't care. But I'll tell you what I do care about: evening up the score. I believe the good book says 'an eye for an eye.'"

"Don't do this, Harrison!"

"You will call me Officer Majors! You think you're such a hot shot. I played football at your high school five years ago. We won regional and I got this ring!" Harrison held up his right hand.

Shaking with fear Chase said, "That's...that's great, Officer Majors."

"But now, I'm a national joke! All because of you!" He grabbed a handful of Chase's hair pulling his head up tight. Angrily he punched Chase square in the nose, breaking it and deeply splitting Chase's cheek underneath his left eye with his ring.

Chase cried out for help as punches rained down upon his face. He heard someone enter the room and yell, "What are you doing?!"

Chase could tell they were wrestling. He was glad someone had stopped his attacker. Chase couldn't see anything except streaks of light, but he heard Jeff say, "What have you done, Harrison? He's a bloody mess. You were just supposed to scare him!"

Breathing heavily Harrison answered, "You're not the one all over the internet. I think this evens up the score."

Chase heard Officer Majors storm out. He felt the handcuff and zip tie being released. He was led to his bed, where he collapsed and quickly passed out.

◀ ◆ ◆ ◆ ▶

Monday morning Chase got up a little earlier than normal. Nick had given him a 30-day personal worship time guide he was starting today. After a hot shower, he dried his hair and then opened up the study guide.

He read a short story about a missionary who encountered a Christian Native American. The missionary, wanting to know more about what the Native American believed about God, asked him what Jesus had done for him. The old American Indian walked over and picked up a leaf. On the dry leaf was a caterpillar. He lit a corner of the leaf on fire. As the flames began to surround the caterpillar, the old Indian gently reached into the fire and raised the caterpillar to safety. He looked at the man and said, "This is what Jesus has done for me."

Chase loved the story. He understood his recent salvation experience was like what the caterpillar experienced. He then read the scripture below it: "Daniel 3:17 'If it be so, our God whom we serve is able to deliver us from the furnace of blazing fire; and He will deliver us out of your hand, O king.'"

Chase said a short prayer, and then got ready for school.

When he arrived at school, he quickly realized the entire campus was buzzing about the state playoff game and the players who had gotten busted. Talking to friends, Chase figured out their starting first baseman, shortstop, right and left fielders and another pitcher had all been arrested at the party. It made him sad, because he had invited each one of them to the church service Saturday night. Andrew caught him before lunch at his locker.

"Hey Chase. Can you believe those idiots got busted? We're in a world of hurt today. We've lost some of our best guys and this team we're playing won state last year!"

"Yeah, we're going to have our hands full."

"We've played and practiced so hard. They just blew our shot at state."

"Andrew, you can't think like that or we really won't have a chance to win. We're going to have to step up our game. I know the odds are against us, but we're the leaders on this team. We have to believe we can win."

"You're right. It just makes me mad at those guys."

"Think about this. If we hadn't gone to the church event Saturday night, where do you think we would have been?"

"Probably at David's party."

"Exactly. And we would be in those guys' shoes. I'm sure they would much rather be on the field with us tonight than dealing with what they're facing. Let's focus on playing the best we can and leading this team to a victory today."

"You're right. We can do this!"

"We'll have to help the younger guys get over it and focus. Let's grab some lunch, Andrew. We're going to need our energy."

The guys went to the cafeteria. Just like every other school day, the cafeteria was filled with the sounds of energetic teenagers talking and laughing. The smell of pizza, prepared for hundreds of high school students, filled the air. While they were in line, Chase began to get nervous about what he had decided to do.

They got their trays of food and joined their friends at their regular table. Chase's pulse increased as he sat down. After a pause for a deep breath, he bowed his head to pray. After a short prayer, thanking God for his food, he lifted his head up. Andrew was staring at him from across the table.

Chase said, "All in, right?"

Andrew smiled, then quickly bowed his head and said a quick prayer.

Chase was relieved. The world hadn't ended, and none of his other friends even mentioned him and Andrew praying. He enjoyed eating lunch and laughing with his friends.

After school, Chase saw Heather in the hallway.

"Hey Heather. Are you going to be at the game today?"

"Of course! I'm excited to watch you play. How are you feeling?"

"We'll definitely have to step up our game. But you know what? I'm really not worried about it. It's weird. I know it's a big game, but it doesn't feel like it's my entire world anymore. I want to play great. I want to win. But this game won't define me or my worth."

Heather smiled, "Chase, God is showing you how much he loves you. He's giving you wisdom. Don't ever let how you play a sport determine your value. That being said, you better play great today! I want to win state!"

They both laughed.

"I better get down to the field house and get ready. Thanks for the support, Heather. It means a lot."

"Go get 'em, tiger!"

Heather's words made Chase feel like he was floating on air. He thought about her on the bus ride over to their opponent's stadium.

He came back down to earth and began getting into the zone during his pre-game ritual. He went through his stretches and warm-up exercises. Then he got away from everyone and focused his mind on pitching. He had gone through these exercises for many years now, and they helped him prepare mentally and physically for the contest.

Coach Sanders gathered up his team in the locker room.

"Men, I know a lot of your emotions are running high right now. Some of you are mad at your teammates. Some of you are sad they're not playing today. Others of you are nervous about having to fill their shoes. Regardless of what you're feeling right now, you have to overcome it. Today holds a lesson for each and every one of us: life is not fair.

"It's not fair that we aren't playing with our whole team. It's not fair some of you sophomores are having to start today. It's not fair our seniors have an uphill climb today.

"Let me tell you about life not being fair. Life wasn't fair to Michael Jordan in the 1997 NBA finals when he got the flu. But you know what he did? He went out and scored 39 points and won the game!

"Life wasn't fair to Emmitt Smith in the Cowboys' 1993 season when he separated his shoulder. He went on to play through the pain and win the Super Bowl.

"Life wasn't fair to Curt Schilling during the 2004 playoffs. He tore a tendon in his ankle, but with blood soaking through his sock, he pitched incredibly, leading the Red Sox to their first World Series championship in 86 years.

"Guys, you can't allow a setback to determine your destiny. We can win today! If you play your best, you can compete with this team. I believe in each and every one of you! But the question is: Do you believe we can win?!"

A thunderous battle-cry of "Yes!" echoed through the field house.

"Then let's get out there and do it!"

Chase headed to the mound in the bottom of the first inning.

The ballpark was full. Parents, students and college scouts were there to see them play.

The game was tight. Andrew hit a solo home run in the fifth inning, but they left several runners on base throughout the game. The younger guys weren't able to get any timely hits to score any more runs. Chase was pitching well and hadn't allowed any runs.

It was still a one-run lead for Silver Springs going into the bottom of the ninth. Chase struck out the first batter. The second batter hit a shot to left field, but Trey Lawson was able to make an incredible diving catch for the second out. After some questionable balls got called, making the crowd boo loudly, Chase walked the third batter.

The next batter hit the ball hard to the sophomore shortstop, but his game winning throw sailed over the first baseman's head.

With runners at second and third base, Chase got the next batter to a full count.

Andrew came out to the mound.

"This guy's swinging."

"Yeah, I know. I think our best bet is to get him to pop up."

"You got it, Chase. Eat him up."

Andrew returned to home plate.

Chase threw a high fastball. The hitter swung and popped the ball up sky high into left field. Chase pointed straight up into the air and yelled, "Pop up!"

Everyone watched the routine fly ball float toward the sophomore, Trey Lawson.

Chase smiled, knowing he had pitched around some very good hitters and led his team, against all odds, to a victory in the state playoffs.

Then the unthinkable happened. The easy out fly ball bounced out of Trey's glove! He scrambled to retrieve it on the ground as it spun away from him. By the time he grabbed the ball and threw it home, two runners had crossed home plate.

The opponents rushed the field celebrating.

Chase's team was in shock, trying to process what had just happened. A hard-fought game lost suddenly on a routine play.

Chase gathered himself and jogged out to Trey, grabbing him by the shoulder.

"We win as a team, we lose as a team."

"I can't believe I missed that catch."

"It happens, Trey. He wouldn't have been in scoring position if I hadn't walked him."

"Chase, I just blew our chance at state."

"It's gonna be hard, but you have to know it's not all your fault. Come on we need to get in line."

The guys walked over to their team and lined up to shake hands with their opponents. It was a hard loss for everyone.

Chase's coach praised his team's effort and thanked them for playing so hard all season. He reminded them that baseball is a game, and there are a lot more important things in life than winning or losing a ballgame.

Although heartbroken, Chase was glad he had already learned that lesson.

Chapter 6

May 15, 2018

Chase woke up with a terrible headache. This was becoming way too common for him. His face had some sort of bandage covering his left eye. He tried to move and groaned in pain.

"Easy there. Don't try to move. You've been through a lot."

"Where am I?"

"You're in the jail's infirmary. You took a pretty bad fall. I'm the nurse here. We had to stitch up the left side of your face."

"Fall? I didn't fall. That insane cop beat me up!"

"Beat you up, huh? Are you going to snitch on the guy who did it? Snitches usually don't do too good on the inside."

"Snitch? I'm just telling the truth."

"Do what you want, partner. Just a word to the wise: the truth ain't always your friend. But I'm just here to patch you up. Not give you advice."

"Could you give me something for this headache? And ask someone to call my lawyer, please?"

"Sure thing."

A little while later, Chase woke up with his head still pounding. Something moving to his right made him jump.

"Who's there?"

"It's okay, Chase. It's Gabriella Cortez. How are you feeling?"

"I've been better."

"What happened, Chase?"

"Officially, it sounds like I fell."

"Chase, we both know that's not what happened."

"Well I think it's my word against his, and my word doesn't seem to be worth very much these days."

"Lucky for you, there's a witness who is willing to tell the truth."

"A witness? Who?"

"Another Silver Springs officer. Jeff Williams. He's admitting to giving unauthorized access to Officer Harrison Majors. He claims he left Officer Majors with you alone in your cell. When he returned to the cell, he witnessed you being punched repeatedly by Officer Majors."

"He's admitting it?"

"Yes. And he will probably be disciplined for his role in the event. But he felt horrible when he saw what happened to you, and wanted to make things right. This could actually help you."

"Help me? How does having my face bashed in help me?"

"With this development hopefully the judge in your case will feel that you, as a minor, have been mistreated, and a portion of justice has been served. If we can portray that picture to the judge, your sentencing might be much more lenient. They are currently charging you as an adult. If we can get some sympathy, maybe we can swing it back to juvenile court and lesser charges. That's how having your face bashed in by your accuser can help you."

"Oh. I guess that makes sense. When do I go before the judge?"

"You were scheduled to plead this morning, but obviously that's been postponed. Hopefully this afternoon. You are going to plead not guilty."

"Not guilty? But I'm guilty. There's even a video from what I hear."

"Chase, you have to trust me. It's just how the system works. I'm going to get you a deal from the prosecutor, and hopefully help you avoid years of hard time."

"I'll do whatever you say. Can you please have them give me something for this headache?"

"Sure thing. I'll see you in court."

Later that afternoon, Chase woke up from a long pain medicine-induced nap. He got up and went to the bathroom. Looking in the mirror he didn't recognize the person looking back. Most of his head was covered in white bandages. They were wrapped around his head and over his left eye and cheek. His right eye was black and blue, and his nose was crooked. He wanted to cry; wanted to scream. Nothing came out. He just pushed all of his emotions deep down inside of himself.

A few minutes later, he was loaded into a wheelchair, at Gabriella's insistence, and led down a long hallway. Judge Simms had agreed to hear the case in the jail's courtroom due to Chase's injuries.

This was a rarely-used small courtroom reserved for handling violent prisoners they didn't want to transfer or, like in Chase's case, weren't physically able to travel easily. The judge's bench was a small wooden oak desk. The prosecutor and defense had fold-out tables to use.

Chase eyed the lady sitting behind the prosecutor's table. She was wearing a dark suit and typing away on her phone. He looked to his left and saw his dad walking toward him.

"Sorry to hear about your fight. Ms. Cortez filled me in."

Chase had never heard his dad sound so distant. So uncaring.

"It wasn't a fight. I was tied up and beaten. Where's mom? Is she okay?"

"I didn't want her to see you like this."

"Dad, I'm really sorry. I just want all of this to go away."

"We'll do what we can, but you've made some pretty bad decisions. You have to own up to them."

It made Chase angry that his dad was blaming all of this on him. He knew he had made some mistakes, but they weren't intentional.

"I just went to a party! Everything just went sideways from there!"

Gabriella stepped over to them.

"Guys, let's deal with your personal issues later. Right now we need to remain very calm and in control of our emotions."

Chase's dad walked away and took a seat. Gabriella pushed Chase up to the defense table.

A bailiff entered the room and announced, "All rise."

Judge Simms entered the room and took his seat behind the oak desk.

"You may be seated. Case #4316: The People v. Chase Barkley. Chase, you are charged with underage drinking, public intoxication, assaulting an officer of the law, resisting arrest and inciting a riot. How do you plead?"

"Not guilty to all charges."

"Not guilty noted. From what I've gathered this case is gaining quite a following on social media. I'm going to put a gag order in place for everyone involved. Hopefully the media will move on to another story in a few days. These are very serious allegations. I am inclined to set bail at $100,000. Any objections?"

Gabriella spoke up, "Your honor, Chase is a minor. I realize his actions are sensational, because of a video, but he has never been in trouble and should not be tried as adult. I'd like to make a motion to move his case to the juvenile court and physically move him to the juvenile detention center. He has already been assaulted, by a police officer, while here in custody."

The prosecutor spoke for the first time. "Your honor, a member of our law enforcement family was brutally attacked by this young man. He is a threat to younger kids in custody. The state objects to him being tried as a juvenile. He will turn eighteen in June, less than six weeks from now."

"You both make good points. Given he has no prior convictions or arrests, I do believe this was an isolated incident and not a pattern of behavior. Still this was a blatant attack on our law enforcement and cannot be taken lightly. He will remain tried as an adult. He will remain here, under extra protective guard, until the time bail is made or his trial takes place. Any questions?"

Both attorneys said in unison, "No, Your Honor."

He hit his gavel on the desk.

The Bailiff announced, "All rise."

After he and the prosecutor had left the room, Chase, his dad and Gabriella met together in a private room.

"I'm sorry, Chase, but I think Judge Simms had his mind made up before the hearing. I imagine he is getting some pressure not to go soft on you. I'm going to contact the prosecutor's office and see if we can get a deal. Is there any way you can make bail? I can put you in contact with a bail bondsman who can give you the details."

Chase's dad said flatly, "I don't see any way we could come up with it."

Chase was filled with anger at his dad's quick, uncaring response. "Don't worry about it, Dad. I'll be fine."

◀ ◆ ◆ ◆ ▶

Chase got up and did his morning worship guide again. He was still disappointed about how the baseball season had ended, but he wanted to stay dedicated to what he had started with his morning worship. It lifted his spirit to read about a teenage girl who had overcome being bullied and became successful in life. The scripture was from Romans 12:21, "Do not overcome by evil, but overcome evil with good."

He went through the morning with people either encouraging him by telling him he played well, or ripping the team for losing. Chase took up for his teammates whenever someone would talk bad about them. He already felt terrible about losing, and didn't think it was fair to criticize the younger guys. They had played their best.

As Chase entered the cafeteria, he saw Trey, the sophomore who had dropped the game-winning out, surrounded by Clay Tyson and two other guys. As he walked over to them, he heard Clay say, "My little sister could have made that catch. You're such a loser!"

Chase lost his cool storming over to them, "I didn't see you out there, Clay! You think it's easy to make plays in that situation? It's not! But Trey made several good plays yesterday."

"He didn't make the most important one."

"Oh and you think you would have?"

"I think you need to get out of my face!"

By this time a crowd was gathering. Chase looked around at the crowd. "If you or anyone else says another thing about Trey, you're going to have to deal with me! It's ridiculous to blame a game on one play or player. But more than that, you're picking on a sophomore who was forced to play before he was ready for that kind pressure."

"I'm about sick of you taking up for this punk. You are as much of a loser as he is."

"At least I'm out there trying, competing. What are you doing? Nothing but talking trash about guys who are out there doing what you wish you could do."

Clay threw a punch at Chase! He ducked to his right, simultaneously grabbing Clay's right arm and, using his momentum, slammed him to the ground. A whistle began to blow as teacher's rushed into the melee.

Twenty minutes later, Chase was sitting in the principal's office waiting room with only the school secretary in there with him. Principal Jones opened her door.

"Chase, please come into my office. Are you okay?"

"Yes ma'am. I'm sorry. I know better than to fight at school."

"What happened?"

"I'm just tired of everyone picking on our younger players because we lost. It's as much my fault as it is theirs. I was taking up for Trey."

"That's what I've gathered from talking to the other students who witnessed the event. Chase, on one hand, I'm proud of you taking up for your younger teammates. That shows character and leadership. On the other hand, how you took up for him is unacceptable. There's several ways you could have taken up for Trey and diffused the situation instead of escalating it. Luckily for you, Clay threw the first punch, and you are not going to face consequences for defending yourself. I don't want any more problems from you."

"Thank you, Principal Jones."

The rest of the day went by without incident.

Chase went home and went straight to his room. As he sat his backpack down, he noticed his personal worship guide laying on his nightstand. He reached over, picked it up and read, *"Do not overcome by evil, but overcome evil with good."*

He felt like a failure. God had prepared him this morning with wisdom, but he hadn't paid attention.

Chase grabbed his phone and dialed Nick.

"Hello?"

"Hey Nick, this is Chase Barkley."

"Hey Chase! How you doing, buddy?"

"Not so good."

"I know yesterday's loss was a tough one."

"Yeah, it was. But that's not why I'm calling. I blew it today."

"What do you mean?"

"All morning, people were picking on the younger guys about losing. At lunch, I ran into a group of them making fun of Trey. I took up for him, but I lost control and ended up in a fight. It wasn't any big deal and I'm not in trouble, but I think I could have handled it differently. I think God wanted me to handle it in a completely different way."

"Chase, there's a time for everything, including fighting. But wisdom will allow you to avoid a fight unless it is necessary. Take tonight and think about the situations you encountered today. Think about how you could have handled them differently. How could you have been an example to help others?"

"I just feel like I failed today as a believer."

"Chase, failing a test doesn't make you a failure. Some of the greatest wisdom in life comes from failing. But fail forward. Learn from your mistakes, and become a better person tomorrow because of your mistakes today."

"Thanks Nick. That makes a lot of sense."

"No problem. You hang in there and I'll see you at church tomorrow night."

They hung up, and a little while later Chase went to eat supper.

His dad's anger was evident, "It's so disappointing those guys made such stupid decisions and couldn't play yesterday. They totally let down our team. If I was their dad, I would disown them."

Chase asked, "Disown them? For making a mistake?"

"Oh, Chase. Your father is exaggerating," his mom said.

"I don't know. Those hoodlums cost us a state title. Chase, I still think you pitched well enough to get Shelton to offer you."

"Dad, I'm really not too worried about that right now. I mean, I hope they offer, but if they don't, things will work out."

"Things will work out? Chase, I don't think you realize what the opportunity to play for Shelton offers. They could develop you into a dynamic pitcher. The sky's the limit with them."

"I know. I'm just concentrating on today, and trying to do what God wants me to do right now."

Chase's mom spoke up, "You're really getting into this church thing, Chase."

"I wouldn't call it a 'church thing', but yeah I'm trying to become the man Jesus wants me to be. It's not easy though."

Chase's dad observed, "He didn't help you win yesterday. But you did pitch well, so maybe God did help you some."

"Do you really think God is concerned about how I pitch or which high school team wins? I think He's got bigger things to worry about. Don't you, Dad?"

"I don't know. Pitching well can get you into Shelton. Getting into Shelton can get you to the big leagues. Seems like God might be interested in a major league pitcher."

"You think God is more interested in major leaguers?"

"Who's not?"

Frustrated with his dad, Chase excused himself to go to his room. He flopped onto his bed, deep in thought. His dad seemed to only be concerned with his success on the field. Chase wanted to figure out a way to express his faith more clearly, but it was all so new to him. Hopefully Nick was right about failing forward. He would continue to try, and trust God would help him where he needed it.

Chapter 7

May 16, 2018

Chase's night was restless. He was filled with anger at his dad, and his head hurt really badly. He was beginning to wonder if he would ever get rid of his headaches. Reflecting on how the doctor at the hospital told him he had a concussion, even before he got his face pounded by Harrison, made him wonder what additional damage had possibly occurred.

A jailor brought Chase his breakfast. Under any other circumstances, he probably wouldn't have touched the cold pancakes and warm milk, but he was starving. Chewing his breakfast caused a dull pain in his stitched-up left cheek.

After finishing the bland meal, he laid down on his bunk. An emptiness settled upon Chase in the isolated prison cell. Alone and abandoned, it was as if he was in a nightmare he couldn't wake up from. How had his life come to this? It was hard to believe just a few days ago he was a popular multi-sport athlete admired and envied by most of his classmates.

He thought about his mom and dad. How could they just abandon him like this? He knew his dad was hurt. Disappointed. They had always been his biggest supporters. He realized he had taken them, like so many other things in his life, for granted.

Chase's thoughts went to his friends. He wondered how Andrew was. Had he avoided jail? He remembered kissing Misty. How filled with lust he had been. He wondered why, because she really wasn't what he wanted in a girlfriend. She was a pretty girl, but very shallow. Not like Heather. Oh, Heather. She was beautiful, through and through. He thought about how she was probably praying for him and everyone involved. Praying. To who? God?

Where was God in all of this? It made Chase angry to think about God. Why was God punishing him? Chase thought back to the service where he almost gave his life to Jesus. Was he being punished for not following through? He decided if that's how Jesus operates, he didn't want anything to do with Him. He could make his own way without God, Jesus, his dad or anyone else. Anger crept into Chase's soul.

Across town, Gabriella Cortez was meeting with the state prosecutor. "Hello, Gabriella. Thank you for meeting me this morning."

"It's my pleasure, Carrie."

"How are things going in the public defense world?"

"Very well, thank you."

"This incident with Chase Barkley is becoming a real mess. I hate you are caught up in the middle of it trying to defend him."

"There's no need to feel sorry for me, Carrie. Although he made some bad decisions, he's a first-time offender who made an adolescent mistake. I think we can get the charges reduced to something more reasonable."

"Gabriella, you weren't even able to get him moved to juvenile court. Why do you think the sentencing will go any better?"

"I think the judge has some pressure on him from city officials and the law enforcement community to punish this young man. Which is understandable. But you wouldn't have called me here today unless you were worried about something with this case. My guess is your superiors are worried about the fact a police officer restrained, tortured and beat Mr. Barkley, a juvenile, while he was in custody."

"Gabriella, you're reaching now. How could that information even get out with a gag order in place?"

"Carrie, the truth always finds a way. Of course, I would never break a gag order. But the details of the attack will naturally come out to the public when Chase files his lawsuit against the officer and the police department. Which we're working on now."

"Interesting. So what would it take to get your client to plead guilty and accept what he's done? The sooner we end this, the better for everyone."

"Chase pleads guilty and gets probation."

"Gabriella, there's no way he doesn't serve some time. Too big of a story for him to just walk. We can't set that precedent."

"Okay. What's your offer?"

"Chase pleads guilty. Does his time at minimum security prison in Davenport, only 30 minutes away from his home here in Silver Springs. It's a nice new facility. He'll even get GED classes. We'll drop all charges, except assaulting an officer. Three year sentence, but eligible for parole in only six months. Permanent gag order concerning Harrison Majors, and he will be fired from the force. Chase signs a waiver clearing Harrison Majors and police department of any wrongdoing."

"Why would he do that?"

"He could pursue a lawsuit. He might even win. But I guarantee you he will spend at the very least eight to ten years in a maximum security prison before there's any chance of parole. We just want this to go away for everyone involved. It's the best deal you're going to get. And it benefits everyone involved."

"I'll talk to Chase this afternoon, and let you know his decision. When would we be able to get him processed and everything complete?"

"It is our priority. Judge Simms would fast track everything and we could put this to rest."

"Thank you, Carrie. I'll share your offer with Chase. It was good to see you."

"Anytime, Gabriella. I'll be looking forward to hearing from you." Gabriella went to the city jail at 2:00 that afternoon. She considered the prosecutor's offer and knew it was the best deal she could get for Chase. Although she wanted him to avoid any jail time, she knew going in that was going to be a long shot.

She checked in and was escorted back to an office used for attorney-client visits. It was a dingy grey room with a metal table in the middle bolted to the floor. A chair sat on either side of the table, and a camera in the corner of the room was pointed toward them with its little red light shining. She opened her briefcase and reviewed some papers while she waited on

Chase. A few minutes later the door opened and he was escorted into the room. He took his seat and the jailor looked at Gabriella, "I'll be right outside if you need anything."

"Thank you. Oh, Chase, you're still all bandaged up. Are you okay?"

"I still have a headache, but I'm making it."

"I'll make sure you have a doctor visit this afternoon. I went by and met with the prosecutor, Carrie Martin, today. They are making you an offer."

"Really? Is it a good one?"

"All things considered I think it's the best we could hope for. Here are your choices. Option one: we go to court and fight it. Honestly, we probably lose. The video and evidence are totally against us. You are sentenced to ten to fifteen years in a maximum security prison. You can still sue Harrison Majors and the police department for wrongdoing and personal injuries. We may or may not win, and if we do, it will be tied up in courts for years.

"Option two: you take their deal. They drop the majority of the charges. You get a three year sentence, but you're out on parole in six months. You'll go to a minimum security prison, which is a much better situation for you. But you waive any wrongdoing against Harrison Majors and the police department.

"The decision is yours to make, Chase. I strongly recommend you take the deal. The risk-reward factor here is huge. You could spend the best years of your life behind bars if we lose."

Chase sat silently processing the information.

"So he just gets away with beating me?"

"I was told he would be fired from the police department. So he gets some punishment."

"I'll take the deal. It's probably the best decision, I guess."

"It is. Chase, I tried to get parole only, but they wouldn't budge. It's only six months and then you can get back to your life."

"No Gabriella, that's where you're wrong. My life will never be the same again. But I'm learning I can handle a lot more, on my own, than I thought I could. I'll survive."

◀ ◆ ◆ ◆ ▶

Chase was up early the next morning working through his personal worship guide. After finishing it and spending a few minutes in prayer, he followed the smell of bacon to the kitchen.

His mom was standing in front of the stove. "Good morning. How did you sleep, honey?"

"Good morning, Mom. I slept like a rock. Breakfast smells great!"

"You eat up, young man. You only have one more week of school and you'll be graduating. I can't believe how fast time flies."

Chase's dad entered the room, "And hopefully you'll be moving on to Shelton University!"

"Good morning, Dad."

"Morning, son. We should be hearing something in the next day or two from Shelton. Coach Ric said it should be this week. They have to make a decision soon."

"Hopefully we'll hear good news, Dad."

Chase finished his breakfast and headed to school. He turned down his radio and prayed most of the way. He asked God to give him a clear path to follow in his college decision. While he knew Shelton was a fantastic opportunity, something inside of him didn't have peace about going there. If offered, how would he explain to his dad he felt like Crossland was a better decision?

As Chase turned a corner going to homeroom, he saw Clay Tyson. He walked toward Clay, knowing what he had to do.

"Hey, Clay."

"What do you want?"

"Clay, I'm sorry. I should have handled things in a different way yesterday."

"Huh? Yeah, well I guess we both could have handled it differently. Why are you apologizing?"

"I handled the situation wrong. We've gone to school together for a long time. Even though we're not close friends, I don't want to end school this way."

"Okay. Well, I guess that makes sense. Seems like it was just the other day we were playing kickball at the elementary playground."

Chase laughed, "Yes it does. Those were fun times. Clay, I've recently started going to church over at Grace. They're having youth tonight. Would you be interested in going?"

"You're inviting me to church? I don't think so. But I'll think about it. I've got to get to in-school suspension. Talk to you later."

"See you later, Clay. And seriously, think about coming by tonight."

The guys headed to their classes.

Chase prayed for an answer to where he should attend college throughout the day. He wondered how many other students were excited about graduating, but anxious about what life would hold beyond these familiar high school walls.

Chase was excited to get to church that evening and catch up with Nick. He felt like he learned something every time he talked with Nick about his faith. As he walked in, he looked around the room for Clay, but didn't see him.

The service began with a funny video and then the worship band played. Chase was learning that he enjoyed worshipping God in song. Somehow the music tapped into something deep within Chase he didn't even realize was there just a few weeks ago. Nick explained this was his soul being awakened to worshipping God. Chase didn't understand it, but he certainly felt it.

Nick taught a lesson from a book in the Bible called 1st Corinthians. He compared running a race to the Christian life. This guy Paul said just like runners train to win a race, people should train in their faith to win. Chase liked the comparison. It made sense to him.

At the end of the service, Nick announced the deadline for the student ministry summer trip was coming up. They were going in June to a week-long Christian conference for teenagers in Destin, Florida. Chase whispered to Andrew that they needed to sign-up.

After church, Chase, Andrew, Heather and Tonya were talking. Nick called Chase over to him.

"Hey Chase, did you get things straightened out at school?"

"Yes sir. I apologized for my part in the fight. Clay seemed to understand and accept it. I even invited him to church tonight. Didn't see him here though."

"That's great, Chase. Did you take some time to reflect on how you could have handled yesterday's situations differently?"

"I did. There were several things I could have done better. Hopefully next time I'll know."

"That's exactly right. We are going to make mistakes. But if we learn from them, we can avoid making them again."

"Nick, will you pray about something for me?"

"Of course. What is it?"

"I should be hearing something from a college soon. I'll have to decide pretty quickly, but I want to go where God wants me to go. And I want my parents, especially my dad, to be happy with my decision. I'm hoping God will open the door I need to go through, and close the others."

"That's a great prayer request. And I will definitely be praying for God to lead you to the right college."

"Thanks Nick! Oh, put me and Andrew down for the summer trip! It sounds fun!"

"You got it!"

As Chase was walking into his house, he checked his e-mail. There was a new message from Coach Ric at Shelton University. His dad was sitting in his recliner and his mom was folding a load of clothes on the couch.

Chase yelled, "Dad! I got an email from Coach Ric!"

Chase's dad hit the off button on the TV and sat up straight.

Smiling he said, "This is it! Go on. Read it."

Chase took in a deep breath and hit the open button with his thumb.

He read out loud, "Dear Chase Barkley, It has been an honor to recruit you. You are an outstanding athlete, and have a lot of potential to become a great college pitcher.

Unfortunately …Unfortunately, we have decided to go in another direction and will not be able to extend a baseball scholarship to you at this time. Good luck and God bless you. Sincerely yours, Coach Ric."

Chase's words trailed off. Although he didn't feel God leading him to go to Shelton, he was surprised by how disappointed he felt. His dad, on the other hand, was furious.

"An e-mail? He couldn't even give you a phone call? You pitched great in your last game, and if you would have had any run support…"

"Dad, it's okay."

"It's not okay! It's ridiculous! They should give us a chance."

"Dad, thank you for caring about me, and investing so much in me. I can't imagine anything else we could have done."

Chase walked over and hugged his dad.

"It's just not fair, Chase."

"I know, Dad. But you have taught me how to handle tough situations. I'll get through this."

Chase's mom said, "You boys sit down. I'm making some chocolate chip cookies and we're having some family time."

They sat in the living room together. After a while, Chase's dad settled down. They ended up laughing, talking and reminiscing until late in the night. It was one of the best nights Chase could ever remember with his parents.

Chase finally said, "I guess I better get to bed. I love you, Mom and Dad. Thanks for all you've done for me. I'm learning I can handle a lot more, with God, than I thought I could. I'll survive."

Chapter 8

May 19, 2018

Chase was sitting on the side of his uncomfortable prison bed when the buzzing of his cell door interrupted his thoughts. Moments later, the heavy door swung open.

"You have a visitor. Come with me."

Chase stood up and followed the guard to the visitor area. They went through a security door that opened up into a long line of booths with thick, grimy Plexiglas windows. Each section had a germ-ridden black phone on the wall to the side of it. Chase walked down the line until he saw a familiar face. He was surprised to see Nick sitting there. He held his hand up acknowledging Chase.

As Chase sat down, he reached up and grabbed the phone. Nick reached over and picked up his phone as well.

"Chase, it's good to see you."

"Hey Nick. What are you doing here?"

"I just thought I'd check on you and see how you're doing."

"I'm still alive."

"How's your hand healing up?"

"It still hurts a lot. The doctor says it's getting better. My face isn't so lucky. I'm obviously scarred for life."

"Chase, I'm sorry these bad things have happened to you. I know you're a good kid. Life sometimes goes in directions we didn't plan."

"This is definitely a direction I didn't plan. I still can't believe I ended up in here. Have you heard anything about Andrew? The last time I saw him was when David's party got busted."

"Andrew got arrested. He fought with the police who were arresting you. Lots of students were arrested out there. Most of the baseball team. David Baker and Matt Tyler, from your football team, also got arrested. Both of those guys got out the next day. David had to make bail, but Matt was released on his own recognizance."

"Is Andrew in as much trouble as me?"

"I don't think so. They're blaming most of the trouble on you and David. They said the two of you were the leaders. You made speeches or something, and provided moonshine to the baseball players there."

"Moonshine? Is that what he gave us?"

"So you didn't know what it was?"

"No. I had no idea. I didn't plan on giving a speech either. Everyone was chanting my name, like at a pep rally, so I just congratulated my team and said we would try to win state."

"Chase, it sounds like you didn't have any bad intentions. You were just in the wrong place at the wrong time. Unfortunately, you can't go back and change your actions. But you can change from this point on and end up in a much better place."

"What do you mean?"

"Chase, What I mean is that God isn't throwing you away. He wants to forgive you and fix your life. He cares about you. If you'll put your trust in him, He will be there for you."

The mention of God caring about his situation infuriated Chase.

"If God cares so much about me, why did he allow all of this to happen?! Why is He still allowing all of this happen to me? No, Nick. I don't buy that God cares about me at all. If He's even real, I don't want anything to do with Him. I can make my own way."

"Chase! Don't write off God. You'll regret it."

"If you see Andrew, tell him I'm sorry. Don't bother coming by again." Chase hung up the receiver and walked away.

Back in his cell, he began to cry. His sorrow turned to anger. Slowly his tears were dried up by hate. He resolved in his heart to only worry about himself from now on.

His lunch was delivered to his cell. He noticed there were three envelopes laying on the tray beside his meal. They were all already opened. Hatred filled Chase at the thought of someone else reading his mail. There was no privacy in jail. After eating about half of the cold, bland stew, he picked up the white envelopes.

The first one was from Andrew.

Chase,

Dude the other night at the party got crazy. Whatever was in that shot David gave us tore everyone up. Most of us can't remember anything clearly after we had those drinks.

I can't believe you broke your hand! I hope it gets better soon, and doesn't mess up your pitching. My lawyer says I should be able avoid any jail-time, but a coach from Crossland said I may lose my offer. I have no idea what I'll do if that happens.

This is terrible! Stupid David tried to run, but the cops tracked him down pretty quick. Misty keeps asking me about you. What a psycho.

The baseball team got killed in the first round of the state playoffs. Coach Sanders wouldn't play anyone who got arrested, so it was mostly sophomores and freshmen. They almost had to forfeit.

My parents are so mad at me. I'm grounded forever. They told me I needed to stay away from you, but you know that's never going to happen. We'll always be best friends. They even said I might be asked to testify against you. I told them they were crazy if they thought I would ever do that.

We'll get through this and figure things out. Hang in there, bro!

Andrew

It was good to hear from his best friend. He was sad to hear Andrew might lose his scholarship. He had worked so hard to earn it. The next letter was from his dad.

Chase,

I'm not even sure who you are anymore. These past few days have been horrible for me and your mom. You had every opportunity in the world to be a success, but you've blown it. The coach at Shelton contacted me to let me know you obviously won't be offered a scholarship. Crossland and the other smaller schools who were interested in you have also withdrawn their offers. I guess you have your reasons for what you did. I'm disappointed you have thrown away everything we worked so hard for. I hope you make better decisions in the future.

Dad

Chase wondered how his dad could become so distant and cold in such a short amount of time. It was like he was a different person. He expected his parents to be disappointed, but this was much more than he ever imagined possible. Chase wondered if his dad would ever forgive him. A part of him worried they might never get past this. Chase looked at the final letter. It was from Heather.

Chase,

I'm so sorry to hear of your situation. I know you are not a bad person, and didn't intend to hurt anyone. I can't imagine what it's like where you are right now.

How is your hand? I heard you broke it. I'm praying God will heal you physically, emotionally and spiritually. Keep hope alive and don't give up. This test can make you stronger if you allow God into your life.

Everyone struggles at some point. Disease, sickness and unfair circumstances can tempt us to give up on God. They can also make us seek Him. My grandma always told me it's how we respond to our trials that matters the most.

Chase, please open your heart to Jesus and allow Him to heal you. I'll keep praying for you.

Your friend,
Heather

Chase thought about what Heather said. Could he allow God into his life? Could he place his faith in Jesus? Chase wrestled with the idea of God in that cold, damp jail cell. After a long time of thinking about his situation, he finally came to his decision: no!

There was no way he would be foolish enough to trust in a God who would allow this bad situation to happen to him and his friends. Chase hardened his heart against God. For better or worse, he would make his own way.

◀ ◆ ◆ ◆ ▶

"Mr. and Mrs. Barkley, it's very nice to meet you. I'm Nick Cunningham, the youth pastor at Grace Fellowship Church."

"It's nice to meet you too, Nick. Please come in."

"Chase has told us so much about you. It sounds like you two have really hit it off. I'll let him know you are here."

"Mr. Barkley, you should be very proud of your son. He's a natural leader and lots of fun to be around."

"Thank you. I am very proud of him. He works hard in the classroom and on the field. We were hoping he could go D-1, but it looks like he will have to settle for Crossland."

"Honestly Mr. Barkley, I get the impression he's embracing going to Crossland. Rooming with his best friend Andrew, and having some other friends attending there, will give him a great support system. I find that's a recipe for success in college. I'm sure you remember how difficult transitioning into this phase of life can be."

"Yes I do. It's not easy. I'm glad to hear you think he'll be in a healthy situation."

Chase and his mom walked into the room.

"Hey, Nick. Good to see you buddy."

"You too, Chase. Your dad and I were just discussing you heading to Crossland."

"Yeah, I think it will be cool."

Chase's Mom asked, "So Nick, you wanted to talk to us about some things with Chase and the church?"

"Yes ma'am. You've already filled out the paperwork for the student beach trip coming up in a few weeks. Here's an information packet. If you have any other questions, don't hesitate to contact me. My cell number is also in there."

"Thank you, Nick."

"The other thing Chase wanted me to discuss with you was his opportunity to be baptized tomorrow in our church service. Chase has acknowledged Jesus as the Lord of his life and he wants to obey the Bible and be baptized. We recently had several students get saved and tomorrow morning we're going to be baptizing quite a few of them. Would it be okay if Chase gets baptized along with them?"

Chase's dad answered, "Chase is old enough to make his own decision. Chase is this what you want to do?"

"Yes sir."

"Fine with me. What time will the service be, Nick?"

"Ten o'clock in the morning. Will you be able to make it?"

Chase's mom answered, "We wouldn't miss it for the world!"

"Great! Chase, be sure to bring a change of clothes, and I'll see you in the morning. Thank you for allowing me to visit. You have raised a fine young man."

"Thank you. See you tomorrow."

The next morning Chase's family rode to church together. It felt unusual, but in a special way. Chase was happy they agreed to come see him be baptized.

When Chase had heard the Bible teaches that followers of Jesus are supposed to be publicly baptized, he wanted to obey immediately. He even asked Nick to run him down to the river and do it right away. Wisely, Nick declined his impulsive request, wanting to give Chase's parents the opportunity to be there and celebrate when he was baptized.

Chase had been praying his mom and dad would experience the love of Jesus in a powerful way when they visited church that morning. The place was packed for the large baptism service. Chase and Andrew's families sat on the same row. As the music began playing, the boys were excited to worship Jesus in song.

After the music, Pastor Tad made his way to the front of the church to preach. He shared the story about John baptizing Jesus from the book of Matthew. Tad emphasized how Jesus is not only our Savior, but also our example of how we are supposed to live once we are saved. Toward the end of the sermon he invited everyone coming for baptism to make their way back to the baptistery.

Tad finished his message explaining how our King, Jesus, submitted to the will of His Father, and how we will be blessed if we do the same. The band came up to play, and Tad invited anyone who wanted to become a follower of Jesus to come forward. Three people went forward and bowed down at the altar.

After they had finished praying, the lights went down in the church. A spotlight lit up the baptistery. Nick stood there.

"Recently, we have had many people acknowledge Jesus Christ as their Lord and Savior. Today we are celebrating new life in Christ through the ceremony of baptism. The Bible teaches us to repent of our sins, believe in our hearts Jesus is Lord, and call on His mighty name to be saved. After this, we are commanded to be baptized. This morning we have nineteen kids, youth and parents who want to make this public profession of their faith! Praise the Lord!"

The auditorium clapped and cheered.

A young girl came into view, making her way through the water toward Nick. He took her hand and helped her. Then her mother stepped into view as well.

"I had the pleasure of talking with 11-year-old Caroline Gales last Tuesday afternoon. We discussed what it means to put our faith in Jesus. She explained to me how she realized she was a sinner and needed a Savior.

While we were talking, her mother Cathy Gales also acknowledged her need for salvation. What an awesome story of God's redeeming love."

The church cheered. Nick took Caroline and turned her sideways to the audience with one hand on her shoulder.

"Caroline, who is Lord and Savior of your life?"

She proudly answered, "Jesus!"

"By your public profession of faith in Jesus, I baptize you now, my sister, in the name of the Father, the Son and the Holy Spirit."

She put one hand over her nose and grabbed her forearm with her other hand. Nick lowered her completely under the water and then quickly raised her up from it.

Several "Amens" were heard as the church shouted, clapped and cheered.

Then he repeated the process with her mom. One by one, Nick baptized people of a variety of ages, incomes and backgrounds. Matt Tyler, the center from the football team, was excited and animated as he arose from the water's depth. Andrew went after him, and then Chase was next. He moved through the water toward Nick.

"This is my good friend, and new brother in Christ, Chase Barkley. Chase didn't know I was going to say this today, but nine of the teenagers who were baptized this morning said Chase had influenced them to follow Jesus. Chase, God is already using you to advance His Kingdom. I can't wait to see the impact your life will have in the future!

"Chase, who is the Lord and Savior of your life?"

"Jesus!"

"By your public profession of faith in Jesus, I baptize you now, my brother, in the name of the Father, the Son and the Holy Spirit."

Chase grasped his nose and his forearm. With one of Nick's hands on his back and one holding his forearm, he leaned backwards allowing himself to be immersed in the water. He felt completely emptied of himself in the depths of the water. Powerfully, he rose back up breaching the surface of the water into brand new life. Chase felt clean inside and out. He turned and hugged Nick.

"I'm proud of you, Chase."

On the way home Chase was excited to hear his mom and dad had really enjoyed the service.

"Chase, that preacher of yours tells a good story. I enjoyed his sermon."

"I think so too, Dad."

"I used to love going to church when I was a little girl. Maybe we should try to go again sometime, honey."

"I wouldn't mind. The people there today were a lot friendlier than the churches I've gone to in the past. Chase, was the water cold?"

"No, Dad, it was comfortable."

"That's good. I'm proud of you following through with your commitments. Nick is a good guy."

"Yeah, he is. I learn something new every time I hear him teach. I want to thank both of you for being there this morning. I know you like to sleep in on Sundays, but it means a lot to me."

"We might just give this church another try. Your mom enjoyed going, and I didn't think it was half bad myself."

Chapter 9

May 31, 2018

"Big day today, Chase."

"Yeah, I know, Gabriella. I can't wait to get to my new cage."

"It's not that bad. You could be headed to a max prison instead of the country club in Davenport."

"Country club, huh. I'll let you know how much I enjoy it after my first round of golf."

"Trust me, Chase. Compared to where you could be going, this is a country club. Are you ready to remove your bandages from your cheek? The doctor said it's time to get them off for good."

"I hope the medicine he's been applying helps. It looked terrible last week."

"I bet it has!"

"I don't. They butchered the stitches in here. I'm still going to look like a freak."

"Come on, Chase. Let's get them off and see how much better you look."

Chase slowly peeled off the bandage from underneath his left eye across his cheek.

Gabriella smiled, "It looks much better. The swelling has gone down and it's healing up."

Chase reached up with his right hand and gently rubbed his fingers across his cheek. He could feel the indentions where Harrison Majors ring had torn his skin apart. Chase looked down at his left hand, still in a cast. He felt like a monster. Like he was trapped in someone else's broken body.

Gabriella asked, "Do you want me to get a mirror so you can see the progress?"

"No. Don't bother."

"Okay. They should be here to transport you anytime now. Chase, stay out of trouble and you'll be out of there in six months. You can do this! Have you heard from your parents?"

"My mom came by once. She cried the whole time. I asked her not to come back. She has written me some letters."

"What about your dad?"

"No. He's pretty much disowned me. I really don't care."

"He'll come around. These situations are hard on families. Don't write him off just yet. Chase, you still have the potential to have a great life. This is hard, but you can overcome it. Get your GED completed and when you get out you can get a job and get your life back on track."

The door buzzed and a guard opened it.

"Chase Barkley. It's time to go."

Gabriella hugged Chase.

"Hang in there, young man! And you have them call me if you need anything."

Chase was led outside. He squinted in the bright sunlight, and was surprised how weird it felt to be outside. He had been locked-up inside for over a week. A short walk later he got into the backseat of a police cruiser and settled in for the ride to his new home.

As they drove through town, Chase looked at everything with a new perspective. There was his favorite burger joint where he and his friends used to hang out. Chase smiled as they passed the gas station where he used to regularly fill up his truck and grab a Gatorade after practice. And there was his high school. He didn't realize how much he missed it. His memories from there felt even more special now. There was a sign hanging out front. What did it say?

As they got closer Chase read it under his breath, "Happy Graduation Day, Seniors!"

A dark cloud engulfed Chase as he realized today was supposed to be his graduation day. He should be celebrating with his friends. Instead, he was on his way to prison. He knew he was missing something he could never get back. A little more of who Chase was died in that moment.

Thirty minutes later they pulled up to the front gate of the Davenport minimum security prison.

Several buildings freshly painted beige sat about a mile off of the highway. The perimeter of the prison was enclosed by a tall chain link fence covered with spiraling constantine razor wire. Nothing but fields surrounded the facility.

The driver rolled down his window, scanned his badge and the gate slowly swung open. He eased through and rolled toward the prison. Pulling up to the building on the right he parked and sang out, "Home sweet, home."

Chase remained quiet.

"Here's how this is going to work. I'm going to open your door. You're going to step out of the vehicle. We'll enter the door immediately in front of us. That's where you will be processed into this facility. There's nowhere to run and hide, so don't even think about it. If you cooperate here, things will go good for you. If you don't, then you'll be transferred to a maximum security prison. I promise you on my mama's grave, you don't want to end up there. Understood?"

"Yeah."

Chase cooperated and entered the prison office. His papers were checked out and he was fingerprinted and photographed again. Then he was led down to an office. The guard knocked on the door.

From behind the door, Chase heard a man's deep baritone voice, "You may come in."

The guard opened the door. Chase cautiously entered the office. The warden didn't immediately look up from his computer. Chase and the guard stood in awkward silence as the seconds ticked by. Finally he clicked his mouse and looked up.

"Thank you. Guard Richards, you may wait outside."

The prison guard stepped out of the room and closed the door behind him.

"Mr. Chase Barkley. I'm Warden Samuel Cochran. Welcome to Davenport minimum security prison. Don't let the term 'minimum security' make you think this is some type of low security facility. We have tabs on you at all times, and no one has ever escaped from any prison where I have been the warden. Nor will they. There will be zero tolerance for insubordination, fighting or anything else that causes trouble here. Do you understand everything I've explained so far?"

"Yeah."

"You will respond to me and the staff with, 'yes sir' or 'no sir.' Is that clear?"

"Yes sir."

"Good. Mr. Barkley, you have the choice to do your time here the easy way or the hard way. If you follow the rules, you'll find this isn't too difficult of a place to survive. I was just reviewing your file. You have a three-year sentence. If you cooperate your sentence can be shortened with parole. Keep your nose clean and you'll make it through here, young man."

"Yes sir."

"Guard!"

The security guard opened the office door.

"Get Mr. Chase Barkley to his living quarters."

"Yes sir! Come with me."

Chase followed the guard out of the warden's office and back outside.

"You're going to be housed in building no. 3. Your building is your team. You will eat and sleep together. We are putting you on kitchen duty. Three members of your team are already assigned there. They will train you."

The guard opened the door and led Chase inside. The building held twenty-four men. There were six rows of bunk beds lining each wall. All of the inmates were wearing identical beige polyester scrubs and canvas shoes. They moved to the end of their beds and lined up to listen.

"This is Chase Barkley. He is now a member of team no. 3. I expect you to welcome him as one of your own. No problems! Chase, follow me."

They walked down to the next-to-last bed on the right.

"Chase, you will be on the top bunk here. This is inmate Micky Floyd. He is your bunkmate and he's now in charge of orienting you to our facility. Micky, do a good job and show Chase the ropes. Get him changed out of these hideous orange coveralls and into his Davenport scrubs. I don't want to hear of any problems. Understood?"

"Yes sir."

"Drop those coveralls off by the office on your way to eat. Lunch is in twenty minutes."

The guard left Chase with his new team: the building no. 3 Davenport minimum security prisoners.

Micky looked like he was in his fifties with thick bright white hair and tanned leather-like skin.

"Welcome to the joint, kid. What happened to your face?"

Chase instinctively reached up and rubbed his fingers across his scars.

"Run in with the law. But I did break his nose."

Micky laughed hard, sounding more like a high-pitched cackle that quickly turned into a hacking cough.

Once he caught his breath he said, "Those smokes are gonna kill me someday. Here's the basics. Be where you're supposed to be, when you're supposed to be there. Do what you're supposed to do. Everything else will work out."

"Seems simple enough."

"It is simple. Doesn't mean it's easy. Guys will try to play a kid like you in here.

"This ain't like the big house, but it can be rough. You'll want to make the right friends around here. Stick with me kid and I'll show you the ropes. Now get changed. It's getting close to chow time."

◄ ♦ ♦ ♦ ►

"Big day today, Chase!"

"I know, Andrew! I can't believe we're graduating in just a few hours!"

"And this fall we will be roommates at Crossland!"

"I can't wait to get up there. But we have a little ceremony and celebration going on tonight before we rush off to college!"

"Yes! I talked to Tonya. She and Heather are going to the party at the church after graduation."

"I know. I talked to Heather earlier."

"So you were actually able to talk to her. Uh, oh, ugh, Heather, I, uh, want to, uh..."

Chase hit Andrew.

"Ow! Ease up on my throwing arm. I know it's not golden like yours, but I need it to be able to throw the baseball back to you."

"I thought catchers were supposed to be tough. Anyway, tonight is going to be fun. Dinner with my folks. Graduation ceremony. Then the all-night party at church. I hear they're giving away some awesome prizes for the winners of the games we're playing. Lots of college-friendly gear. Gaming systems, flat screen TVs and tons of gift cards."

"How do they get all of that stuff to give away?"

"Heather said they get lots of it donated. Stores can write it off. The church also buys some of it. Nick told me it helps keep kids off the streets and away from wild parties. Makes sense, after seeing what David's party did to our baseball season."

"And we can rack up on some free stuff!"

"Yeah, that too, Andrew. You better get home and get ready. I have to shower before we go eat. Catch you at graduation."

Chase rode with his parents to his favorite burger joint. His dad had offered to take him to the local steakhouse, but Chase thought this sounded like more fun. They talked, laughed and enjoyed eating together. Chase realized things were about to change. He knew he was blessed to have such wonderful parents.

After their meal, Chase's dad disappeared. When he returned he was holding a wrapped gift.

Chase smiled. "Thanks! You guys are the best!"

"Go on and open it!"

Chase tore into the package. Wrapping paper flew into the air as he ripped the gift open.

"A new laptop! It's perfect! This will be great for college. Thank you so much!"

A few minutes later they loaded up and drove to the school for graduation.

His parents hugged him and wished him luck. They went inside the auditorium to get a seat, while Chase headed backstage where all of the graduates were getting ready. It was chaos back there as teachers were trying to organize students alphabetically. The excitement was palpable flowing through the crowd of students. Finally it was time to march out. Miraculously, everyone was in order.

As they marched to their seats, Chase spotted his parents in the stands and waved to them. Thirteen years of hard work was coming to a final culmination. Great memories of teachers, friends, tough classes, hard work and competitive games flooded Chase's mind. Emotions were raging inside of him as this chapter of his life was coming to a close.

The auditorium rose for the playing of the national anthem, the Pledge of Allegiance and the school's alma mater. Speakers shared words of wisdom and funny stories. A video played honoring a retiring teacher. Then one-by-one they called out the student's names. Chase got a lot of cheers as he walked across the stage and received his diploma.

Afterward, his class made a circle and threw their graduation caps high into the air. Families quickly filled the auditorium floor searching for their loved ones. Cell phones were snapping pictures and videoing the entire event. Chase found his parents and hugged them. He had a friend take some family photos. He took several pictures with lots of different friends, coaches and teachers as well.

The auditorium slowly cleared out as families exited. When it was time to leave, Chase stopped and took a good long look at his school. This was the last time he would be here as a student. He thanked God for the blessing of his education, friendships and great times he had experienced here.

He and his parents talked all the way home about the graduation ceremony. Chase hugged his mom and dad, thanked them again for his computer and headed to the church.

As he entered the youth building late that night, he was amazed at how they had transformed the facility. There were brightly colored game booths set up all around the gym floor. He approached the entrance where a couple of ladies welcomed him.

"Hello! What's your name, young man?"

"I'm Chase Barkley."

Handing him a pile of tokens, one of them explained, "You will use these to play games. The better you do at the games, the more tokens you will win. We'll have an auction later tonight for prizes. We'll also have a big bingo game where you could win some cool stuff. Have fun!"

Chase thanked her and went inside. He walked through the crowd of students past a table covered in pizzas, chips and desserts. He saw Andrew and Tonya playing a football toss game.

"Winning lots of tokens?"

"Hey Chase! Andrew has made one so far. I can't remember how many I've made."

"She's made four. Four! I think she should play quarterback next year at Crossland instead of you."

"You may be right."

Heather walked up to the group, "Hey guys! Sorry I'm late. What's going on here?"

"It seems Tonya is going to play quarterback at Crossland next year instead of me, because of this game. There's some major changes happening here tonight!"

Heather smiled. "Well I have a major change to announce."

Andrew asked, "Are you going to play running back next year at Crossland?"

"No, silly. But I will be attending Crossland next year with the three of you!"

Tonya screamed and hugged Heather. "I still haven't been assigned a dorm. You want to room together?"

Heather smiled. "Of course!"

Chase asked, "When did you decide? I thought you were going to Gulf Coast College?"

"I was accepted to both. I've been praying really hard about it, and I feel like God wants me to attend Crossland. My parents also felt good about it. Pretty cool, huh!"

Chase smiled. "Very cool."

Andrew said, "Hey, That's great and all, but I've gotta win some tokens!"

Tonya pushed Andrew. The group laughed and moved on to the next game.

Later they made their way to the prize tables. Chase had heard right. The group was impressed with the flat screen TVs, laptops, gaming systems and lots of gift cards available. All the students attending were guaranteed to get a gift. The church and community made this graduation party a big event to help keep kids safe and off the streets on graduation night.

Chase saw Matt Tyler and several other guys from school. They talked and laughed for a while. It was a fun night.

Everyone played bingo at 3 a.m. Nick was the emcee. He told lots of jokes and entertained everyone for an hour. The kids were really into it and having fun. Chase ended up winning the grand prize, a laptop computer, during the final cover-your-card round.

They had the auction and finished giving out all the prizes at 5 a.m., and then a big breakfast was served. As everyone finished eating, they slowly began saying their goodbyes and loading up their treasures to take home with them.

Chase said goodbye to his group. Walking toward his truck outside in the parking lot, he spotted Matt and caught up with him.

"What did you end up with, big guy?"

"Hey Chase. I got a $50 gift card to Taco Bell, and a $25 McDonalds gift card. I was hoping to get a laptop for college. But tonight was a blast, and I'm walking away with $75 in free fast food!"

Chase knew Matt's family didn't have a lot of money. Matt had told him the only way he was going to college was on the scholarship he had worked hard to earn. He was attending Central State College on an academic scholarship in the fall.

"Matt, I really wanted that $50 Taco Bell gift card. My parents gave me a laptop earlier tonight as my graduation gift. You want to trade that gift card for my extra laptop I won tonight?"

"Get outta here, man! You could sell that computer for over a thousand bucks."

"Matt, you've protected me on the football field since we were in middle school. Make the trade. I already have a laptop. What am I gonna do with two? What I really need is some Mexican food. I'm too skinny to play quarterback in college."

Matt thought for a second, "Deal! You really are too skinny. But you're the best!"

The guys exchanged their gifts.

"Matt, you probably just saved my life. I can eat at Taco Bell for a whole semester on $50!"

Chapter 10

June 17, 2018

As Chase mopped alone in the kitchen, his thoughts drifted back to the discussion he had earlier with his GED teacher. His instructor had explained to Chase that judging by his grades, he could probably pass the GED test without even studying. To qualify to take it, he only had to complete the pre-test portion. Chase informed him he wouldn't be coming back to the class. He could care less about listening to a teacher or looking at a book. Even though it would be easy for him, Chase wouldn't go through the motions to get his GED. He was apathetic about his life and his future.

He was glad he had volunteered to finish up the mopping alone today. The peace and quiet was a nice change of pace. His kitchen duties, unloading the deliveries and cleaning up after meals, was mindless work.

His thoughts were interrupted when he noticed the door was open. He looked around.

"Hello. Anyone there?"

No answer. He went back to his chores. Minutes later a voice startled him.

"Hey, kid. I hear you have a pretty good left hook."

Alarmed, Chase quickly sized up the man who had snuck in behind him. He was a white guy with a shaved head, lots of tattoos, probably in his late twenties, and weighed about twice as much as him.

"What do you want?"

"Just want to talk. Nothing wrong with talking is there?"

"What do you want to talk about?"

"They call me Tank. I need someone to break a black dude's face. His name is Cedric. He's in your building, so I figured you would be the perfect guy to do it. I saw your video."

"Why would I attack someone I don't even know?"

"Because I asked you to, Chase Barkley. Judging by your face, you're tough enough. You can even hit him with that casted hand. That should hurt him. If you take care of this situation, you'll be in good with me and my boys. Otherwise, you may have a rough stay here."

"Why don't you take care of him yourself?"

"I could. But me and my crew think this is a good chance to see what you got. Think of it as an initiation. We don't let just anyone in our gang."

"I'll think about it and let you know."

"Unfortunately, Chase, I'm going to need an answer now. Cedric took something from one of my guys and payback needs to be pretty quick. Like today."

"Well then, Tank, the answer is No. I'm not really looking for a crew. You can take care of Cedric yourself."

"You sure about that?"

"Yep."

"Bad decision!"

The huge man rushed him. Chase swung his mop trying to defend himself. It broke against Tank's side, but the big guy tackled him to the ground. Chase pounded away with his right fist, trying to cover up his head and face with his broken left hand. He felt like he was getting sacked in a football game again, except this time the guy wasn't getting off of him. Tank maneuvered himself on top of Chase. He covered his face and head with his arms, so Tank hit him repeatedly with body blows. After what seemed like an eternity, Chase was relieved to feel Tank's weight lift off of him. He heard Tank laughing as he left the kitchen.

Chase eventually got up off of the floor. His side was hurting and it was hard to breathe. He was moving around slowly when a guard arrived.

"What happened to you?"

Chase struggled to breathe while talking.

"I...I slipped on the wet...floor and...the mop broke...when I fell."

"Yeah, sure you slipped. Let's get you to the infirmary."

The X-ray tech helped Chase stand up in front of a square white device against the wall. He positioned Chase and told him to hold still. Chase heard him say to take in a breath and hold it. He did his best through the pain. Several X-rays of his chest and ribs were taken.

A little while later the doctor came in to see Chase.

"Looks like good news. No broken ribs. Lots of bruising though. I'll give you something to help you heal up. Did you hit your head?"

"No. But...I have a headache. My last doctor...said I had a...concussion a while back. Should I worry...about that?"

"Probably not. But I'll keep you here overnight. We'll see how you are in the morning. Try not to talk too much. I can tell it hurts. Any chance you want to tell me who beat you up?"

"I told you...already..."

"I know, I know. You slipped on the wet floor. I can promise you the warden won't like that answer. I'll try to keep him out of here until tomorrow. Now, swallow these pills and get some rest."

The medicine knocked Chase out. He slept surprisingly well the rest of the day and all through the night.

The next morning, he woke up and carefully moved around. He felt remarkably better. His sides were still sore, but he was breathing much easier. His doctor gave him another dose of his medicine.

Bacon, eggs and toast were brought to him for breakfast. After finishing the delicious meal, he laid back down to rest.

A little while later he heard the door to the infirmary swing open and several footsteps enter. Warden Cochran's deep voice carried through the hallway. Moments later, the warden stood at the end of his bed with muscular guards flanking him on either side.

"How are you feeling this morning, Chase?"

"I'm feeling much better."

"Good. Chase, this is unacceptable behavior. I can't stand the thought of any of my inmates getting beaten up on my watch. I'm going to take care of this unpleasant situation. Discipline is the cornerstone of keeping order here. Now tell me who did this to you."

Chase wanted to say it was Tank who beat him up. He believed the warden cared about him and wanted justice. But he knew he couldn't snitch. It was the code of prison. A stupid code, he thought, but one he had to live by now.

"Thank you for caring about me, but it was an accident. I was mopping and slipped."

"Young man, there's not a soul in this room or in this prison who believes that lie. I do not allow crime to go unpunished in my prison. Now you tell me the name of the person who attacked you."

"Honestly, Warden, I slipped and fell."

Tension filled the room as Warden Cochran stared at Chase. Rage emanated from him. His speech was measured and stern.

"Son, I'm going to ask you one last time. If you do not give me the name of the person who beat you up, you will be receiving their punishment. Do you understand?"

"Yes, sir."

"Good. Now tell me: Who was it that did this to you?"

Chase was silent. He knew his next words would have harsh consequences.

"I fell."

"Guards, get this prisoner to the hole! Seventy-two hours of solitary confinement."

The warden spun on his heels and was gone. Yanking Chase from his bed, the powerful guards practically drug him all the way to another building. Once inside, he was led to a corner room and thrown inside. Landing on the concrete floor hurt his ribs. There was no light and the room smelled like a sewer. The cell was hot and stuffy. Eventually, after laying there for a long time, he began feeling his way around. The only items he found were a metal bucket and a blanket. Both smelled disgusting.

Regardless, Chase had to use the blanket to protect himself from the hard floor. He doubled it up and laid on it. Anger burned inside of him as he began imagining all the different ways he could get even with Tank.

As he laid there in his filthy cell, he eventually drifted off to sleep. Later, he woke up in a panic, forgetting where he was. It didn't bring much relief when he remembered.

Two knocks on the door grabbed Chase's attention. Suddenly light flooded into his pitch-black world as the door was swung open. He threw his hands up to block the sudden bright light from stinging his eyes.

A prison guard stepped in and exchanged his bucket for a fresh one. Another guard sat a bowl down on the floor, just inside of the door. "Here's your meal."

They quickly swung the door closed, extinguishing the light. Chase's whole existence was immersed in darkness.

◀ ◆ ◆ ◆ ▶

The bright sunshine forced Chase to put on his sunglasses as he helped load the vans for the youth trip. He was super excited about leaving for the beach with his church's youth group. After the morning service, they loaded up eight 15-passenger vans and headed their convoy toward Destin Beach. The kids laughed, sang and told stories during the five hour trip. There were eighty-five youth and fifteen adults in their group.

They arrived at their beachside condo and unloaded. It was built for groups of this size and had a large dining area on the ground floor where they could all eat together and gather for meetings. Some kids quickly nicknamed the community room "The Pit."

Nick gave them their room assignments and told them to unpack and meet back at "The Pit" in thirty minutes. The Student Blast Conference would be held in the convention center a short distance away.

Thirty minutes later, everyone was back in the big assembly room. Nick stood up with a microphone.

"Who's glad to be here?"

The kids cheered.

"Great! Listen up to your schedule. Then you can hit the beach for a few hours!"

The kids cheered once again.

"When we dismiss from here, you have free time for three hours. Stay with your assigned team and adult counselor at all times. You can swim in the pool or ocean, play volleyball or ultimate frisbee on the beach, lay out or just chill. Be dressed and ready for worship in here tonight. Our youth band is going to be leading us in worship this evening.

"Beginning tomorrow morning, we'll follow the same routine each day.

Breakfast at eight, and then we'll go to a morning session at the conference center. We'll have free time every afternoon here at the beach. Evening sessions are at 6 p.m. back at the conference center. Each night when we return, we'll break up into our small groups for a discussion time.

"Each of you received a notebook to take notes and journal in this week. I want you to be sure to keep up with your journal and use it. I promise you God will reveal things this week you will want to remember. Bring your Bible and notebook with you when we head over to the Student Blast Conference.

"Don't forget your sunscreen! I don't want you to ruin your week by turning into a lobster."

The kids laughed. Nick prayed and dismissed them to go have fun.

Chase and Andrew's group played beach volleyball, and then skim-boarded in the ocean waves. Heather and Tonya laid out for a while, and then laughed at the guys wiping out trying to skim-board.

Later that evening, the youth group got back together in "The Pit." Heather sang in the band, helping lead the youth group into a special time of worship. Chase went to bed happy that God had allowed him to come on this trip.

The next morning, Chase and Andrew got up a little early to take a run on the beach and do their Bible reading. After breakfast, they headed to the

Student Blast Conference. Chase was amazed when they entered the auditorium. There were over a thousand youth there. Nick led the group to a section where they all sat together.

The worship band came out and led them in some fun songs of praise. A group of actors came out and performed an immaculate skit based on a pirate theme. The "good versus evil" idea was evident, and the performance was incredible. It contained drama, comedy and action. Chase was impressed they could keep the attention of over a thousand students the whole time. The skit had a cliffhanger, so he figured they would see it play out each day. The band returned and led them into a time of deep worship in song. Chase felt the same feeling he had felt the night he was saved.

After the worship band exited the stage, a guy came out and introduced himself as Yancey Irving. He told them stories from the Bible and explained how they could apply the lessons from those stories to their lives. He was very talented at speaking to big groups of kids.

Chase had his notebook out, scribbling as fast as he could. He was glad Nick had given it to him, because he wanted to remember the great things Yancey was sharing.

After the morning session, they headed back to the condo. The afternoon was spent playing on the beach with the kids in their youth group.

The evening session was as good as the morning had been.

After his small group discussion, Chase caught up with Nick.

"Hey Nick. Man this trip has been great!"

"I'm glad you were able to come with us. I can see a lot of the younger guys looking up to you."

"Really? There's a lot of good guys in our group. Is that why you mixed up younger and older guys in each small group?"

"I tried to get two or three leaders in each group. And guys who would hopefully relate to each other. That's why Mitch is in the group with you and Andrew. He's the ninth grade quarterback and relates to you two."

"Nick, you put a lot of thought into this trip. I've heard you say several times that we would hear from God this week. How you are so sure God will show up?"

"Chase, do you remember how I wouldn't allow students to bring their cell phones, iPads or any books other than their Bibles?"

"Yeah. A few of them were upset. I have to admit, it's kind of weird not having my phone with me."

"I know, Chase. I've experienced camps as a student and for several years now as a youth minister. I have seen over and over that when we get away from our routine, spend time in the Bible, sing praises to the Lord and focus on the things of God, He shows up.

"At almost every camp I've been to there's been a time when you knew the Holy Spirit was there. So while I realize kids will get upset at me for asking them to sacrifice their electronics for a week, it's worth it when I see them experience Jesus. And I've seen it so many times, I have come to trust God to reveal himself. In the book of James, it says, 'Draw near to God and He will draw near to you.' I simply trust God to keep his Word.

"I've also learned kids connect to one another when they aren't distracted with their electronics. It only makes sense if you think about it.

"Ironically, we make some of our best connections where there isn't any Wi-Fi."

Chase laughed. "That's funny. And it makes a lot of sense."
"You're growing as a Christian, Chase. You have a lot to learn, but you are doing great. One lesson that is hard no matter how mature you are in your faith is that you can trust God's Word. The sooner you learn that lesson, the better. But it's a lesson you have to keep learning and relearning as you grow."

"I'd like to say I get it, but I think there's a lot more to it than I understand. But I want to get it!"

"And that's enough. If you desire to grow, God will be faithful to answer those prayers."

"Thanks for taking time to teach me these things, Nick."

"It's why I'm here, Chase. Hey, let me run something past you. I'm going to ask if anyone wants to give up their free time at the beach on Wednesday to go do a service project. It wasn't on our agenda, so I'm only taking volunteers instead of making it mandatory. It's a need that was made known to me by a friend today. Would you be interested in going?"

"What kind of service project is it?"

"We're going to be helping a church a few miles away. We will serve food to the needy and afterward help do some painting for them. If we have enough kids volunteer, we'll also work on their playground."

"Man, I'm in! And I guarantee there are several others who will jump on board. What good is learning all this stuff about Jesus if we don't help other people?"

"I was hoping you would feel that way! Let's hit the sack. It's been a great, exhausting, wonderful day!"

"Yes it has!"

Chapter 11

June 21, 2018

Darkness engulfed Chase's entire existence as he laid on the cold concrete floor in solitary confinement, wondering if he would ever get out of this filthy prison cell. His time in here all alone had tested the limits of his sanity. His only interaction with other people had been the short visits from the guards changing his bathroom bucket and leaving him a bowl of stew. Only twice had his stew been warm. They didn't even give him a spoon, so he had to hold the bowl to his mouth with both hands and drink it.

Chase begged the guards to tell him how much longer he had left, but they ignored his questions. They only spoke a sentence or two during each encounter. He began to wonder if he had misunderstood the warden say he had given him a 72-hour sentence. Surely it had been much longer than that already.

Chase spent his time reminiscing about his life; how he had enjoyed playing sports and going to school. Although he hadn't had many girlfriends because he was so focused on sports, he thought about the girls he had dated. He hadn't ever gone all the way, but he had fooled around with some of them. Who would be interested in dating an ex-con now?

His thoughts turned to the future. School was out of the question. He had no desire. He would have to find somewhere to live. Would his dad take him back? Probably not. He didn't want to go back home anyway.

What kind of job could he get? It would probably be something low-level since he didn't graduate. Having been in sports all of his life growing up, he hadn't worked much. Cutting grass and washing cars for some of his neighbors was about all he had ever done. He'd have to figure something out.

Regardless of where his thoughts went, eventually hate and bitterness carried him back to planning revenge on Tank. He became consumed with the desire to hurt him. Maybe even kill him.

As he pondered on how to take out his nemesis in the pitch-black darkness, two quick knocks on the door startled him. He instinctively rolled to face away from the door quickly covering his eyes.

"Chase Barkley, your 72 hours in the hole are up. Come with me."

Chase slowly sat up and then struggled to his feet. Squinting hard to protect his eyes he walked out of "the hole." As his vision adjusted, he could see the guard was leading him back to building no. 3. They arrived and the guard buzzed the door open.

"It's 11:00 now. You'll be going to lunch at your regular time. Warden Cochran said to let you know he's disappointed in your decision. He will remember this in the future. Chase, we don't want any problems out of you from here on out. Keep your nose clean.

"Off the record, you did your time well. The hole can break men in here. You held it together better than most first-timers. Now, get in there with your team."

"Okay...I mean, Yes, sir."

Chase walked inside and toward his bunk. Several comments were made, mostly positive, about him returning from his time in solitary confinement. Micky grabbed Chase's shoulder.

"Kid, you survived! I was worried about you. Word is Tank messed you up bad. And you didn't rat him out. Smart move! Glad you listened to me when I told you about snitching in here."

Several guys were standing within earshot to see if they could hear Chase's side of the story. He knew he had to act the part of a tough guy to keep any credibility.

"Seventy two hours in the Hole was a nice break from this group of losers. And it smelled better in there."

The place busted out in laughter.

Micky said, "Judging from how you smell, they moved the hole to the bottom of an outhouse. Geez kid, you stink. Go hit the shower before lunch."

Another inmate said, "Good job, kid. I figured you for a rat."

"Me? A rat? Nah. But I'll tell you what I am. I'm a dude who gets revenge. And that's a promise."

Several guys hooped and hollered.

Chase headed to the end of the building where the bathroom and showers were located. After a hot shower, he felt like a brand-new man. His ribs were healing up and feeling better, which he was very happy about.

Chase got Micky alone as everyone headed for lunch in the dining hall.

"Micky, I gotta ask you for a favor."

"What is it, Kid?"

"I need to get my hands on a shank."

"A shank? No! That's a bad idea. What you're thinking about is going to take you places you don't want to go."

"Micky, you know I can't let this go. I have to hit him back. I'm not big enough to fight him fair. It's my only play."

"Kid, this is a minimum security prison. It's a country club compared to the big house. If you do this, that's where you'll be headed. And for a much longer stretch then you have now. Let this go and it will blow over."

"I can't. I don't know why, but I can't let it go. So either hook me up with someone who can get me a shank, or watch me get killed by Tank."

"Okay, kid. I'll see what I can do. Let's go eat. It's catfish Friday!"

"It's Friday? What's the date?"

"June 21st. Why?"

"Well Micky, it's my eighteenth birthday. Maybe they'll have a cake in there for me."

"Happy Birthday, kid. Getting out of the hole must have been your birthday wish come true!"

"Best gift I've had in a while. Come on, let's go eat. I'm famished."

The next day during the afternoon break in the yard, Micky came over to Chase.

"When did you start smoking, Kid?"

"I guess today."

Micky laughed and broke into one of his coughing fits. He quickly lit up a cigarette. After a few drags, his coughing stopped.

"Bad habit to start. But you're old enough to make your own decisions. I still can't believe you went into the hole before your eighteenth birthday."

"Guess I'm an overachiever. Any luck on the shank?"

"I got a meeting set up with a guy. He's going to want something big in return for it. And no matter what, you have to stick to the story you made it yourself and never mention his name. Otherwise you're a dead man walking."

"Whatever. Sounds like a deal. When do we meet?"

"Right now. Follow me."

The two men walked around the corner of a building. Micky pointed to a group of black men standing by a storage building.

"Chase, I highly recommend you turn around and leave. When you dance with the devil, you don't get to lead!"

"I'm doing this, Micky."

"Okay, kid. Walk over there and tell them you're Chase Barkley and you want to speak with Lucky."

"I owe you one."

Chase walked over to the group of guys, who slowly surrounded him.

"What do you want, White Bread?"

"I'm Chase Barkley. I'm here to see Lucky."

"Want to see Lucky, huh? Wait here."

The largest of the inmates stepped into the building. After several minutes, Chase began to get nervous. Finally the door opened again.

"He'll see you now."

After being patted down, Chase walked inside. He was shocked to see a skinny white guy wearing glasses sitting behind a desk.

"Chase Barkley, I understand you wanted to see me. By the look on your face, I think you expected someone else?"

"Uh, no. I mean yeah, but it's fine."

"With the black gentlemen outside, I think you were expecting an African-American man, maybe a thug or gang-banger type? Expectations can be a dangerous thing, Chase. In fact, you are here meeting with me today because you have certain expectations, but they are not going to be realized."

"What do you mean? I thought we had a deal?!"

"Young man, exactly what do you have to deal? You have no money, no power, no prestige. You are looking for a handout of an item that you don't know how to use properly and will certainly lead back to me."

"Then why did you agree to meet with me?"

"I like the fact you didn't snitch on Tank, even after the beating he gave you. You handled yourself admirably in the hole as well. Your scarred-up face tells me you have absorbed some pain, but your hands, or should I say un-casted hand, tells me you aren't from the streets.

"You know you need to deal with Tank, or he and his boys will torment you. I can solve your problems without getting you killed in here or sent to death row."

"Why would you help me? Like you said, I have nothing to offer."

"Oh, but my boy, you do. But only if you work with me. You work in the kitchen where there are regular deliveries. If you can handle moving some items from the kitchen to another area for me, I can get Tank and his crew to leave you alone."

Chase thought about his options. Everything inside of him wanted to kill Tank. Lucky was right though. This would allow him to live peacefully until parole.

"OK, Lucky. You got a deal. Get Tank off my case and I'll deliver whatever comes in for you."

"You are a very smart young man. I'll give you the details as you need them. If you are caught, you must never utter my name, or you will have more misery placed upon you than you can imagine. Do I make myself clear?"

"Yeah, we have a deal. I'll make your deliveries, just call me FedEx."

109

Lucky laughed hysterically.

◀ ◆ ◆ ◆ ▶

Emerald green waves crashed against the sandy beach where Chase and Andrew sat. The rest of the group was spread out all along the beach.

"Chase, this has been an incredible week. I feel like I've grown so much as a Christian. It's hard to believe we didn't even go to church a few months ago."

"I know. Isn't it amazing how Jesus has changed our lives? I loved the worship band and Yancey's teaching this week. Nick said we're doing well, although I feel like there's so much more I want to know and learn."

"I'm glad he decided to let us help at the church. It was hard work, but it felt great to be helping them. Honestly, if we had just gone to the camp it would have been a fantastic week. But helping those people made me feel like we were putting into practice the things we were learning."

"I know what you mean, Andrew. When Nick first asked me about going out there and serving, I was excited to go but I wasn't sure if anyone else would want to give up a day at the beach to go serve. How cool was it that our whole group volunteered to go help?"

"After your talk Tuesday night, how could anyone refuse? You had our whole group cheering and yelling, excited to go serve. I felt like it was a halftime speech!"

"Hey, I was excited! And why wouldn't they want to go serve others? It was fun. I enjoyed painting the swing sets and then watching the kids play on them. Did you see their eyes light up when they saw the bright new playground?"

"Especially little Chris. That kid is a pistol!"
Both guys laughed.

"Chase, are you worried about moving off to college?"

"It's going to be a big change. I'm glad we're rooming together. I talked to Nick about some college ministries we can connect with."

"I think it will be good. Just different. I'm glad Tonya and Heather are going to Crossland. I really like Tonya. She's such a breath of fresh air compared to most girls."

"Andrew, remember what Nick told us about dating boundaries and keeping our minds pure? It's tough."

"You got that right! Are you going to ever be more than friends with Heather? You know, now that you can actually talk to her."

"Ha, you're so funny. We need to keep our status as 'friends' for now. She's amazing, but I need to focus on growing into the man God wants me to be. Then maybe I can handle having a girlfriend. You know, all the temptations."

"Chase, you're going to have to keep me accountable to do the right things. The freedom we'll have in college will be even more tempting."

"Yeah Andrew, it will be. But think about how awesome this week has been. If we stay connected to Jesus and help each other, we can continue to grow into the men God created us to be."

Andrew smiled, "I like the sound of that! You ready to go hit the waves? It's our last beach day!"

The guys ran down the beach to the rest of their group playing in the surf.

After supper, Nick caught up with Chase.

"Wanna go for a walk on the beach before our final service starts tonight?"

"Sounds good, Nick."

The guys walked down to where the waves were gently rolling onto the white sand. Birds flew haphazardly up and down the beach. The blazing heat of the day had subsided, and the wind coming off the ocean made it a pleasant afternoon for a walk.

"It's pretty cool your parents and Andrew's have started coming to church."

"Yeah, I never thought I'd see my dad actually excited about going to church."

The guys laughed.

"Nick, do you think God cares about me playing sports? I mean there's a lot more important things in life I could spend my time doing than playing a game."

"I believe Jesus loves you. And since He loves you, he gives you the opportunity to pursue things you enjoy like sports. If those things become more important to you than your relationship with Him, then you have a problem. But I believe Jesus uses things like sports and hobbies to allow us to reach other people with the same interests. So your sports, if kept in perspective, can become a ministry for you."

"Good point. I've never thought about it quite like that. I can actually worship God by doing the things I enjoy. Thanks man!"

"Chase, let me ask you a question now. What's the number one thing you've learned this week?"

"Oh man, there's so many things. Yancey taught us a lot. You shared some great stuff in our small groups. Helping that church taught me the importance of not only knowing about Jesus, but actually putting my faith into practice."

"I'm glad you learned so much, Chase. But if you had to narrow all the worship, the lessons, the serving down to the number one thing God revealed to you this week, what would it be?"

Chase walked quietly, deep in thought for a while. Finally he looked over at Nick.

"If I had to narrow it all down, it would be this: Jesus is worth it. No matter what I have to do to follow Him, He will be worth it. Many kids didn't want to come on this trip, because it was a sacrifice. Even though it was at the beach, they felt like a church trip wasn't worth going on. But I've heard several who decided to come at the last minute say they're glad they did. Turns out, Jesus was worth it.

"At first many in our group didn't want to give up a beach day to go serve at the church. It doesn't make sense to go work when you could play on the beach. But when we were done, everyone was glad they went and served. Jesus was worth it.

"Holding my hand up for the first time during worship wasn't easy. But after I sacrificed my pride and experienced a new, deeper level of worship, I knew Jesus was worth it.

"I know next year I'll have much more freedom and temptation. God has a path for me and if I stick to it, regardless of what I have to give up, I have to remember Jesus is worth it."

"I can't tell you how awesome it is to hear you say that, Chase! Cling to what The Lord has revealed to you this week. There will be ups and downs in your life, but if you hold onto Jesus, you're right, it will be worth it!"

The guys headed back to the condo. After supper, the youth band, including Heather, led worship in "The Pit". Nick shared a few thoughts and then asked if anyone wanted to share with the group about their week. Several students got up to talk about how God had impacted their lives. It was a refreshing time of bragging on the greatness of Jesus. Andrew, Chase and Heather all shared.

After Nick had closed the evening service with prayer, Heather asked Chase if they could talk. After getting permission from Nick, they walked out onto the beach. It was a clear night with a bright moon shining and a canopy of stars twinkling above them. The sound of the waves rhythmically washing up on the shore drowned out all the other noises.

Heather turned to Chase.

"I've enjoyed this week with you."

"Me too. This has been a great week in a lot of ways. There's a part of me that hates having to leave."

"Camps are usually like that. After spending a great week with God it's hard to go back to your routine at home."

"Have all the camps you've gone to been like this?"

"No. God has always been faithful to show up in some way. It's always been in unique ways with each camp. But this week has been the best. You had a lot to do with that."

"What do you mean?"

"Chase, watching you grow and stepping up in our youth group has been wonderful. The talk you gave the other night about going to serve at the church was inspiring. All the guys want to be like you, and all the girls would love to date you."

"Heather, I'm not interested in dating any of them."

"Oh, really? There's lots of cute girls in our group. And next fall there will be plenty of college girls who will be interested in a cute boy like you."

"What are you talking about? I'm only interested in you!"

Chase froze. He hadn't intended on telling Heather he was interested in her, even though he knew it was obvious to anyone watching.

"You're interested in me, Chase?"

"Well, uh, yes...yes I am! I think you are amazing. It's just right now I'm such a new Christian, and I want to become a guy, no, a man, who's good enough for you. You deserve the very best, and until I can be that for you, I don't want to mess up what could be an awesome relationship. I don't..."

Heather suddenly grabbed Chase in a tight hug. She held her head to his chest and began sobbing. Chase stood there holding her, confused. Finally he spoke.

"Did I say something wrong?"

Heather pulled back from him slightly and looked up into his eyes through her tears.

"No, you silly, stupid, wonderful boy."

"I didn't mean to make you cry."

"It's fine. What you said was perfect. Thank you."

She leaned back into Chase. Finally she broke away from him and they walked back to the condo.

Heather was smiling and happy. Chase was still confused, not totally sure of what had just happened. But he was clear about one thing. Holding Heather was amazing.

As they walked back into "The Pit" the lights suddenly came on and everyone yelled, "Surprise!"

Chase was shocked!

Everyone joined in singing Happy Birthday. Heather led Chase up to the front where they were lighting candles on his birthday cake.

It was the best birthday Chase could imagine!

Chapter 12

August 18, 2018

The suffocating humidity wrapped around Chase like a blanket as he pulled the garbage cart out of the kitchen's backdoor into the hot, muggy day. After unloading the trash bags into the dumpster, he took his traditional smoke break. Lighting a cigarette, he thought back about his time here. He found prison life mundane. A very routine existence. Every morning he would eat with his team from building no. 3. After breakfast, his job in the cafeteria consisted of cleaning up the kitchen and doing the dishes with his crew of three other men. Between meals on delivery days, he would stock food and kitchen supplies. More important to him was his side job for Lucky, delivering boxes marked with a red 'X' to the drop spot. He knew it was vital for his safety to do this job well.

After making his deal with Lucky, Chase learned every detail of how the kitchen operated. He knew the other guys on kitchen duty would gladly give up any work they could, so Chase volunteered to unload and sort all the deliveries. Once he had the shipment organized, they simply had to stock the shelves with the already-sorted piles. Chase also volunteered to handle the dreaded garbage duty. He gladly did the majority of the work, and they never questioned his motives.

Chase's system was simple. As he would sort the delivery, he would separate Lucky's specially-marked boxes into their own pile. Later, he would drop Lucky's pile into a trash bag and take it out with the rest of the garbage. After tossing the real trash into the dumpster, he would walk over to a black tarp lying beside a storage building and place Lucky's delivery underneath it. Setting all of this up turned out to be easier than he expected.

As he took a drag off of his cigarette and wiped the sweat from his forehead, Chase recalled how his heart was pounding the day of his first drop. The sorting and loading of the boxes went as planned. After filling the trash cart with bags of garbage, he tossed Lucky's bag in and pulled the big cart out of the back door. Once outside, Chase emptied the real garbage bags into the dumpster. He decided to have a quick smoke before placing his special delivery under the black tarp only a few feet away. As he lit the cigarette, the back door of the kitchen swung open. Tank and one of his guys swaggered out.

"Hey punk. What are you doing out here by yourself?"
Chase prepared for another beating. "Lucky's deal is worthless," he whispered under his breath.

"I'm just taking out the garbage."

"The garbage taking out the garbage. Ha! Good thing you've got some protection. I'd wear you out again otherwise. I'm supposed to let you know we have a truce. So whatever deal you made was worth it. Just don't cross me or my guys. Otherwise, I might be breaking that truce against your already-wrecked face."

"Why don't you get out of here, Tank, before you say something you'll regret?"

"I'll say whatever I want! I got other things to take care of right now. See ya around, punk."

As Tank walked away, Chase was elated. If he hadn't paused to smoke, Tank would have seen him making his drop, which would have ruined everything. And he had avoided taking another beating. Things were finally going his way. He knew he had to be as careful as possible now. All of his plans and safety hinged on successfully making his secret deliveries unnoticed.

Chase thought back over all these events as he stood behind the kitchen finishing his smoke. Since then, Lucky and Chase had developed a great relationship. Lucky began supplying him with cigarettes, as a reward for doing such a good job with the deliveries. The nickname "FedEx" stuck with Chase after his joke about being Lucky's new delivery guy. The name was kept just between the two of them, because Lucky didn't want anyone knowing where he got his contraband.

After Chase finished his smoke, he headed back to his building. Micky caught up with him.

"Hey, kid. How's the world treating you today?"

"Like a king, Micky. Like a king."

"I bet, kid. Hey have you heard about the guy they lined up to come speak for the church service tonight?"

"No. I'm not real interested in hearing about how Jesus can save my soul. Now, if this guy could tell me how to get out of here a little sooner, he might be worth listening to."

"I thought you might be interested in this fella. You told me you liked baseball, right?"

"Yep. Baseball is a great game. I might have had a future in it, if I would have gotten some better breaks. Why?"

"Well this guy, Hayden 'The Hitman' Holmes, is supposed to come talk at the church meeting tonight. Guards say they're meeting in the kitchen to have enough room for everyone."

"'The Hitman' is coming here tonight? That's so cool! He led the league in home runs three years straight. He won two gold gloves playing first base early in his career, but his specialty was the long ball. Man, could he hit."

"Sounds like you know a lot about him."

"Anyone who plays baseball knows about him. He's definitely one of the all-time greats. How did they get him to come talk to a bunch of felons?"

"No idea, Kid. Maybe you can ask him tonight."

"I hate the idea of going to a church service, but I can't pass up a chance to see the 'The Hitman' in person."

Chase got cleaned up quickly so he could be early for the service. Several guys were gathered around his bunk talking about Hayden Holmes's visit tonight. Chase forgot where he was for a little while, as passionate arguments took place over who was the greatest baseball player of all time. Baseball statistics were the ammunition fired back and forth to make their cases.

A little while later, Micky and Chase entered the crowded kitchen to get a seat. Guards were keeping order and controlling the movement around the room. Once seated, the prisoners were not to move. Chase worked his way up as close as possible to the front. A few minutes later, Warden Cochran stepped up to the microphone, his deep voice filling the room.

"Everyone quiet! Thank you. As many of you know, we have a special guest here tonight. He is a man I admire as much for the life he leads in his community as his play on the baseball field. Hayden 'The Hitman' Holmes is a man we should all respect. He overcame racism and poverty to become one of the greatest baseball players in history. We also have another great man here with us this evening. Johnnie 'Red' Brouwer is back tonight. As many of you know, Red comes out here regularly. He'll be playing his guitar and leading us in worship this evening.

"While these men are here, I expect you to be on your best behavior. Absolutely no cursing. Any outburst and you will be removed and punished accordingly. Now, please join me in welcoming Johnnie 'Red' Brouwer and Hayden 'The Hitman' Holmes!"

The two men walked out in front of the crowd, one carrying a guitar and the other a baseball bat. The gathering of inmates hooped and hollered!

"Hello, gentlemen. I'm Red. Let's kick things off with some good 'ol gospel music."

He began playing his guitar and singing "I'll Fly Away." After several other upbeat gospel songs, including "Chainbreaker" by Zach Williams, he stopped and prayed.

Chase hated to admit it, but he enjoyed the music and felt something he hadn't felt in a long time. It was that strange feeling he had experienced at Grace Fellowship Church last spring. It filled him with a mixture of sorrow and anger all at the same time.

After praying, Red welcomed 'The Hitman' to come speak. As he stepped forward, the congregation of inmates began chanting his nickname, just like the crowds at baseball stadiums had always done.

"Hit...Man! Hit...Man! Hit...Man!"

Smiling, he held his hand up for silence and the crowd cheered!

"Thank you for making me feel so welcome tonight."

The crowd cheered again and then settled down. Hayden shared about his days playing baseball and the challenges of rising to the top of his sport. He talked about how he grew better by practicing daily and playing better competition. Finally, he related all of this to following Jesus.

Chase wasn't sure what he was feeling, but his emotions were running high. He didn't give it much thought when he stood up and shouted, "I have a question!"

A guard quickly stepped over to grab Chase, but Hayden said, "It's ok. I'd like to hear the young man's question."

Chase asked, "You're one of the greatest, most successful hitters in history. You dominated college baseball setting records that still stand today. You also held the best slugging percentage in the pros when you retired. It's obvious your natural talent and hard work got you there. Why do you give credit to this fairy-tale Jesus you can't even see?"

The guard grabbed Chase's arm as the crowd instantly began murmuring. Hayden spoke above them, "No. It's fine. That's a very good question."

The guard released Chase's arm, but stood alert, ready to drag him out.

"He's right. I have never actually seen Jesus. I have a question for you, young man. You said I set records in college that are still around today. When I played in college, video wasn't common, and we only played on TV in the championship game. I would guess you never saw me play in person. In fact, I bet you weren't even born during my college days. So, how do you know I even played in college?"

Chase answered, "I mean, it's in the record books. Other people saw you play and recorded the stats."

"So you're trusting the eyewitness of other people, who you have never met and many of whom aren't alive today?"

"Well yeah, I guess so."

"That's exactly what I'm doing by putting my faith in Jesus. I'm trusting people who recorded events and passed them down. Others gathered their testimonies and letters into what we call the Bible. Not only that, but I'm also trusting in a living God who reveals Himself to us today. It sounds foolish to those who aren't saved, but it is the power that I live by. And there is evidence in the way I live that I am changed. And you can be too. By simply repenting of your sin and believing in Jesus as your Lord and Savior."

Chase sat down.

"Thank you, young man, for asking such a great question. I hope I was able to answer your concerns."

Chase couldn't disagree with anything Hayden had said. But instead of the answer drawing him closer to following Jesus, Chase hardened his heart and became even more bitter towards God.

A few minutes later, several men responded to the opportunity to acknowledge Jesus as their Savior, while Chase sat there in anger.

◀ ◆ ◆ ◆ ▶

"One more time! Everyone runs the full one-hundred yards. Fast as you can. This is where winners are made! Go on my whistle!"

At the whistle, Chase ran as hard and fast as his legs would carry him. He crossed the goal line gasping for air with sweat pouring down his face.

His football coach, Coach Maddux, had pushed this football team harder than Chase thought was possible. He was from the state of Texas and, like most Texans, very proud of it. Wearing his cowboy hat, he gathered up his team.

"Huddle up men! I'm proud of how you've practiced! Sam Houston wasn't any prouder of his troops than I am of you! It will show on the field beginning next Saturday. Things will be changing around our campus with the rest of the students arriving this weekend. Stay focused! I don't want any off-the-field issues to keep you from playing next week. I'll see you Monday afternoon at three to begin our first game-week practice!"

The team responded with a powerful roar!

"Bring it in!"

The team gathered in a big huddle, all raising their helmets into the air.

The team captain yelled, "Who are we?!"

A thunderous reply answered, "The Eagles!"

"Will we quit?!"

"Never!"

"Why not?!"

"We are trained! We are tough! We are together!"

The whole team was jumping up and down, and yelling as loudly as they could.

Two quick blasts from Coach Maddux's whistle made the players slowly disperse toward the locker room.

After a shower, Chase and Andrew walked to their dorm.

"I'm glad that's our last practice before game week, Chase. Two-a-days the past couple of weeks has been brutal!"

"I know, but we're in the best shape of our lives. I thought high school football practice was tough. It's nothing compared to this. Are you going to try to catch a nap before we help the girls move in?"

"I'm slamming a protein shake and crashing! Their drop-off time is 3:00, so we have a few hours until they get here."

"Sounds like a great plan to me, Andrew!"

The guys slept a couple of hours and then walked over to the girls' dorm.

On their way over Andrew looked over at Chase. "Can I ask you something?"

"Of course, Andrew. What's up?"

"It's just this whole Christianity thing seems to be so easy for you. You're killing it and I don't feel like I'm doing as good as you are. I still struggle in some areas, and it's really hard for me to understand a lot of things in the Bible."

"Oh man, it's tough to understand tons of stuff in the Bible. And I struggle too, Andrew. I guess I just don't show it."

"Yeah, I guess so. You're just so natural at it. I want it to be more like that for me."

"Andrew, you're doing great, man. Your friendship has helped me stay on track a whole lot of times since I've been saved."

"Really? It doesn't seem like it."

"Remember what Nick told us about Satan using lies to make us feel like we're not good enough. I think that may be what's happening. I'm glad Jesus is allowing us to go through this together. I need you to push me to grow as a Christian, just like you push me on the field."

"Just like the devotional talked about this morning! Iron sharpens iron."

"Exactly, Andrew. You just keep doing your best and trust God to grow you. I'm proud of the man you're becoming."

Andrew was smiling and feeling much better as the guys got to the dormitory.

"Man, there's a lot of people moving in today. I just got a text from Heather. They're almost here."

"I'm glad! It's been over two weeks since I saw Tonya."

"You mean you haven't enjoyed my company as much as hers? I'm a little hurt, bro."

"She's a lot softer and smells much better!"

The guys were laughing as Tonya's family slowly pulled up to the sidewalk through the crowd of kids and parents unloading cars filled with stuff. Heather's family pulled in right behind them.

The guys gave them time to park and begin getting out of the car. Chase walked over to the driver's side door to shake Heather's dad's hand.

"Hey, Mr. Hopkins. It's nice to see you."

"Hello, Chase. Thanks for helping us move Heather into her dorm. Looks like chaos around here."

"I've heard it would be. Hey, Mrs. Hopkins."

"Hello, Chase. Looks like you have survived practicing in this hot weather."

"Yes ma'am. They make sure we stay hydrated. But it has been tough."

Heather stepped around her mom and gave Chase a hug.

"Hey there, stranger."

"Hey, Heather! It's good to see you."

Mr. Hopkins interrupted, "I guess we better start unloading."

Chase broke his gaze from Heather. "Oh, yes sir!"

Heather's mom gave her husband a look and mouthed, "You be nice!"

He rolled his eyes and laughed.

Chase and Andrew carried load after load up to the girls' room. Gathering the last boxes, Andrew looked at Chase.

"Why did they have to get a room on the top floor?"

"I know, man. My legs are on fire. But the elevators are way too slow with so many girls moving in."

"This is the last one for Tonya."

"Yeah, this is it for Heather, too. I think we're going to go eat with Heather's parents when we're done."

"Good deal. We're going out too. I'll catch up with you after we eat."

"Cool. Okay, let's get these last ones up there."

When the guys got the last of the girl's luggage up to their room, they saw both of the girls dads were sitting down in their dorm room. They teased the boys about taking so long to get the last load up. Chase and Andrew looked at one another and laughed. They were too tired to bother with any comebacks.

A little while later, everyone agreed they were ready to go eat. The families said their goodbyes, and Chase rode with the Hopkins to Chili's. They talked about everything from decorating Heather's dorm room to Chase's odds of getting any playing time this fall. They enjoyed their meal, and drove back to the dorm.

When they got out of the car Heather's dad said, "Chase, why don't we go for a walk and you can show me around the campus. The girls can have some privacy and finish unpacking."

"Sounds good, Mr. Hopkins."

The guys started walking while Heather and her mom went into the building.

"Chase, how are you doing up here away from your family?"

"We've been so busy, I really haven't had time to get homesick, yet."

"That's good. I'm sure your family misses you."

"I've talked to them every day. They're coming up for our game next week, even though I probably won't play. Mr. Hopkins, can I ask you a question?"

"Sure, Chase."

Chase took in a deep breath and composed himself.

"With your permission, I'd like to eventually ask Heather to be my girlfriend. I know this is kinda weird, but I feel like I owe you the respect of asking you."

"That is very admirable, Chase. Moving away from home brings a lot of freedom and responsibility with it. Kids are excited, but a lot more vulnerable than they realize. Especially emotionally. Tell me this: what does it mean if you become Heather's boyfriend?"

"I would consider it a deeper relationship where we are still friends, but focus more on getting to know one another. It would also mean not pursuing other people."

"There are a lot of other pretty girls up here."

"None as pretty as Heather. She's beautiful on the outside, but her real beauty comes from deep within her soul. Her love for Jesus and how she cares for other people is amazing."

"Chase, you have my permission to date Heather. I expect you to honor her and protect her. Even if that means you're protecting her from making bad decisions with yourself. Do you understand?"

"Yes sir. Thank you. I know we won't be dating for a while, because we both need to adjust to college life."

"Just take things slow, Chase, and they will fall into place. If you and Heather are meant to be, you'll know it."

Chase and Mr. Hopkins walked back up to Heather's dorm room. The girls were unpacking and laughing together when they arrived.

Heather said, "Tonya just texted. She'll be back in about twenty minutes."

Mr. Hopkins said, "Why don't we pray as a family, and then we'll let Chase head back to his dorm. We should give the room to Tonya's family, so they can have some personal time together before they have to leave."

The four of them grabbed hands, and Mr. Hopkins led them in a heartfelt prayer for God's grace and protection to be upon the students. After they prayed, Chase left to give them a few minutes alone to say their goodbyes. He knew it would be hard on them, but he was excited to have Heather's dad's permission to date her. Now he just had to get Heather to agree.

Later that evening, Chase and Andrew went over to the girl's dorm room. A cheerful girl with red hair checked them in at the front desk at 8:00. She told them curfew was at 11, and they needed to leave before then. They took the elevator up to the fifth floor and knocked on the girls' door.

"Hey guys! Come on in. Thanks for helping us move in today. I know it was a lot of work."

"No problem, Tonya. Andrew needed some extra leg work anyway."

"Whatever dude! My legs are already sore. I dread waking up tomorrow."

After making some popcorn and getting everyone drinks, they started a movie.

"We decided to get that new boxing movie you guys have been wanting to see. Just to say Thank you."

"Aw, you're so sweet, Heather. Chase is so lucky to have you."

"Quit being a wise guy over there, Andrew. Or I'll have Tonya smack ya."

Tonya playfully hit Andrew and everyone laughed. The group was happy to be back together again.

Fifteen minutes into the movie, Tonya whispered, "Heather, Andrew is passed out cold."

"So is Chase!"

"I guess they're exhausted."

"Yeah. They've been hard at it for several weeks now. I think they need to rest."

"We can let them sleep until 10:45 then we have to kick them out."

"Can we, at least, turn off this terrible movie and watch something good?"

Both girls giggled.

Chapter 13

December 15, 2018

"I can't believe you're getting out of here, kid!"

"Yeah, Micky. I'm finally getting out of this rat hole."

"I've got eight more months and I'll be out. Maybe I'll look you up. We can go watch a baseball game together like normal folks."

"I'd like that, Micky. Hey, thanks for taking care of me in here. You taught me a lot. I appreciate it."

"No problem, kid. Now stay out of trouble and go make something of yourself."

A guard stepped into their building.

"Chase Barkley, are you ready to go?"

"Yes, sir! Thanks again for everything, Micky."

"Yeah, kid. Go get 'em."

Chase followed the guard to the main building of the minimum security prison. He was escorted into an office.

"Chase! It's so good to see you."

"Hey Gabriella. Thanks for being here."

"It's my pleasure. We need to review your parole rules once again and get all the documents signed. Have you heard if your parents are picking you up today?"

"I haven't talked to them in several months. I know my mom is heartbroken and my dad hates me."

"Chase, you need to cut them some slack. This is a major life event for them too. I know they still love you."

"I don't. But to answer your question, no, they won't be picking me up today."

"Would you like to ride back to Silver Springs with me? I can drop you off wherever you like."

"Thanks Gabriella. I could use a lift."

"Let's get all this legal stuff taken care of and get you out of here."

Later that day, Gabriella pulled up in front of Chase's house.

"You stay out of trouble and check in with the parole officer at your scheduled times. Chase, you're still very young and have so much potential. Please don't waste your life."

"Thanks for everything, Gabriella. You've been the one person I could count on through all of this mess. I'll do my best not to disappoint you."

Chase got out of the car, and waved goodbye as she drove away. He turned around and faced the house where he grew up. Filled with emotions, he walked up to the front door and knocked. It felt so weird knocking on the door he had thoughtlessly ran in and out of his whole life. He heard movement and the door opened.

"Chase! You're home!"

His mom grabbed him and held him as tight as she could. It felt good to be in his mother's arms. She wept. They stood there holding each other, unconcerned about anything else in the world. Finally, she stepped back and looked at him.

"Oh, honey, your face."

She reached up to touch his scars. He put his hand over it quickly.

"It's okay, Mom. It doesn't hurt."

"I still think you're handsome."

"Thanks, Mom. How are you?"

"It's been hard. Come in. Are you hungry?"

"I could eat."

"I'll make you a sandwich. You have gotten skinny."

"Yeah. Prison food isn't the best."

"Was it hard there?"

"I did okay, Mom. I'm tough."

They talked as Chase ate. Being home again with his mom was the happiest he had been in a long time. They heard the garage door open.

"Just sit right here, Chase. Hey, sweetheart! How was your day?"

Chase's dad walked into the kitchen, "It was....when did he get here?"

Everything inside of Chase instantly changed. Walls flew up and anger crouched, ready to spring.

"Chase got home about an hour ago. We were catching up."

"Telling her all about the grand prison life, huh?"

"I just came by to pick up a couple of things. I don't want to bother you. You smell like a brewery. Careful or you'll get a DWI and end up in prison like your delinquent son!"

"You're one to lecture me! Get your stuff and get out of my house."

Chase got up and went to his old room. He could hear his mom chastising his dad for the way he was acting. When Chase opened his bedroom door, he was shocked. All of his stuff was boxed up and sitting in piles. His bed was stripped, and all of his trophies and pictures had been removed from the walls. His world, his space, his home was gone.

Chase grabbed a duffel bag and backpack. He loaded up some jeans, T-shirts, socks, shoes and underwear. He grabbed his favorite baseball hat, and shoved one picture of himself in his senior baseball uniform into the pocket of his backpack.

Chase took one last look around the room and shut the door. He walked back into the living room, where his parents were bickering and walked over to his mom.

"I love you, Mom. None of this is your fault."

He hugged and kissed her and walked toward the front door.

"No hug or kiss for your old man? Maybe you'd rather slug me. You're pretty good at that!"

"What's happened to you? You're drunk and not acting anything like the man I knew."

"Hate to disappoint you. But I guess you started it. I couldn't be any more disappointed in you!"

"Don't worry, you won't have to see me again. I hate you!"

Chase slammed the door and ran as hard and fast as he could away from his home. Tears streamed down his face. He didn't know where to go. Instinct took over and he began walking across the neighborhood.

A few streets over, Chase walked up to his best friend's house. He needed to see Andrew. Chase knocked on the front door. Andrews's dad opened it.

"Chase Barkley, It's been a while. You look like you've lost fight or two. What do you want?"

Chase could hear the animosity in Andrew's dad's voice.

"I was wondering if Andrew was home?"

"No, Chase. Andrew doesn't live here any longer. After the two of you got arrested, Andrew continued to make bad decisions. We haven't seen him in weeks."

"Oh. I haven't heard from him in a long time either. Do you know where he might be?"

"The last I heard, he was living over in North Ridge. In some apartments off 7th Street. Please don't come by here again."

The door closed in Chase's face. He couldn't believe it. This was the man who used to play catch for hours with him and Andrew. He was like a second dad. And now the second dad who had basically disowned him in less than an hour.

North Ridge was a town four miles north of Chase's hometown. It was poverty-stricken and dangerous. Chase stuck his thumb out as he walked toward North Ridge. About a mile into his walk a guy driving an old beat-up pickup stopped.

"Where you headed?"

"North Ridge, 7th Street."

"Hop in. I'm headed that way."

Chase jumped in the truck. They drove until they crossed the bridge going into North Ridge.

"This is as close to 7th St. as I'm going."

"Thanks for the lift."

Chase got out and started walking again. The further he walked, the worse the neighborhoods got. When he crossed the railroad tracks, he remembered how his parents used to warn him to never go over to North Ridge alone. It was getting late and he needed to find his friend.

Chase finally got to the apartment complex. It was run-down and dirty. He began wandering around the dilapidated buildings, looking for any sign of Andrew. He asked a couple of people if they knew him, without any luck. Chase was crossing the parking lot to try another set of buildings when a loud, rusty Trans Am swung around a corner, almost hitting him!

Chase jumped out of the way and angrily shouted obscenities at the car. It squealed to a stop and sat idling. Chase couldn't see into the car through the blacked out tinted windows. Suddenly the driver's side door swung open, and a guy jumped out running straight at him.

Chase dropped his duffel bag and prepared to fight! He was shocked when he realized it was Andrew!

"Chase! What are you doing here?"

"Andrew, you almost killed me, you punk!"

The guys grabbed each other and laughed. They had really missed one another.

"Andrew, I hope you have somewhere I can crash."

"Dude, I am set up! Grab your stuff and throw it in the car. We have a place in the next building up."

"Who's we?"

"You remember Matt Tyler, the center from our football team? We have a place together. It's a bachelor pad!"

"Honestly, right now I don't care if it's a dump. I just want to get off these streets. I've walked for miles and this is not the best neighborhood to be walking around in at night."

"You look tough with those cool scars!"

"You think so? Thanks. I need to look tough around here."

"It's not so bad. You'll get used to it!"

"Yeah, Andrew. I don't know if that's a good thing or not."

◀ ◆ ◆ ◆ ▶

Chase threw his backpack into his truck and walked over to Andrew's vehicle, where he was loading up the last of his luggage.

"Great semester, dude! I can't believe how fast it went!"

"It was great! I'm happy to be done with finals though!"

"I know! Think about all that's happened, Andrew. You got to play on special teams and got reps at running back in some games. We connected with the college ministry. We both had good semester GPAs."

"You had a 4.0! And you started and won our last three games at quarterback. If you hadn't pulled your hamstring, I think we would have won that last playoff game."

"I hated being injured! But getting to win those games was awesome! We'll be better next season. And amazingly Tonya hasn't dumped you...yet."

"Yet? At least Tonya is my girlfriend! You got permission from Heather's father to date her, and still haven't made anything official!"

The guys both laughed.

"I know it's weird, but you know we agreed we shouldn't focus on a dating relationship right now. We're involved in so many other things."

"It doesn't matter anyway, Chase. When you do hang out socially it's with her. And you're not seeing anyone else, so you're basically dating."

"So why are you so worried about us making it official?"

"Because it's weird, man!"

"Whatever. Awesome semester. You lead and I'll follow you home to Silver Springs. It will be nice to sleep without listening to your snoring for a few weeks!"

The guys drove home and split up when they got to their neighborhood. Chase parked and ran through the front door yelling, "Mom! Dad! I'm home."

Chase's parents came rushing into the living room.

It's so good to have you home!"

"Thanks, Mom."

"Did you have a good drive back?"

"I did, Dad. I followed Andrew. Oh, we're going to the college worship service in Springhill on New Year's Eve!"

"Goodness gracious, Chase! Let's get your bags unpacked before I hear anything else about you leaving again, young man!"

"Yes ma'am. I'll drop my backpack in my room and go get the rest of my stuff out of the truck."

Chase walked down the hall to his room. He opened the door and stared nostalgically at all of his trophies, posters and pictures. Everything was just as he had left it. He didn't realize how much he missed his room until now. He had spent so many years in here growing up.

His dad bumped him from behind. "Move it or lose it, sport. I grabbed your other suitcase. This thing is heavy!"

Chase threw his backpack on his bed and took the luggage from his dad.

"Thanks, Dad. I would have gotten that."

"Hey, I'm not too old to carry in some luggage. Do you feel like a game of catch? We have about an hour before supper."

"Sounds great! Meet you in the backyard in five?"

"See you there."

Chase opened his luggage and tossed some dirty laundry in the hamper. Then he unzipped his backpack and grabbed his baseball glove out of it. Sitting down on his bed, he reached over and picked up a picture from his nightstand. It was him in his senior high school baseball uniform covered in dirt after a game. It was his favorite picture.

He had pitched a shutout and won the game sliding into home plate, just beating the tag. It wasn't pride that made him love that picture. It was the memory of how it felt to bring joy to everyone he cared about. He liked winning, but deep down he loved making his parents proud of him as well.

Chase hopped up and went outside to meet his dad. As he ran out the backdoor, his dad threw him the baseball. He tossed it back, beginning another round of the game they had played since Chase could barely walk. It was during these times Chase felt closest to his dad. Many of life's toughest challenges had been discussed during a game of catch.

"I was starting to wonder if you were coming out?"

His dad tossed the ball back to him.

"I just got caught up in some old memories. It's weird not living here anymore."

"Having some homesickness?"

"No you and Mom coming to my football games helped that a lot. Just coming back brings back a lot of good memories. I'm really lucky to have such great parents."

His dad overly exaggerated, "Yes! Yes you are!"

They both laughed. Chase tossed the ball back to his dad.

"Seriously though, Chase, the greatest joy we can have as parents is seeing you doing well. We're very proud of you."

"Thanks, Dad. I'm glad you and Mom joined Grace Church. Are things still going good there?"

"Yep. Your mom and I love it. Pastor Tad is a great teacher. It's amazing how much we've learned in the past few months. You know we're in a small group meeting over at Heather's house. Andrew's parents recently started attending too."

"How cool! Our college group's parents are all hanging out and studying God's Word together just like we are."

"I got some more news for you. Your mom and I are getting baptized while you're home on break."

"For real? That's awesome!"

"Andrew's parents are too. We're all getting dunked on the same day. Sunday the 23rd. We thought we would surprise you kids."

The ball landed in Chase's glove. "Well, I'm surprised. And I'm proud of you."

A little while later Chase's mom opened the back door, "Supper will be ready in ten minutes!"

His dad put the ball in his glove and walked over to him.

"Chase I have to talk to you about something else."

"Is everything okay, Dad?"

"Yeah. I just need to talk to you about something. Over the past few months, I've realized how out of balance I've been as a husband and father. As the leader of our family, I shouldn't have spent so much of our family time focused on you and sports."

"You've been a great dad."

"I appreciate that, Chase. But your mom and I allowed our relationship to revolve around you. Honestly, if we hadn't gotten into church and figured this out in a healthy way, I'm not sure what would have happened. Raising you became our only priority and we didn't have anything else when you were gone. It's not your fault at all. It's ours. And actually it's a common problem between many parents when kids leave home. But we are dealing with it and are happier than ever."

"That's good to hear. You had me worried there for a minute. Why are you telling me all this, Dad?"

"Chase, you have a certain expectation of what normal family life is, because of how you were raised. I don't want you to make the mistakes I did. They were honest mistakes, but still unhealthy. Remember how upset I got when you didn't get an offer from Shelton? I can't imagine how I would have reacted if it would have been something worse. If you put God first in your life, everything else will be supported on a firm foundation. Pastor Tad taught me that little bit of wisdom. Now, let's get inside before your Mom has to tell us again. Race ya!"

His dad jumped up and they raced to the house, just like they had done so many times before. Once inside, they washed up and sat down at the dinner table.

His dad said, "Okay, I know this is new, but your mom and I pray before we eat now. So let's all bow our heads."

Chase bowed his head and smiled. His dad's simple, thoughtful words warmed his heart. He was proud of his dad.

Around ten that evening, Chase got a text from Nick. Since his parents were getting ready for bed, he agreed to meet him.

They were glad to see each other and caught up over some delicious, late-night Waffle House. The subject rolled around to dating life.

"How are you and Heather doing, Chase?"

"That's something I wanted to talk to you about."

"Okay. What's up with you two?"

"Well, to be honest, I'm real confused. I want to move forward in our relationship, but things are good right now and I don't want to mess them up."

"So you're still officially 'friends,' but you would like to be 'dating?'"

"Yeah, I know it sounds silly, but I don't want to mess it up."

"Chase, I think you've been very wise up until now. You have concentrated on building a healthy relationship with Heather as a person while you have grown in your walk with God. Most kids rush into physical and emotional relationships way too soon that are unhealthy. But it sounds like at this point you're beginning to make decisions based on fear, and not on truth."

"Fear? No. Well...maybe."

"Chase, it's important to be a leader and trust God in your decisions. The Bible says in 2nd Timothy that God doesn't give us a spirit of fear or timidity, but of power and self-discipline. If you pursue Heather with pure motives, I'm sure things will work out exactly the way God wants them to."

"I think you're right. You know, I have 300-lb. linemen trying to crush me when I play football, and that sweet little girl scares me ten times more than they do!"

The guys laughed.

"I'll be praying for you, Chase. You're doing good. Let's get together again soon!"

"You got it, Nick."

Chapter 14

December 24, 2018

"Andrew, I can't believe I have to work at the stupid gas station today. What a lousy way to spend Christmas Eve."

"You're lucky to have a job, Chase. I had to call in some favors to get them to overlook your felony."

"Whatever. It's a crummy job at a gas station in North Ridge. How many employees do they have without a record?"

"I don't know. Who cares? It's not like you have any other plans anyway."

"I know. It just stinks. What are you and Matt doing?"

"Matt's spending the night hanging out with those guys over off 4th Street. They're bad news. He better watch it. My mom asked me to come by. I don't know if I will. My dad acts like such a jerk when I come around anymore."

"I know the feeling. My dad was drunk again the last time I called Mom. He mouthed off during our whole conversation. I'll miss them on Christmas though. It's so weird how quickly life has changed. Andrew, do you ever wish we could go back to last spring and change some of the choices we made?"

"Nope. Because we can't. Anyway, we're doing pretty good. Nobody is around to tell us what to do. Now that you're here and working, the bills are divided by three instead of two, which is great! We'll get ahead on bills soon. Maybe we can go somewhere for spring break. Like to the beach or something."

"Yeah, maybe. I got to get ready for work. I get off at 11 tonight. Are you gonna be around?"

"Probably. You need to get a burner phone so I can text you. They sell those cheap ones at the gas station. I'll leave a note if I go anywhere."

"Trust me, I can't wait to have a phone again. Try to be here. I don't want to spend Christmas alone."

Chase got ready and walked to his new job at the Quick-Mart gas station. It was in a rough area, only a few blocks away. Tonight he was working with a guy named Jake.

A few minutes after 10, the bells on the glass door jingled, as two girls walked in giggling. One of them looked over at Chase and stopped in her tracks.

"Chase Barkley! Is that you?"

Chase was shocked to see Misty Dobbins.

"Hey. What are you doing here?"

"What am I doing here? You get over here and give me a hug! It's been forever since I've seen you!"

Chase stepped around the counter and hugged Misty. "It's been a long time."

"Yes it has. I've heard all kinds of rumors. What really happened to you?"

"Oh, I'm fine. Just had to deal with everything from the night of David's party."

Misty smiled and reached up to touch Chase's face. "I remember that night! You look completely different now. These scars are sexy."

Chase caught her hand and gently pushed her away from touching his scars. Although he hated her pointing out his wounds, he was flattered and happy they weren't a turn-off.

"I've had to get a lot tougher. Life isn't like it was in high school."

"Tell me about it! I'm not in college anymore! I had a little too much fun. Turns out, you have to pass some classes to get to stay there. My parents are being totally unsupportive about it all."

Misty laughed hysterically.

"So what are you going to do?"

"They said I could go to community college this semester, and if I do well there I can go back to a real college. Community college! Can you imagine? How embarrassing."

Chase laughed at how ridiculous she was acting. "Misty, have you been drinking?"

"No! But now that you mention it that's why we're here. This is my cousin, Claire."

Claire was leaning over the counter flirting with Jake. Hearing her name, she looked over and smiled at Chase.

Misty had everyone's attention as she continued, "Claire is 21, but she forgot her ID. You can overlook her forgetfulness can't you, Chase?"

Chase looked at Claire, "It's not up to me. You'll have to convince Jake."

Claire leaned back over the counter and took Jake's hand. "Pretty please, Mr. Jake. I can give you my phone number, and I'll show you my identification later, if that would help."

Jake smiled, "I think we can work something out."

The bells on the gas station door jingled loudly as a man quickly stepped in wearing a black mask and holding a gun!

"GET YOUR HANDS UP!"

Everyone was caught off guard. The girls screamed. Chase stepped back and raised his hands into the air. The gunman turned his attention to Jake behind the counter.

"Open the cash register and put all the money in a sack. Now!"

Jake quickly obeyed and handed him the Quick-Mart plastic bag full of cash and change.

"Good boy. Now get over here with your friends. Everyone on the ground! Facedown!"

The group all laid down on their stomachs. They heard the bells on the door jingle loudly again, and as the man ran out of the store he yelled, "Merry Christmas, you filthy animals!"

Jake quickly jumped up and tossed Chase the keys.

"Lock it up! I'll call 911!"

A few minutes later, the police arrived and interviewed all the witnesses. It was midnight by the time they wrapped everything up.

Misty smiled at Chase. "It's always exciting when we hang out."

Chase smiled, "Yeah, I guess it is. Are you headed home now?"

"I guess so. Where else would I go?"

"I don't know. My place isn't far from here if you wanted to come over."

"Chase Barkley! If I didn't know better I would think you were hitting on me."

"Maybe I am. You interested in dating an ex-con? Your parents may not like it."

"I'm not real concerned with what they like right now. How about me and Claire crash at your place tonight."

"Sounds good. Let me grab something. I'll meet you at the car."

Chase went back inside for a few minutes, then climbed into Claire's car with a Quick-Mart sack. They drove the short distance to Chase's apartment. As they walked inside Misty asked, "What's in the bag?"

Chase pulled out a bottle. "I thought some strawberry wine sounded festive!"

The girls both giggled. Chase walked into the kitchen and found a note from Andrew saying he wouldn't be home until the next day. Chase was happy the girls were there with him. He poured each of them some wine in a Styrofoam cup. They were taking turns telling their version of the nights exciting events.

As Misty was in the middle of her story, Chase interrupted her. "Home Alone!"

"What?"

"He said, 'Merry Christmas, you filthy animals!' That's from the movie Home Alone!"

They all laughed hysterically. The wine was having its desired effect.

"Let's see if we can find a Christmas movie."

Chase turned on the TV. "Looks like It's a Wonderful Life is on."

Claire sat in the recliner. "I love this movie."

Misty turned off the light and grabbed a blanket off the back of the couch. She kicked her shoes off and laid down. She patted the couch beside her, inviting Chase over. They snuggled up close together.

Chase held Misty as they watched the movie. They laughed when they heard Claire begin lightly snoring. Misty turned toward Chase. His smile faded as he looked deep into her eyes. Their mouths met in a passionate kiss.

Later that night, Chase laid on the couch holding Misty who had fallen asleep. He reminisced about this strange day. Surviving an armed robbery and ending up with Misty was an unbelievable end to an otherwise mundane Christmas Eve. He was glad she was here, mostly because he didn't want to be alone. He didn't know what would happen in the days to come, but for tonight he was happy.

◀ ◆ ◆ ◆ ▶

"Dad, I can't believe it's already Christmas Eve! This semester break is flying by."

"Holiday breaks are like weekends, Chase. They always go by way too fast!"

"I'm proud of you and Mom getting baptized yesterday. And Andrew's parents too. What an awesome service!"

"It was a great day."

"That was funny when Andrew's dad came up out of the water, and yelled so loud! I think it caught Pastor Tad by surprise."

"I think it caught everyone by surprise. He is so happy and excited about following Jesus. So what are your plans tonight, Chase?"

"I'm going to eat supper at Andrew's, and meet you at the 9:00 Christmas Eve service. I'll try to get there early so we can visit with everyone before it begins. I'll plan on coming home afterward, and we can open presents in the morning!"

"Great! We'll meet you at the church."

Chase got dressed and went to Andrew's. They talked to Andrew's parents about the previous day's baptism service while they ate supper.

The boys arrived at Grace Fellowship Church at 8:30. As they walked toward the front door, a man in a policeman's uniform approached Chase.

"Excuse me, young man."

"Yes, sir?" replied Chase.

"I don't know if you remember me or not. My name is Harrison Majors. I believe I pulled you over earlier this year."

"Yes! Officer Majors. I remember you pulled me over for running a stop sign. But you let me off with a warning."

"That's right. We talked about you playing in the state baseball playoffs."

"Yeah. That didn't turn out so good."

"I was there! You pitched a good game. When I pulled you over that day, you invited me to visit church here at Grace. I didn't really consider it at the time. But a few days later, my temper got the best of me, and I almost made some really bad decisions. I realized I had anger issues and needed help. I remembered you talking about this church, so I came and visited with Pastor Tad. Long story short, I got the help I needed and I'm a new man because of it. Now there are several other officers who also attend here, because of you inviting me that day. Thank you for being bold. It really made a difference!"

"Wow! That's a God thing! I had no idea what a difference simply inviting you to church could make. I just wanted to share Jesus with everyone I could!"

"I'm happy you did. It's good to see you. I'll let you get inside."

"Thank you, Officer Majors!"

"It's Harrison. And Merry Christmas!"

Chase and Andrew walked into Grace Fellowship Church together. Nick was standing there welcoming guests.

"I remember you two walking in here together like this about seven months ago on a Wednesday night. A lot has changed since then."

Chase gave him a hug. "A whole lot has changed!"

Andrew hugged Nick as well, and the guys talked for a while.

A few minutes later Heather, Tonya and their families entered the beautifully-decorated church foyer.

When Chase and Andrew's parents arrived, everyone greeted one another and then made their way into the sanctuary to get seated. Ushers handed each person a candle as they entered.

A string orchestra softly played "Silent Night" as Chase's eyes adjusted to the dimly-lit room. The fragrance of pine trees filled the air. The little green freshly-cut trees stood at attention along the back of the stage, dressed in white lights and tinsel.

Several young children wearing their pajamas sat with their parents throughout the church; an air of excited anticipation flowing from their young souls filled the sanctuary. A short time later, a couple walked onto the stage and began reading the Christmas story from the Bible. The church choir followed the story of the nativity singing several Christmas songs accompanied by the string orchestra. It was a beautiful time of worship.

Following the worship in song, Pastor Tad took his place before the gathering of families, loved ones and friends.

"When I was 12 years old, a few weeks before Christmas, my father lost his job. My parents, being very wise, made plans for us to go serve the poor at a shelter on Christmas Eve. They knew by having us serve others, we would see how blessed we were, even though presents for us would be few that year.

"After our family had served food for a couple of hours, we sat down and ate with the very people we were there to serve. We had the most pleasant evening laughing and talking with one another and the people there. The Lord revealed to me that night what was truly valuable in this life.

"I discovered on that Christmas Eve my love for serving people, which eventually became my purpose in life.

"Tonight, I pray you know and believe in the love of Jesus. He gave up heaven to be born of a virgin in a dirty stable, because of His love for you. He is the light of the world, and darkness will never overcome the light. As I share the light from my candle, the light grows, and the darkness diminishes."

Pastor Tad lit his candle by the large one up on the stage. He then stepped over and lit other people's candles. As more and more candles were lit, the church became much brighter. They began singing, "Joy to the World."

In the lobby after the service Andrew rushed up to Chase. "Man, I need to run out to the CVS store over in North Ridge."

"Now? It's Christmas Eve. No way."

"Chase, it won't take 30 minutes and they have this hair thing my mom really wants. Everyone has been sold out, but I just got a text saying the CVS store in North Ridge just got a shipment. If we go now, we can make it before they close at 11."

Chase and Andrew quickly told everyone bye and took off. As they crossed the bridge going into North Ridge, Chase realized he needed gas. They pulled into a gas station a few minutes after 10.

Chase filled up and went in alone to pay. As he was standing at the counter, he heard a familiar voice. "Chase Barkley! Is that you?"

"Misty? Wow girl, it's been a while. How are you?"

"I'm great! This is my cousin, Claire."

"Hey Claire, Nice to meet you. How is college going, Misty? Enjoying your Christmas break?"

"Yeah. I'm not sure if I'm going back to school. I might do something else."

Chase could tell Misty was hiding something.

"Misty, college is tough for everyone. Don't worry if you're struggling. It will all work out."

She could tell Chase really cared. "Thanks, Chase. You've always been so sweet."

The bells on the door jingled loudly as a man in a black mask with a gun stepped inside.

"EVERYBODY GET YOUR HANDS UP!"

Chase stepped up and pushed the screaming girls behind him. The robber pointed the gun at Chase's face, "Don't be a hero! Get your hands up! NOW!"

About an hour later, Chase was telling his story to the police and his parents.

"...then the guy made us all lay down on our stomachs. He made Jake, the cashier, fill up a plastic sack with the money from the register. Then he swung the door open and yelled, 'Merry Christmas, you filthy animals!' I've heard that before. Wait! ...Home Alone! That's where I've heard it."

The policeman laughed.

Andrew had been in the car on his phone and almost missed the entire event. He had looked up just in time to see the burglar running out of the store.

Everyone was happy the boys were safe.

When Chase got home, Heather was there waiting for him. She ran up and threw herself into his arms.

"What in the world were you doing in North Ridge this time of night? And on Christmas Eve?"

"Let's get inside and I'll tell you the whole story."

They went inside and Chase's parents went to bed. After telling Heather his story, it was well after midnight. He walked her to the door. Chase pointed up. "Look. Mistletoe."

Heather turned and put her arms around his neck. "Chase Barkley, you are one sneaky boy."

Chase smiled. "Heather, tonight when that guy pointed his gun at my face, all I could think about was how much I love you."

Chase slowly leaned in to Heather. Their lips finally met for the first time in a long, passionate, loving kiss. Finally, Chase pulled away.

"Heather, will you be my girlfriend?"

Heather looked Chase in the eyes and stated, "I already am."

Chase had never felt more attracted to this confident, beautiful, amazing girl.

As Chase laid down in bed, he said a prayer thanking Jesus for His protection and for Heather.

This Christmas was much different than any he had ever experienced. He was thankful he had survived the life-threatening robbery and thrilled to have finally kissed Heather. Oh what a kiss to remember. He didn't know what would happen in the days to come, but for tonight he was happy.

Chapter 15

December 31, 2018

Chase took a long drag off of his cigarette. Seconds later, he released a huge cloud of smoke and exclaimed, "We're gonna totally rock out tonight! New Year's Eve, Andrew. I'm ready to party!"

"Me too! When are Misty and Claire coming over?"

"They said around eight. We can hang out a little while, and then walk down to the river and watch the fireworks. I think a band is playing down there somewhere."

"I can't believe you're seeing Misty. I still think she's crazy. But I do like her cousin Claire. Maybe the psycho gene only runs on Misty's side."

"Quit talking bad about Misty. We've had a good time this past week. She's cool."

"Chase, you've enjoyed making out with her the past week. I get it. Just don't get serious with her. I'm telling you, you'll regret it."

"Whatever. Hopefully I'll close the deal with her tonight. Anyway, I'm a grown man. And I'm a free man. I can do whatever I want."

"Tell that to your parole officer."

Chase jumped up and grabbed Andrew, tackling him to the ground. They rolled around on the floor wrestling. Chase finally flipped Andrew over and pinned him. Chase laughed.

"Say Misty isn't crazy."

"Come on, man. Let me up."

"Say it."

"Okay, okay. Misty is only a little crazy."

Chase pushed Andrew harder into the floor. "Not good enough, Andrew."

"Okay! Okay! She's not crazy."

Chase released Andrew. They got up laughing, trying to catch their breath.

"Alright, man. You date her all you want. But don't come crying to me when she goes loco on you."

"Deal. Let's clean this place up before they get here. We've got ladies to impress!"

They spent the afternoon picking up their apartment and watching sports. Around seven, they got cleaned up and ready to go out. The guys put on their favorite shirts and jeans, and way too much Axe cologne. There was a knock on the door at 9:00.

Andrew opened it and Misty entered the apartment singing out, "Hey guys!"

Claire walked in right behind her. She hugged Andrew. Chase didn't get up from watching his football game.

Misty walked over and stood in front of the TV.

"What are you doing? I have money on this game."

"I'm more important than your football game, right?"

Chase stood up and grabbed Misty. He swung her around and gave her a big kiss. She laughed hysterically.

"Of course you are. Why are you so late?"

The girls looked at each other and burst out laughing.

Andrew asked, "Did I miss something? Because that was a question, not a joke."

Misty squealed, "Show them, Claire! We're gonna party tonight, boys."

Claire pulled two bottles of tequila out of her purse. Misty squealed again. Andrew smiled. "Cool. Where did you score those goodies?"

Misty proudly answered, "We snuck them out of Claire's mom's house! My aunt has ton of liquor. She'll never miss it!"

Claire added, "It's true. She'll just think she drank it and go buy some more. So, are you thirsty, Andrew?"

"Yes, yes I am. I say we have some drinks and then head down to the river about 11. We can take some blankets and get a good spot down there. What's up with the game, Chase?"

Chase was gripping the back of the recliner, focused on the TV. Without looking away he answered, "Bulldogs are attempting a 48-yard field goal. If they make it, I lose. Miss it, and I win a 100 bucks."

Andrew grabbed the remote control and turned up the volume. Now everyone was focused on the game. They anxiously watched and listened to the announcers.

"Here comes the snap. It's a good hold. The kick looks long enough. And it's...WIDE RIGHT! WIDE RIGHT! He missed it..."

The kids were jumping up and down, screaming and hugging each other. Chase pumped his fist, yelling and celebrating.

"Set up the drinks, Claire! I'm ready to party!" shouted Chase.

Each teenager took their turn drinking a shot of the potent alcohol. They laughed at the faces each other made as the liquid burned their throats.

After her second shot, Misty grabbed the remote control and turned over to a New Year's Eve countdown show. They had a popular boy band performing. She turned the TV up as loud as it would go. Andrew rushed over and yanked the remote from her, quickly turning it back down.

"Hey, psycho! We have to live here. I'd rather not have everyone hate us!"

"Shut up, Andrew! It's New Year's Eve! Everyone living in this dump is either high or out partying."

Chase stepped between them. "Calm down! Both of you. Let's get ready and go watch the fireworks."

Claire said, "I don't know, Chase. These are pretty good fireworks right here."

There was dead silence. Then they all busted out laughing together.

Misty insisted everyone take another shot before they left. Chase and Andrew grabbed a blanket and they began the short walk down to the river. They laughed and joked about each other's struggle to walk straight.

There were already several groups of people gathered all around the park. Misty picked an empty spot for them and they spread out their blankets. The band was playing and the group enjoyed listening to them while waiting for the fireworks.

A single white streak of light shot into the sky at 11:40. It sounded like a bomb going off when it exploded. Everyone cheered as the sky lit up with blasts of bright colors streaking and cascading all around. Everyone would "ooh" and "ahh" at particularly impressive explosions. There was a big finale, lighting up the night sky just before midnight.

The excited crowd cheered and clapped loudly as the sky once again became silent. A member of the band announced over the PA system it was almost midnight, and then began a count-down.

"Fifteen seconds to New Year's....ten, nine, eight..."

The crowd loudly counted down to the new year in unison. Andrew had his arm around Claire. Chase was holding Misty. "Three, Two, One! Happy New Year!"

The guys kissed their girls as the band began playing "Auld Lang Syne." The joyous crowd of people joined in singing and celebrating. A short time later, the group began making their way back to the apartment. Misty stumbled and ran into a parked Honda Civic. The car alarm blared and the lights started flashing.

Chase grabbed Misty's hand and they stumbled as fast as they could away from the noisy alarm. As they turned a corner Misty stumbled into a couple coming toward them on the sidewalk.

The guy barked, "Watch out, you stupid drunk."

Chase was immediately infuriated, "Don't call my girlfriend stupid, punk!"

As the guy stepped up to reply, Chase punched him with a left hook. The guy collapsed to the ground and Chase began kicking him and shouting obscenities at him. Misty and the guy's girlfriend were trying to pull him off of the now unconscious young man.

Finally, Chase realized what he was doing and stopped. He grabbed Misty's hand and they ran.

Arriving back at the apartment, they were laughing about the night's excitement. Once inside, Misty insisted everyone have another shot. A few minutes later, Andrew and Claire disappeared into Matt's room. He was staying with some friends for the holiday. Chase and Misty went to the other bedroom.

Chase sat beside Misty on his bed. "I'm glad you're here tonight. You look amazing."

Slurring her words, Misty replied, "Thank you. I heard you tell that rude loser that I'm your girlfriend. Then you defended my honor. I'm all yours tonight, Chase Barkley."

They began to kiss. Suddenly, Misty pulled away from him. Wide-eyed she jumped up off the bed, took two steps toward the door and began throwing up everywhere. The sight and smell hit Chase, causing him to gag, fighting the urge to throw up himself. He spent the next hour cleaning up Misty and his carpet.

◀ ♦ ♦ ♦ ▶

Chase stepped up to the free throw line on this sunny but chilly last day of the year.

"We've both got an S. Next one to get a letter loses. Free throw, backboard."

He shot the ball with a high arc and it bounced off the backboard, swishing back through the net.

Chase smiled and passed the ball to Andrew.

Andrew focused on the basket and began his shooting motion. Chase interrupted.

"Andrew! Wait!"

Andrew stopped suddenly. "What?"

"You know what makes this shot so hard, Andrew? It's because you practice free throws all the time. Having to adjust to hitting the backboard gets you mentally off your game. It scrambles all your muscle memory."

"Quit trying to get inside my head, Chase. I know what you're doing. I do it to batters all the time when I'm catching."

Chase laughed. Andrew lined up and took his shot. The basketball went high into the air, coming down short of the backboard, hitting the back of the rim. It bounced high and away from the goal.

"That would be HORSE for you, Andrew! You didn't even hit the backboard."

"Whatever. You cheated with all that talking. I'll get you next time. So, on a different note, what are you and Heather's plans again? I can't believe you're not riding to Springhill with everyone."

"We signed up to serve at the Helping Hands New Year's Eve supper downtown. They were short on volunteers. We'll miss riding over with everyone and eating at the hibachi grill before the show. It starts at 9:00 and we should be there by 10:00, so we'll miss the first hour. We're good with that though. It will still be a great show."

"Helping Hands. Isn't that the place where Heather's family volunteers? They help a lot of people downtown, don't they?"

"Oh yeah. They have a Sunday meal each week, give out boxes of food, assist people getting their GEDs, help them find jobs and all kinds of other stuff. Several nights during the week they'll have a worship service or class to benefit the downtown community. The guy who runs it is awesome. I'm excited to serve there, and then meet up with everyone in Springhill. It should be a great night!"

Andrew slapped hands with Chase, "See you two tonight around 10 then. Be careful."

"See you at the concert."

Later that afternoon, Chase picked Heather up and they went to Helping Hands. They enjoyed serving and eating supper with the people there. After eating, they told Heather's parents bye and hopped into his truck to drive to Springhill.

About two hours into the three hour trip, Chase felt his steering wheel suddenly begin jerking. He gripped it tighter, slowed down and guided his

154

truck off the road. Getting out he found his front passenger side tire blown out. It took him about twenty minutes to change the flat and get back on the road toward Springhill.

"Well, Heather, we're going to get there a little later than we planned."

"It's fine. I'm just glad I have an athletic boyfriend who can change flat tires."

"Boyfriend. I like how that sounds coming from my...girlfriend."

Heather laughed at how cheesy they were acting when suddenly the truck began violently jerking again. Slowing down and pulling onto the shoulder, Chase got out and walked around the vehicle. Heather rolled down her window.

"What's wrong now?"

"You're not going to believe this. My spare went flat. And I have no cell service. This isn't good."

"What should we do, Chase?"

"Midland isn't far. About a mile or so. I guess we can walk up there and find a phone. Or you could wait here on this dark, creepy highway all alone. Your choice."

"Dark, creepy road alone or stay with my big, strong boyfriend to protect me? I'm coming with you!"

Chase grabbed a flashlight out of his glove compartment and locked up his truck. He and Heather bundled up and held hands as they walked toward Midland in the chilly weather. She started singing and he joined in as they walked beneath the brightly-shining moon and stars.

As they neared the town, they could see a business on each side of the road with their lights on. An Exxon gas station was lit up on the left side of the road, while a diner had a neon sign flashing "Open 24/7" in its window across the street.

"I still don't have a signal, Chase."

"Me either. So gas or diner?"

"Oh, let's go to the diner. I could use something hot to warm me up."

As they walked across the parking lot, Chase's phone rang.

"Looks like I finally have a signal. Hello?"

"Chase, it's Andrew. How close are you? We have an intermission, so I thought I'd check on you. Figured you would be here by now."

"We had two blow-outs and a long walk to Midland. We're fine, but we're not going to make it to Springhill."

"Two blow-outs? That's bad luck, dude. Want me to come get you?"

"No. That's okay. I'll call my dad. You have fun and tell everyone 'Happy New Year' from me and Heather. And I appreciate you offering to leave and come get us."

"Okay, if you're sure. I'll have my phone on if your dad can't make it for some reason."

"Cool. Later." Chase hung-up.

He immediately dialed his dad and explained the situation.

"Mom and Dad are on their way. Looks like it will be a little after midnight before they will be able to get here."

"Good, we'll have our own little New Year's Eve celebration in Midland!"

The diner was empty except for one lone customer sitting at the counter and a waitress behind the bar. Red and green Christmas lights were still hanging from the ceiling around the place, and a Top 40 country music year-in-review countdown played in the background.

They grabbed a booth and ordered. Enjoying their time together laughing and talking, they didn't notice the old man get up from the counter and walk over to them.

"Excuse me. I don't mean to interrupt. I just wanted to tell you it's wonderful to see two young people who are obviously so in love. Enjoy every minute of it."

Chase answered, "Thank you. Happy New Year."

"It's been a little over four years since I've had a Happy New Year. But thank you."

Heather said, "I'm sorry to hear that. Would you like to join us?"

"No, I don't want to ruin your night."

"We're just waiting for Chase's parents to come pick us up. We had some car trouble. Please, have a seat."

The old man slowly scooted into the booth across from Chase and Heather.

"I'm Harold. I was wondering why two young kids like you would be spending the holiday in this little town."

"Nice to meet you, Harold. We're suckers for a good greasy cheeseburger and fries. If you don't mind me asking, why has it been four years since you've had a good new year?"

Harold looked down at his hands crossed on the table. He paused long enough for Chase to wonder if he should have asked the question. Finally he answered, "Just after Christmas four years ago, my Gene passed away from cancer. We were married 56 years. She was my everything. We had three kids. All of them have moved away to bigger cities where there are better jobs. I understand why they left. They stay in touch, but life is empty without my Gene. She was an amazing woman."

Heather had tears in her eyes. "I'm so sorry. She sounds like a wonderful person. What was she like?"

Harold spent the next 30 minutes sharing all about him and his late wife's life together. How he and Gene got married just before he went to basic training in the Army. How they struggled at times and thrived during others. He laughed a lot and shed some tears.

Chase and Heather listened and enjoyed his stories.

"Thank you kids for listening to an old man's rambling. It's a quarter 'til midnight. I'm going to drive up to the church cemetery and visit my Gene. Happy New Year!"

"Happy New Year, Harold."

The waitress stepped out from behind the counter and made her way over to the booth, taking Harold's place.

"I'm Hope. I haven't seen him smile since Gene's death, until tonight. You two are something special."

"Nice to meet you. I'm Heather and this is Chase. I think sometimes people just need someone to listen and care about them."

"Trust me, honey, I know people. And you two have a gift or something."

"We simply try to love people like Jesus would love them."

"Love them like Jesus. Why?"

Heather spent the next few minutes explaining the gospel of Jesus. How anyone who repents of their sins, confesses with their mouth that Jesus is Lord and believes in their heart God raised Him from the dead will be saved.

Hope asked, "So I can be saved? Even though I have a baby, and I'm not married?"

"Yes! All you have to do is admit you are a sinner. The Bible says every single person has sinned. Repent of your sin, which means turning away from sin and following the way of Jesus. Believe God raised Jesus from the dead to forgive you of your sins, and acknowledge Jesus as Lord. If you believe Jesus is Lord and He wants the best for you, then you'll want to follow Him. You can learn how to do that by reading the Bible. You can talk to God, and you'll grow and change to become more like Jesus. His love is amazing!"

"I want to! I know I've made lots of bad decisions, and I want the forgiveness you said Jesus will give me. Will you help me?"

Heather lovingly reached across the table and took Hope's hands into her own. As the clock struck midnight, a new year and a new life began.

Chapter 16

May 30, 2019

"Mr. Barkley, could you join me in the office."

"Sure thing."

Chase followed his boss Howard Nettles into the gas station office. The cramped area contained only a small desk covered in papers and receipts, a night deposit vault and a couple of chairs. Chase sat down in the dingy chair beside the desk where his boss was sitting.

"What's up, Mr. Nettles?"

"Mr. Barkley, first I want to say how much I appreciate you regularly picking up extra shifts. Being a team player is important, both to me and to your coworkers."

"Thank you."

"Unfortunately, I have some other issues we need to discuss. Last Saturday when you got off at 3 p.m., the cracker section didn't get stocked before you left. I'm going to have to write you up for that, and..."

"You're getting onto me because the crackers didn't get stocked?"

"Correct. Also, the trash didn't get pulled behind the register. As you know..."

"Are you kidding me?! I worked a double Friday night through Saturday afternoon! Jake called in and I had to cover overnight for him. It was crazy busy and I barely had time to go to the bathroom! And you're gripping about some stupid crackers not getting put out on the shelf!"

"Mr. Barkley, you need to calm down. There is a simple checklist of things that need to be done before you leave, and..."

Chase was furious.

"I've worked doubles without complaining! I take up the slack for everyone around here! I earn minimum wage, and you're writing me up for not getting some crackers put out! I'm done! I QUIT!"

Chase jumped up, raring his fist back. Howard Nettles quickly ducked and covered his head to protect himself. Chase paused and then powerfully swung his arm across the piles of papers on the desk. They flew everywhere, floating in the air slowly to the floor, as he stormed out of the office.

The last thing Chase heard as he exited the gas station was Howard Nettles yelling, "Don't ever come back here again, or I will call the police!"

Chase began to run. His anger fueled him as he sprinted as hard and as fast as he could. Several blocks later, his body gave out but his anger remained. He made his way back to his apartment.

As he walked across the parking lot, he noticed Kattie Anne standing outside smoking. She lived in the complex next to his. They had talked a couple of times.

"Hey, Chase. What are you up to?"

"Nothing. Just getting some fresh air."

Kattie Anne blew a big cloud of smoke and said, "Yeah, me too."

They both laughed at her joke.

"Can I bum a smoke?"

"Sure, honey. Are you not working today?"

"I think I'm going to get a new job. My financial consultants have informed me the gas station doesn't offer the retirement plan I desire."

Kattie Anne laughed. "I had no idea. I figured it was a lucrative career."

"Stealing cigarettes was about the only benefit I ever received. If I really wanted a lucrative career, I would get back into baseball. You know I was on track to get into the big leagues before I hurt my hand."

"Really? A professional baseball player. That's pretty cool."

"It would have been awesome. But I'll still be successful. Nothing can stop me!"

"I like your confidence, Chase."

He moved in closer to Kattie Anne as they continued to talk and laugh. With all the fighting between him and Misty the previous months, it was refreshing to have a civil conversation with a girl.

160

She invited Chase to come inside with her. Flirting led to kissing, and it escalated quickly from there. The fighting with Misty, the recent loss of his job and all of his frustrations about life were replaced by the passion of the moment.

Later that afternoon, Chase was finishing up the spaghetti for his date with Misty. He had some roses on the table, which he bought more out of guilt than affection for her.

Misty arrived and gave Chase a big hug.

"Dinner smells wonderful! How's my sexy guy?"

"I'm good. Things went bad at work today, though."

"Oh no, what happened?"

"Old Man Nettles got on me pretty hard. He was being a real jerk. I was tired of working there anyway, so I quit."

"You quit? What are you going to do now?"

"I don't know. I'll find something. I don't really feel like talking about it. Are you ready to eat?"

"Yes. I'm famished. Oh, you got me flowers!"

Misty ran over to the table and opened the card. She held the flowers up to her nose and inhaled their beautiful aroma.

"Well, aren't you Mr. Romantic this evening?"

Chase smiled and walked over to her and bent down to give her a kiss. Misty put her hand up to his chest as he leaned in. She inspected his neck intently.

"What's on your neck?"

Chase jerked his hand up, covering where she was looking.

"I don't know. Maybe I cut myself shaving."

"No, I'm pretty sure that's a hickey on your neck!"

Chase's mind raced. How could he get out of this one? Maybe it wasn't so bad. He and Misty fought all the time anyway. This could be a good time to end it with her.

"I don't know what to say, Misty."

"You don't know what to say?! I paid your rent last month! I stole from my parents to give you money to live on, because you work at a gas station. A job you're not even smart enough to keep!"

"Whatever, Misty."

"WHATEVER?! Why you..."

Misty began attacking Chase. Screaming obscenities as she slapped and kicked him wildly, until he grabbed her and tossed her onto the couch.

"Calm down!"

Misty was crying. Chase knew it would be a tough break-up, but the hardest part seemed to be over. Misty finally regained her composure and stopped crying.

"Okay, Chase. I'm calm now like you told me to be. I'll need you to remain calm as well when the police arrive."

"Police?! What are you talking about?"

"Domestic abuse, Chase. I mean, you can't go throwing a girl around like that without consequences."

"You were slapping me and going crazy!"

"Tell it to the judge. Maybe he won't revoke your parole. But we both know he will."

Chase didn't know what to do. How had he allowed Misty to have this much power over him? He couldn't go back to jail!

"Misty, you know you don't want to call the police. We just had a little fight. You know I only care about you."

"That's a bit hard to believe, Mr. Cheater!"

"I didn't cheat on you! A girl was hitting on me. I did have a moment of weakness, but it's not because I wanted to cheat on you. It's because I care so much about you."

"What? That doesn't even make sense."

"Misty, I love you with all my heart. I realized today how much you mean to me, when I turned that other girl down."

"Really?"

"Yes, silly. She threw herself at me, but all I could think about was you. That's why I made your favorite meal and bought you these flowers. I wanted tonight to be perfect."

"Why would you want tonight to be perfect?"

"Because Misty, I want to ask you to marry me. Make my dreams come true, baby. Please say yes. Be my wife."

"Oh, Chase! Yes, Yes, Yes! I love you too. We're going to be so happy together."

She jumped up and rushed into Chase's arms. They embraced. As he held her, the relief of avoiding returning to jail washed over him. His relief was quickly replaced with regret, wondering how in the world he had ever ended up engaged to Misty Dobbins.

◄ ♦ ♦ ♦ ►

"Chase, can I see you in the office?"

"Yes, sir!"

Chase followed his college baseball coach Jimmy Hill into the small office in the baseball complex in Cary, North Carolina. The Crossland Eagles baseball team had won its conference and advanced through the 48-team NCAA Division 2 tournament to today's final championship game. They were preparing to play against the reigning national champion, the University of South Columbia Pirates.

"Chase, how are you feeling?"

"Good, Coach."

"This moment isn't going to be too big for you is it? You've pitched well all year. We're going to need you today."

"I feel like you have prepared me for this opportunity. I'm ready!"

"Great. The plan is to start Lopez. He will hopefully be able to get us through the fifth or sixth inning. If that happens, we'll bring you in for an inning or two, depending on the situation. You just get out there, relax and get us some outs. These guys are great batters, so if they get a hit or two, don't let it shake you. Collins will hopefully close it out in the ninth for us. Chase, I'm proud of how you have played this year. Let's finish strong."

"Yes, sir!"

Chase went back into the locker room. Andrew sat down beside him as they made their final preparations.

"Coach talk to you yet, Chase?"

"Yeah, just got done. How about you?"

"Yep. Told me to be ready. I probably won't get in though. I'd sure like to catch for you today if you get in to pitch."

"Me too. You'll be the starter next year after Rozen graduates. You've played well when you've gotten playing time."

"Oh, I know. He's an all-conference senior. It's his time. I'd just like to be out there with you. But I know the main thing today is to finish this run with a title!"

"That's right!"

"Andrew, I'm going to step out for a minute and meet Heather. You know, our pregame ritual."

"Okay. I talked to Tonya a little while ago. You have seven minutes before coach's pregame talk."

Chase stepped out of the locker room and saw Heather down the hall.

"Hey, Chase! You ready for the big game?"

"I am. I'm more excited than nervous."

"Good! You just play your best and that's enough."

"Thank you. I've only got a few minutes. You ready?"

Heather took Chase's hands into hers and they bowed their heads.

"Jesus, Heather and I thank you for the opportunity to pray to you once again. As I give my best effort today, help me to find joy in competing in the sport You have gifted me to play. Win or lose, we will praise Your name. Amen."

Heather prayed, "God, your Word says that whatever we do, to do it with all our hearts as unto You. Allow the practice Chase has put in to be evident when he has the opportunity to play today. Give him strength and peace out on the field. It is in the all-powerful name of Jesus we pray, Amen."

Heather then reached up and kissed Chase on his right cheek, then his left. After a quick kiss on the lips, they lovingly put their foreheads against one another.

"Love you, Heather."

"Play your best today."

With their foreheads still pressed together, they smiled at one another in a loving, peaceful moment.

Heather gave Chase a quick kiss.

"You gotta go. Love you!"

As Chase walked away, he shouted, "Win or lose, meet me on the mound after the game. I want to get a picture of us!"

"You got it, baby!"

Chase hustled back to the locker room. Coach Hill was just calling the team together. He gave an impassioned speech about playing smart and rising up to the moment.

The game was scoreless going into the bottom of the sixth inning when a close play at home plate caused a violent collision between the runner sliding home and the Eagles' catcher, Rozen. The runner was safe, giving the Pirates a one-run lead. To make matters worse, Rozen wasn't getting up.

The trainers were working on him when Coach Hill called out, "Andrew, you're up!"

Andrew quickly threw on his catcher's gear. They had two outs, but there were two runners in scoring position. After a short discussion with Lopez on the mound, Coach Hill called the bullpen for Chase to come into the game as well.

The two best friends quickly got onto the field to warm up. Rozen received a round of applause as he walked off with assistance.

Chase hurled the first pitch by the batter for a called strike. Two pitches later, they were out of the sixth inning, with Chase and Andrew feeling great!

Chase blew through the next two innings without giving up a hit, but the Eagles were unable to score. Going into the top of the final inning, they were still down 1-0 when Andrew got up to bat.

He hit the first pitch to the wall for a double. The following two batters struck out. With the game on the line, the next batter hit a home run, giving them a 2-1 lead!

Coach Hill walked over to Chase in the dugout.

"You look great out there. Do you have enough left in the tank to finish this thing?"

"I feel good, Coach."

The Eagles' next batter struck out, ending the inning.

Chase walked to the mound. After striking out the first two batters, he had a full count on the final batter between him and the NCAA Division 2 championship.

Chase shook off Andrew's first pitch selection. Andrew reluctantly called for a fastball. Chase went into his wind-up. He released the pitch as hard as he could throw and watched the batter swing at strike three!

The Eagle players stormed the field in celebration. They dog-piled Chase on the mound. Once the celebrating died down, they lined up to shake hands with their opponents. The trophy presentation was fun, and Chase received the Most Valuable Player award of the championship game.

Afterward, he saw his mom and dad talking with Heather and her parents. He went over and hugged all of them.

"Heather, are you ready for our picture?"

He took her by the hand and walked to the mound with several people scattered all around the infield. Andrew and Tonya made their way over along with all of their parents.

As they got to the mound, Chase took Heather by the hands and faced her.

"Heather Hopkins, you are the most wonderful person I've ever known. I can't imagine life without you. You have my heart. I would like to ask you for your hand."

Chase knelt down on one knee and held out a ring.
"Will you marry me?"
Heather burst into tears, nodding and saying, "Yes."
The crowd cheered as the couple stood and embraced.

Chapter 17

April 24, 2020

Chase and Andrew ate their lunch on the loading dock, enjoying the beautiful spring weather. They had recently landed jobs with a delivery service loading trucks. It was hard work, but they were excited because it paid well.

"I'm ready to move into our new place this weekend, Chase."

"Me too! I can't believe we've lived in that dump as long as we have. Since Matt got busted, he won't be around for a while. I told you hanging out with that gang was going to catch up with him. Hate it for him, but we'll have a much better place now. And we're going to have a pool!"

"I can see some awesome pool parties in our future! Is Misty still going to help us move?"

"Who knows? She spends so much time wasted these days I never know what she'll be doing. Which is fine with me. I just have to keep kicking this wedding down the road."

"I warned you she was crazy."

"She's okay sometimes. I keep thinking she'll get tired of fighting all the time and move on."

"Well you better be careful seeing those other girls. She'll lose her mind if she catches you again."

"Trust me, I know. You're one to talk. How many girls are you seeing right now?"

"Not enough!" Both guys laughed.

"Throw me those chips if you're not going to finish them, Andrew."

"You don't need them. You're getting a gut!"

"What? I'm in better shape than you are."

"No way, dude!"

"I've always been a step faster than you, and you know it!"

"How about we put some money on it? Five bucks says I can beat you!"

The guys sitting around heard the challenge and began taunting them to race. A few minutes later, they were lined up in the parking lot ready to run. Another worker raised his arm up and yelled, "On your mark, get set, GO!"

They started out even. Chase slowly pulled ahead. Several of their coworkers were outside cheering them on. Just before the finish line, Chase felt something pop in the back of his right ankle. He collapsed onto the asphalt screaming in pain.

After quickly checking on him, Andrew ran and got his truck. Several guys loaded Chase into the passenger side. Andrew drove as fast as could to the nearest emergency room.

They rushed Chase back into a trauma room. About 45 minutes later, a nurse came and found Andrew in the waiting room.

"Mr. Barkley would like for you to come back to see him."

"Is he okay?!"

She explained as they walked, "He's given me permission to share his medical information with you. Chase tore his Achilles' tendon in his right ankle. His doctor is afraid it pulled away from where it attaches on the bottom of his heel. We're going to do a MRI to confirm this, and if it is torn away from the bone, we're going to do surgery to repair it right away."

"Oh no. That's terrible."

"Yes it is. Andrew, he needs lots of encouragement right now. He can recover from this, but it's a long hard road ahead. Stay positive for him. Here's his room. You can go in and talk to him. We'll come get him for his test soon."

Andrew walked into the hospital room.

"Hey, buddy. How you feeling?"

"Not good, man."

"The nurse said you can get over this. You're tough. You'll be okay."

"Yeah. I'll be fine. Man, it felt like someone hit me with a baseball bat in the back of my ankle."

"I hate that."

"They called my parents. I wasn't too sure about some of my medical history stuff, so they called my mom. I told her what happened. She wants to come up here."

"I'm sure her and your dad will be here as soon as they can."

"Dad won't. He was home for some reason today. I could hear him in the background. You know what he said?"

"What?"

"He said that I wouldn't be in this situation if I was playing baseball in college like I should be. I'd be in better shape and wouldn't get hurt like this. I don't know. Maybe he's right."

"Chase, guys get hurt in baseball all the time. Who knows if you would get hurt or not. It's stupid to think about anyway. You're not in college, so what does it matter? Focus on getting better! You'll have a nice new apartment when you get out."

"Thanks Andrew."

"I know why you did this. You wanted to get out of helping me move tomorrow!"

The guys laughed. Chase's MRI confirmed he had ruptured his Achilles' tendon, and it would require surgery to reattach the tendon to his heel.

When Chase woke up from surgery, the nurse told him his mom was in the waiting room. He told her she could come in to see him.

His mom rushed into the room and over to Chase. She leaned over and hugged him as best she could. Kissing him on the cheek she asked, "How are you?"

Chase smiled. Although he would never admit it, he was happy his mom was here with him in the hospital. He still felt groggy from the anesthesia.

"I'll be fine, Mom. You didn't have to come out here."

"Chase, don't be ridiculous. I'll always be your mom. Whenever you need me, I will always be here for you. You rest now. I'll be here when you wake up."

Chase closed his eyes and turned his head. He didn't want his mom to see him tearing up. He relaxed and fell back asleep.

171

Later that evening, Chase woke up. It was dark in his room except for the dim glow from some monitors. He rolled over to try and look around the room.

He was relieved to hear his mom's voice, "Are you hurting?"

"No, just woke up. What time is it?"

"It's 9:00 at night. You came through surgery well. The doctor said you should heal up just fine, but it will take at least six months of recovery time. He'll be by in the morning to explain everything to you."

"Thanks, Mom."

"Chase are you awake enough to talk for a minute?"

"Yes."

"Would you consider moving back home while you recover? It would be much easier, and I could take care of you."

"Mom, you know Dad wouldn't let me. And even if he did, he would make it awful. It's not an option."

"I was afraid you would say that."

"Could you give me just enough money to make it a month or two? I'll figure something out by then."

Chase's Mom hesitated. She didn't want to become an enabler, but her little boy needed her. Why wasn't her husband here taking care of their son? Taking care of her? She hated doing this on her own.

Chase interrupted her thoughts.

"Mom...so can you help me?"

"Yes. I'll give you some money to get you by for a little while. But only until you get healthy again. There's something else I want to talk to you about. Chase, I've been listening to this preacher on the radio a lot lately. He's helped me discover God's love for..."

"No!"

Chase's mother was shocked by the anger she felt emanating from her son.

"No preachers. No Jesus. Nothing about God. Mom, I appreciate you caring about me. I'm glad you've found whatever it is you've found, but I'm

172

not at a point where I want to hear anything about God. If He's even real, He definitely hates me."

"Chase, don't say that."

"My face and hand are wrecked! My ankle is ruined! And my life is a mess! I'm having to ask my mom for money like a bum. I don't want to hear how much God loves me."

"I'm sorry, Chase. I didn't mean to upset you. Please just rest."

"You don't need to be sorry, Mom. Thank you for being here."

Chase's mom reached over and held her son's hand. He slowly drifted back to sleep.

◀ ◆ ◆ ◆ ▶

Chase sat in the red studio chair beside a pretty female reporter on the baseball field enjoying this beautiful spring day. Only a few feet away, a cameraman faced them while recording their interview.

"I'm here today speaking with Chase Barkley, quarterback of the Crossland Eagles in the fall and starting pitcher for them this spring. You are a busy young man, Chase."

"Yes ma'am. I don't have a lot of down time."

"You're also a member of the Bucks Christian fraternity, active in a local college ministry and on the honor roll academically. How do you keep up with a schedule like this and still maintain your grades?"

"I have a great support system. My coaches, parents, teammates, friends and fiancée all help me in one way or another. Honestly, I just take things one day at a time. I try to give my schedule to God and so far it's worked out well."

"Fiancée? That's going to disappoint a lot of girls watching our show."

Chase laughed. "Heather is amazing. I'm lucky to have her."

"So Chase, you were the only Division 2 player named in 'The Athlete' as a player to watch. You led your football team to the playoffs the previous two seasons, won the baseball championship last year and are the favorite to repeat this year. Because of your outspoken faith, some people are calling you the Tim Tebow of Division 2 sports."

"Tim Tebow? I haven't heard that one! I'm just trying to be my best in every area of my life. God gives everyone different gifts. He has blessed me with the ability to throw a ball. I'm just trying to glorify the name of Jesus in everything I do."

"You do a lot more than just throw a ball. Good luck to you and your team with the rest of your season."

"Thank you."

Chase said goodbye to the news crew and went to get warmed up for the game. He was the starting pitcher for the weekend series beginning at noon.

In the bottom of the sixth inning, Chase had a no-hitter going. He struck out the first batter and got the second one to ground out. Having worked the third batter into a full count, he threw a fastball. The batter squared up and put a bunt down between Chase and third base.

Chase sprinted to the ball, bare-handed it and wheeled around to throw out the player at first. When he planted his right ankle, he felt it pop. Chase collapsed to the ground, screaming in pain and grabbing his ankle. Andrew ran from behind home plate to check on him. The trainers were right behind him.

They loaded Chase up into an ambulance and rushed him to the nearest emergency room.

Chase's parents were with him when the doctor stepped in to give them the results of the MRI.

"Chase has ruptured his Achilles' tendon. It's actually torn away from the bone, and I will need to do surgery to reattach it."

"Will I be able to play ball again?"

Chase's dad answered, "Chase, playing ball is secondary to you living a healthy life."

The doctor continued, "This is a tough injury for an athlete. It is possible, in some circumstances, to recover and play again. Chase, the recovery process won't be easy, but I'm sure you'll be up to it. Let's get you put back

174

together before we worry about your rehab. I'm going to go get prepped for surgery. See you in there."

Chase and his parents spent some time in prayer. He was moved to pre-op, then to surgery. Several hours later Chase woke up in his hospital room.

In a raspy voice, he said, "I'm thirsty."

He heard Heather. "Here, sweetheart. Here's some water."

She held a cup of water to his mouth. He raised his head up and took a drink.

"How are you feeling?"

"Not good. It felt like someone hit the back of my ankle with a baseball bat. It's numb now."

"I'm so sorry, baby. The doctor said it was a really bad tear, but he was able to get everything back in place."

"Good. Thank you for being here."

"Get some rest. I'll be here when you wake up."

Chase immediately fell back to sleep. Later that evening he woke up again.

"Heather?"

"Hey Chase, I'm here. How do you feel?"

"I feel okay. What time is it?"

"It's about 9:00 at night."

Heather helped him raise his bed into a more upright position.

"What am I going to do if I can't play ball anymore?"

"We're a long way from worrying about that, Chase. I think you need to try to eat some of this Jell-O and rest."

"You're probably right. Will you still feel the same about me if I can't play again?"

"Chase Barkley! If you think I love you because you can play a game, you're sadly mistaken. I love your soul, your laugh, your intelligence. I love the way you treat me and how you care about others. I love your faith in Jesus and how you strive to be the man He's called you to be. You can get sad, depressed and mad, but I'm going to be right here loving you!"

Chase smiled for the first time since the accident.

"So I guess you kinda still like me?"

Heather put her hands on his cheeks and leaned in until their foreheads touched.

"No, you dummy. I don't kinda like you. I love you. Forever. No matter what."

As they kissed, Andrew and Tonya walked in the hospital room.

"Whoa! Is this some kind of new therapy for a sprained ankle? Oh, Tonya. My ankle hurts. How about a kiss?"

"Sorry guys. The nurse said we could come in."

"It's fine, Tonya. I was just giving Chase a pep talk."

"I could use a pep talk, Tonya."

Tonya hit Andrew's shoulder.

Chase asked, "Andrew, did we win?"

"Yep! No thanks to you. That last throw to first went wide right. Ruined your no-hitter, too."

Tonya said, "Are you sure you want him here, Chase? He's like the worst person to bring to a hospital."

Andrew exclaimed, "Jell-O! Are you gonna eat this?"

Chase laughed. "It's all yours. I can get as much as I want later. Tonya, I wouldn't want to ever be his chaperone on a hospital visit. Good luck."

Everyone laughed. After a while Andrew and Tonya prayed with Chase and then left.

Chase and Heather's parents arrived back in the room a little while later.

After visiting with Chase, her dad spoke up.

"Heather, it's getting late. Chase needs his rest. We will be back first thing in the morning."

"I hate to leave you, Chase."

"I'd rather you go home and get some rest, Heather. I'll be fine. I'm ready to sleep some more anyway. I love you."

"Love you too, baby. Remember what I said."

Chase smiled.

After the Hopkins had left, Chase's dad went to get some stuff from the car. His mom sat down beside his bed.

"You're a very blessed young man to have so many friends who care about you."

"I really am."

"Chase, I know you're worried about getting healthy and playing ball again. I know you'll work hard. Just remember, even if things don't go the way you want them to, Jesus has a plan for your life. He knew you would get injured today. He knows what will happen tomorrow. We'll pray for your full recovery, but no matter what, He loves you and has a plan and a purpose for your life."

"Thank you, Mom. I needed to hear that."

Chase's mom reached over and held her son's hand. He slowly drifted back to sleep.

Chapter 18

June 12, 2021

Chase unlocked the door and limped into his apartment. He and Andrew were still roommates, although Andrew was seldom there. Hanging out at his new girlfriend's place occupied most of his spare time.

Andrew still worked loading trucks, but Chase's injury kept him from being able to stand on his feet all day. He was able to find a job at another gas station in town, where he could sit most of the time. At this station, he spent his time in a small glass booth primarily dispensing candy, cigarettes and lottery tickets.

Trapped in the booth all day felt like a metaphor of his life. The world was going by, but he wasn't able to actually live in it. He felt disconnected, with a clear glass barrier between him and everyone else. Even when he was with a girl physically, he felt alone. There was never any real intimacy or love.

Misty was constantly in and out of his life, depending on her circumstances. They had broken up and gotten back together more times than Chase could count. He hated her, but didn't want to be alone. They were back together at the moment.

He drank regularly to numb the emptiness he felt. Although he was under 21, alcohol was easy to come by in his neighborhood. Anger was his constant companion, residing just below the surface at all times. The slightest thing would send him into a rage. He had been in several fights over things that really didn't matter.

Chase grabbed a beer out of the refrigerator and flipped on the TV. A few minutes later, the door swung open and Misty walked inside.

"Hey Chase. What have you been up to today?"

"Hey. Nothing really. Just working."

"You know you could act a little more excited to see me."

"Sorry, babe. It's just been a lousy day. My foot has been bothering me."

"If you would have gone to rehab like the doctor said, it might be better by now."

"You know I can't afford to take off work or pay for rehab!"

"You don't have to yell at me! I'm trying to show you that I care about you!"

"I'm sorry. It's just frustrating. Do you want to run down to The Rusty Bucket and get a pizza?"

"Sure. Grab my backpack. I have some cash."

"Got it."

Chase threw Misty's backpack over his shoulder and locked the door as they left. They walked the three blocks down to the local bar and pizza joint where they were regulars.

Grabbing a booth, Chase ordered two beers and a pepperoni pizza.

"This is going to be a great month for you, baby! You just had your last meeting with your parole officer. And you have a big birthday coming up! What are we going to do to celebrate?"

"I don't know. I'm just happy to be off parole. I talked to Skip over at the liquor store on 8th St. He said next week when I turn 21, he'll have a job for me. One that will be more money and will get me out of the glass box."

"And to help pay for our wedding, finally. That's so exciting. Oh, here comes our pizza."

They ate and talked more about their plans. Misty excused herself to go to the restroom. On her way back to the table, she bumped into a guy at the bar.

"Watch out, chick! You almost made me spill my drink."

"You watch out yourself! Mr. Loser."

"What'd you call me?"

"I called you Mr. Loser! Loser!"

"If you weren't a girl I'd..."

"You'd what? Step up and show me what you would do!"

Chase had seen the drama unfolding and walked over.

"Just tell your girl to watch out. I don't want any trouble."

"You shut your mouth. Another word and I'll shut it for you."

The guy looked down at his drink.

Chase and Misty went back to their seats. Chase spoke in a harsh, accusing tone, "Why do you always do that?"

"Always do what?"

"Always have to be so mouthy? We were having a perfectly good evening, and you have to go start something."

"Me? I accidentally bumped into that jerk and he yelled at me like I was stupid."

"Whatever, let's get out of here."

Chase threw her backpack on his shoulders and headed out the door. When he stepped outside the guy from the earlier altercation and his friend were standing there.

"Well it's Mr. Tough Guy and his loud-mouth chick."

Chase stepped forward. "Look guys, I should have handled this in a different way earlier."

"Right now, I'm sure you're rethinking a lot of your life decisions, but it's too..."

Chase hit the guy mid-sentence with a right cross. His friend, shocked at the sudden punch, couldn't react in time to block a left jab. Chase quickly kicked the first guy in the stomach, sending him to the ground. He grabbed the second guy and threw him against the brick wall of the pizza shop.

A policeman driving by saw the whole incident. He called for back-up and rushed over, ordering Chase and Misty to the ground. She was hysterical, screaming and crying.

A short time later, several policemen roamed around taking everyone's statements. One of the policemen came over to Chase, who was handcuffed.

"Mr. Barkley, it looks like there hasn't been any major damage done. Our officer saw them approach you and it seems you were defending yourself. I think we can let this one go. Now you and Ms. Dobbins go home and stay out of..."

"Hold on, Brian." Another officer was going through Misty's backpack when he interrupted Officer Brian.

"Whatcha got?"

"Looks like we have some drugs in the backpack. Whose are these?"

Chase looked over at Misty in disbelief.

"Mr. Barkley, you were wearing the backpack. Are these your drugs?"

"I think those guys might have planted them on me earlier."

"Nice try. Chase Barkley, you're under arrest. You have the right to..."

Chase was read his rights. He complied with the policemen and was taken to the North Ridge jail, where he called Andrew. A public defender showed up about two hours later.

Chase was brought out of the community cell into a private room. A thin black man wearing bifocal glasses and a bow tie was sitting at the table typing away on his laptop.

"Have a seat, Mr. Barkley. My name is Eugene Watterson, pleasure to make your acquaintance. I'm your duly-appointed public attorney. With your permission, I'll be representing you in your criminal case.

"I've read the police report. You're being charged with possession of a controlled substance. With your record, I suggest we plead guilty, and try to get a reduced sentence of six months to a year in prison."

"Aren't you even going to ask me if the drugs are mine?"

"We can go down this line of questioning if you would like, sir. You can deny everything and we can fight the charges. But here's what the judge will see. A convicted felon, of police brutality, no less, fighting in the streets of North Ridge with drugs in the backpack he's wearing.

"If you want to argue for your innocence, and run the risk of a longer sentence in jail, I'll fight your battle. But I am obligated to give you the best legal advice as I see it. Thus, I advise you to plead guilty and let me try to reduce your prison time.

"The hour is late. Think about what course you would like to pursue. I will stop by tomorrow morning at 10:00 sharp to find out your decision, Mr. Barkley. Farewell, good sir."

Eugene stood up and slightly bowed. He turned and left the room, leaving Chase wondering about his strange new lawyer.

Chase sat quietly for a moment processing his situation. More time in prison seemed to be his only option. Anger at his hopeless predicament built up inside of him until it boiled over.

Moments later, the guards rushed into the room to find Chase pounding the table with his fists and screaming incoherently.

◄ ♦ ♦ ♦ ►

"Here's where we push it, Chase! I'm dialing up the treadmill elevation and speed. Go as hard as you can...now!"

Chase sprinted as fast as he could. Sweat was pouring off of him, making his muscles glisten as he ran.

"3...2...1...stop!"

Chase jumped with his feet resting on either side of the treadmill. His team's trainer, Coach Fleming, dialed down the treadmill until it was level with the ground and not moving.

"How do you feel?"

Between breaths, Chase managed to say, "Feels pretty good."

"That's enough for today. You're on track with your rehab, but I'm still worried your Achilles' tendon isn't rebounding as strong as I would like. I spoke with your orthopedic surgeon and he agrees."

"What else can I do? It feels pretty good, other than the soreness I have sometimes. But my right calf is still smaller than the left."

"Chase, you're staying on track with your training. We just have to hope and pray your ankle eventually responds. We should know more in a month or two."

"Thanks, Coach Fleming. I'll keep working hard."

"I know you will. I've never seen anyone work as hard to recover from an injury. I mean, you're in here killing it on your wedding day!"

Chase laughed, "It's better than sitting around nervous all day. We should have planned this wedding for 8 a.m. instead of 6 this afternoon."

"You getting cold feet?"

"No, not as far as marrying Heather. I can't wait for her to be my wife. She's my angel. After my injury, when things got dark for me, she was always there.

"On days when I wanted to give up, to get mad at God, she shared love and truth with me. She pushed me and wouldn't let me quit. I'm so blessed to have her. I grew a lot through those dark days, and learned what I really believe during that season of pain.

"Following Jesus isn't about prosperity in this life. It rains on the Just and the Unjust. Heather helped me come to a point where I can honestly say like the Apostle Paul that God's grace is sufficient for me, because His power is perfected in weakness. That's not an easy place to get to."

"Chase, you're on an amazing journey. I'm glad to be part of it. Now, hit the showers, and then meet me in my office."

Chase cleaned up and headed to Coach Fleming's office. As he walked up, he could hear Coach Fleming talking to someone else.

"Chase, come in. I want to introduce you to a friend of mine. This is Hayden Holmes. You might know him by his nickname, 'The Hitman.'"

Chase was at a loss for words. One of his heroes growing up was right here in the same room with him.

Hayden stuck his hand out. "Hi, Chase. It's nice to meet you."

"It's an honor to meet you, Mr. Holmes. I'm a big fan."

"Please, call me Hayden. I'm a fan of yours, as well."

"A fan of mine?"

"Yes I am. Coach Fleming told me about you when you were a freshman. Two-sport athletes as good as you are in both sports are rare these days. I hated to hear about your injury last season. I was in the area today for some speaking engagements, so I thought I would stop by and meet you."

"Thank you! I'm still rehabbing. It's not responding great, but hopefully I'll get back out there."

"I certainly hope so. Coach Fleming has told me how hard you're working. Chase, I don't know if you'll get to play ball again or not, but I do know God isn't finished with you. He has a plan for your life, on or off the field. Don't let this injury define who you are as a man."

"I really appreciate you coming by here today. I know God still has a purpose for me, but it's good to be reminded."

"From what I understand you have a big day ahead of you. Congratulations on your wedding. Get out of here and go enjoy your day!"

Chase shook hands with both men and left. He went back home where Andrew was waiting for him.

"You're never gonna believe who I just met!"

"Doesn't matter. Tell me on the way. We have a tee time in thirty minutes."

"Golf? Andrew, you do remember I'm getting married today, right?"

"How could I forget? I'm the best man! And you're still free until six. We have the whole afternoon. Now hurry up!"

The guys headed over to the golf course. After checking in, they got their cart and drove to the first tee.

Chase exclaimed, "Andrew, you didn't tell me our dads were playing with us."

"Thought I would surprise you!"

The boys pulled up to the tee box.

"Hey! Thanks for the surprise golf game. This will be a great way to spend my last afternoon of freedom."

Chase's dad said, "Today's a special day, son. One I don't think you'll soon forget. Let's get started."

As the guys played the first three holes, Chase told them about meeting 'The Hitman.' They reminisced about all the fun times their families had growing up and playing ball together. The men also shared lessons they had learned about being a husband.

When they drove up to the fourth tee, a man was sitting there alone in a golf cart. It was Nick, Chase's youth minister, who had led him to Christ.

Andrew's dad walked over and shook Nick's hand. "Time for me to go. Nick, would you please join these guys."

"I'd be honored."

Nick got out of the golf cart and grabbed his clubs. Andrew's dad drove off.

Chase walked over to Nick and gave him a hug and said, "Don't wear yourself out. You have to perform a wedding later today!"

"I slept in this morning. Some friends kept me up until after midnight last night after their rehearsal dinner!"

"We had a great time, Nick. We're glad you and Robin could hang out so late. Thanks for being here today."

Chase's dad stepped up to the tee. "We better get moving or we may miss the nuptials."

The guys all laughed. As they played a few more holes, Nick shared with Chase the importance of being the spiritual leader in his home, and how important it will be to love Heather as Christ loves the Church.

On the seventh hole, Chase spotted his high school baseball coach sitting alone in a golf cart. Coach Sanders switched places with Nick and the golf game continued. Different coaches, pastors and men of influence in Chase's life rotated into the golf game as it progressed. Each of them spoke words of encouragement and wisdom into Chase.

When they had finished their game they returned to the clubhouse. All of the different men who had played in the round of golf were waiting there. They gathered around Chase and prayed for him. Chase was a bit overwhelmed realizing how blessed he was to have so many strong, godly men in his life.

A little while after they had finished praying, Chase announced, "I want to thank each of you for investing in me. I've learned something from each of you, by your words and actions, about being a man. One important thing I've learned is to be on time. So I have to go, or I might miss my own wedding!"

The room roared with laughter. Chase and Andrew raced home to get ready. Chase threw his honeymoon luggage into his truck and drove to the church, where his tuxedo was waiting.

They quickly got dressed for some pre-wedding pictures.

At 6:00 Chase stood in front of a packed church full of friends and family. Nick stood with him. Andrew, along with three other groomsmen, escorted the bridesmaids to the front of the church. Chase's heart pounded as the music paused for a moment and the Wedding March powerfully resonated throughout the church.

The doors to the sanctuary swung open and Heather, arm in arm with her father, walked down the aisle toward Chase. She was the most beautiful sight he had ever seen. He silently thanked God for blessing him with such an amazing woman to be his wife.

A few hours later, Chase and Heather Barkley drove away from Grace Fellowship Church to begin their new life together. Chase rolled down his window, threw his fist into the air, and let out a thunderous shout of joy.

Chapter 19

August 17, 2021

Chase laid in his uncomfortable cot thinking about his next move. His eccentric lawyer Eugene Watterson had been able to get his sentence reduced to one year in jail.

Green County Prison was a completely different experience than Davenport had been. This was a maximum security prison with short-term and long-term offenders. There was a dark, oppressive spirit engulfing every part of this facility. Chase knew right away he was in for a tough stretch. The day he entered, he was threatened by three different gangs. He wasn't afraid to fight, but he knew he had to be smart in here or he would end up dead.

A few days later, Chase was approached by some guys offering for him to join their gang. He followed them around the corner to discuss how things would work, when another guy strolled up to them.

"Gentlemen, I'm not sure I have been properly introduced to the newbie."

Chase looked over and was shocked to see former police officer Harrison Majors!

"You? What are you doing in here? I guess you ended up on the wrong side of the fence!"

"Chase Barkley. I knew we would cross paths again one day."

"You ruined my life, you creep! You left these scars on me I have to look at every single day!"

Chase charged to attack Harrison, but two guys quickly grabbed him and pinned him to the wall. Harrison punched Chase in the stomach.

"Shut up and listen, punk! These are all former cops. We have each other's back. You think those scars are bad? They're nothing. It's going to be a long, hard year for you, Chase. I'll make sure of it! Now run along and play."

As Harrison punched Chase in the stomach again, the men released him, letting him double over and collapse to the ground. They walked away laughing.

The attack had just happened yesterday. Chase sat up on the side of his cot unsure what he would do next.

He got up and put on his prison uniform. The walk to breakfast didn't offer any hope with several guys staring him down. Chase decided he would pick the meanest-looking guy in the cafeteria and fight him. At least, win or lose, everyone would know he wouldn't go down without a fight.

Chase kept an eye out for who he would fight as he ate breakfast. Some other inmates sat down at his table. They ignored him, but spoke to one another in hushed tones.

As he took his last bite he decided who he would fight. It would be the huge, muscular Hispanic man with a mohawk. He was covered in muscles and tattoos and looked like he could knock-out a bull. Chase thought to himself, "*This is gonna hurt!*"

He stood up to go pick his fight. Suddenly one of the guys at his table said something that caught his attention.

Chase blurted out, "What did you just say?"

The skinny dishwater-blonde haired man answered, "I wasn't talking to you."

"Right. I know, but did I hear you just say, 'Lucky can get it.' I was in another joint, Davenport, and I knew a guy named Lucky."

The group of inmates cut their eyes back and forth at one another.

"Maybe you should mind your own business. Come on, guys. Let's go talk where we can have some privacy."

Chase watched the guys leave as his mind raced with questions: Was Lucky here? How could he find him? Would he be willing to help him out?

Forgetting about the fight, his mind continued to race as he went to his work duty station in the laundry room.

During his shift he loaded clothes from a giant washer into an industrial dryer. Another inmate beside him was whistling and looked surprisingly friendly.

Chase decided to take a chance, "Hey bro, I'm Chase."

The older black man smiled and fist bumped Chase. "What's up? I'm Mac."

"Good to meet you, Mac. I'm new to this place. You look like you might know who I can see to get things around here?"

"Get you things, huh. What kind of things are you looking for?"

"I'll need smokes. Maybe a new tat. And other stuff that isn't as easy to find."

"If you want a good tat you'll definitely want to see EZ over in cell block D. He's the master of ink! But he ain't cheap."

"Cool."

"Other contraband can be acquired by one of two sources. Steve the Money-Man can get stuff. He's fair, but you gotta be careful doing deals. It can get sketchy. You know, make the deal very clear to all involved. When you go talk to him..."

Mac kept explaining how to deal with Steve. Chase wanted to scream! He couldn't care less about this Steve guy. But he kept his cool.

"Man, that's some great advice. So I think you said there was another guy who could score some stuff, too."

"Oh, yeah. He can get just about anything. But it will cost you. They call him Lucky. He only works by invitation. You have to be in here a while, before he'll deal with you."

"Only VIPs? Interesting. If I ever have the privilege of dealing with him, where can I find him?"

"He hangs with the Mexican Brotherhood. You have to go through them. But I wouldn't recommend it. They're a rough bunch. And you're still WAY too new here to be dealing with them."

Chase had what he needed. He went ahead and continued to get as much information about the prison as he could from Mac. Knowledge was power in prison. When their shift was over, he went out to the yard for afternoon exercise.

After some further investigating, Chase spotted a group from the Mexican Brotherhood in the yard. He took a deep breath and walked over to them.

They quickly surrounded him and he was shocked to find himself face-to-face with the huge man with the mohawk he had planned on fighting earlier.

"You are a very foolish gringo."

"I need to meet with Lucky."

"Foolish and bold. That's a bad combo."

"Look, we can fight if you want, but I need to talk to Lucky. I know he doesn't work with dumb guys, and I know he won't be happy if I beat you up."

The big Hispanic man, along with all of the guys surrounding Chase, burst into laughter. He stared at Chase for a minute and then turned to walk away. He looked back and asked, "Who should I say wants to talk to him?"

"Tell him FedEx needs to see him."

A little while later, Chase was ushered into an office down a side hallway. He wondered how Lucky was always able to establish a business office inside of a prison.

"Chase! My favorite delivery boy! Wow. You have grown up into a delivery man."

"Hey, Lucky! You're a sight for sore eyes."

"Word on the street is you have a problem. Chase, how do you always find trouble wherever you go?"

"I don't know. I guess it's a gift."

"You really should learn how to make friends better, my boy."

"Maybe you can teach me someday."

"Possibly. Now to the business at hand. Your request from me?"

"Protection. Keep these guys off of me. All of the guys in here."

"And your offer?"

"I work in laundry. Not sure what I can offer you, yet."

"Nothing to offer. Needing protection. Seems like we've had this conversation before. Laundry is shipped all over the prison. I can use you. I'll set up your protection. You'll remain my delivery man while you're in here, and then I'll have your obligation of one year of service when you get out. Do we have a deal?"

"How will it work on the outside? You don't know where I live or when I'm getting out."

"Chase, you should know me better than that by now. You reside in North Ridge, and your sentence is for one year. Don't underestimate me, my boy. Now do we have a deal?"

Chase was excited. "Absolutely!"

◀ ◆ ◆ ◆ ▶

"Thanks for meeting me for lunch on such short notice, Nick."

"No problem, Chase. You know I'll always make time for you."

"I really appreciate it. I had an appointment this morning with my orthopedic surgeon. My playing days are officially over."

"Oh, man. I'm sorry. Your ankle still isn't responding?"

"No. Not like I need it to, if I'm going to perform at an elite level. I've done everything the doctors and trainers have told me to do, but it's just a career-ending injury."

"Do your parents know?"

"Yeah. They were at my appointment with me today. My dad was so supportive. He reminded me there's a lot more to life than playing a game. You know my mom. She just loves me no matter what."

"You're lucky to have them. How are you?"

"Nick, you know how hard it hit me last year. It was probably the hardest thing I've ever had to deal with. But I think I'm going to be okay now. I realize God must have something else for me. It's not easy giving up on my dreams, but I'm dealing with it. I just needed to talk to someone."

"You are a phenomenal athlete, but you're gifted in many other ways."

"Thanks. As you know, I've been praying for guidance on what to do if I can't play again. I've considered going into vocational ministry, but I don't think that's what I'm supposed to do.

"I'm going to move out of athletics to focus on what's next. It's been hard watching everyone going through two-a-days while I'm in the training room. Next week is game week, and I'm not involved. It's hard."

"Chase, we'll continue to pray for direction. I'm not sure you should completely get away from athletics. That's a big part of your life. Take some time to think it through before you make that move, okay?"

"I'm supposed to talk to Coach Maddux, my football coach, tonight when I get back to campus. I'll see what he thinks."

"Let me know what you decide. How is Heather?"

"Amazing! I love being married to her. I'm not sure if I could handle all of this without her."

"That's good to hear. Tell her I said hi. Robin and I will be on campus next weekend. Let's get together."

"Sounds great!"

"Let me pray for you before you leave."

On the way out of Silver Springs, Chase found himself pulling into his old high school campus. Memories flooded his mind as he parked by the baseball field.

He walked up and leaned his arms on top of the fence. A smile crossed his face, remembering all the good times he enjoyed here.

Some guys crossing the field caught his eye. Chase didn't recognize any of them, but they certainly recognized him. They excitedly waved him over.

"Hey, Chase! What are you doing out here today?"

"I was in town and thought I would stop by."

"You probably don't remember me. I'm Casey Tyler, Matt Tyler's little brother. Coach has me doing some pitching. I'm getting pretty good."

"I remember you, Casey! You've grown a lot! Show me what you got."

194

Another guy tossed Chase his glove and he went and kneeled down behind home plate. Casey got in his stance on the pitcher's mound. He went into his wind-up and tossed a nice curve ball across the plate.

Chase gave him some pointers on how to get more movement on his pitches. A familiar voice interrupted the guys' impromptu pitching lesson.

"And to what do we owe the honor of having a champion college pitcher visiting us today?"

"Hey, Coach Sanders. Sorry, I was just showing the guys a couple of things I've learned. Most of it was from you."

"From what I observed, it was a lesson well taught and well received. Now, Coach McEntire is waiting for you current students in the weight room. The longer you make him wait, the longer he will make you lift."

The players turned and ran toward the gym, shouting back their thanks to Chase.

"Now, let's have a seat in your old dugout and you can tell me what you're really doing here."

Chase smiled. Coach Sanders could still read him like a book.

"Coach, my ankle isn't going to heal up enough for me to continue playing ball. I'm not sure what I should do."

"Bum ankle, huh? Your Achilles, if I remember correctly."

"Yeah, they fixed it, but I can't get any velocity on my throws. I'm having soreness when I push it. No matter how hard I work it won't respond."

"That's a tough injury. Used to, ACLs were the biggie - ended the careers of lots of fine young men. They can fix those pretty well now. What are you going to do?"

"I don't know. Sports have been my whole life. I mean, even when I got saved, God used sports to allow me to serve Him. I love it. Not in a bad way. I love God much more, but playing sports was my ministry. I don't understand why He has taken it away."

"Maybe He hasn't."

"Coach, I told you, my body is broken. They can't fix me. I can't play anymore."

195

"Well, Chase, you can't play anymore, but you can still invest in people through the sports you love so much. Have you thought about coaching?"

"Coaching? No, not really."

"If you really want to make an impact in people through sports, you still can. It's not easy. A lot of the time coaching can be frustrating, unappreciated, hard work. You'll wonder if a kid who has potential will ever get it. You'll see kids with talent throw it all away on bad decisions. But every once in a while, you'll see one succeed and it will all be worth it.

"Think about who has impacted your life. How does God want you to make an impact? I watched you teaching those boys just now. You have the gift. I've got to get to practice. Good to see you, young man. Good luck."

"Thanks for the talk, Coach."

Chase sat there contemplating what his high school coach said. Later that afternoon, he met with Coach Maddux about quitting the football team. His coach was sitting behind his desk wearing his favorite cowboy hat.

"Chase, come on in, boy, and pull up a chair."

"Hey, Coach Maddux."

"Chase, Coach Fleming gave me the bad news about that ankle of yours. Son, you're tougher than a two-dollar steak, but sometimes being tough isn't enough. I'm sorry you didn't get better news."

"Me too. I still can't get much on my throws because of my ankle. And the soreness is still a problem."

"What can I do for you, Chase? You know we'll honor your athletic scholarship so you can still get your degree."

"Yes sir. And I appreciate you and the school for that. I've really been praying about what to do if I can't play anymore."

"Have you made up your mind on anything?"

"I asked to meet with you today to tell you I was going to quit the football team. It seemed like a good idea, because it's hard to be here and not contribute. But I stopped and talked to Coach Sanders from my high school."

"He's a good man."

"I think so too. He told me I should consider coaching."

"Chase, that's a great idea! Best I've heard all day! You've shown leadership, character and a great work ethic ever since you walked in the door. I'd be honored to help you transition into coaching."

"Really? You think I have what it takes?"

"You will have a lot to learn. Things are different on this side of the whistle. But you definitely have the potential to be a good coach. There are choices you'll have to make, like what sport do you want to coach? Do you want to pursue coaching high school, college or pro? We can work through all those decisions. What do you think, boy?"

"I think it's what I want to do. I've been praying for months and this feels like the right move. Of course, I'll need to talk to Heather tonight. If she doesn't object, could we start right away?"

"I'll get the paperwork together to make everything official with the school. You'll need to talk to your guidance counselor and adjust your classes. Unless I hear otherwise, tomorrow we'll begin the process of building you into the best coach you can be! Son, your future is bigger than the Great State of Texas! Now, do we have a deal?"

Chase was excited. "Absolutely!"

Chapter 20

July 1, 2023

Chase pulled up in front of a seedy apartment complex in his late model Chevy Camaro. The blacked-out windows and loud stereo system, along with some chipped paint on the hood, fit right into this neighborhood. The deal with Lucky had worked out fantastic. He was protected from any harm while in prison, and had become one of Lucky's most trusted delivery guys. Since his release, life had gotten much better. He continued to deliver packages around the region. Lucky liked the fact he was dependable and never asked any questions.

He and Misty had made up. She apologized for getting him busted and was acting better most of the time. They were living together in his newest apartment.

Today he had a delivery of three cardboard boxes for Apt. #245 in this rundown area of North Ridge. Carrying the boxes in a local grocery store bag helped disguise them. Chase was familiar with the complex, having already made several deliveries in the area.

He made his way up to the second story and knocked on the scratched-up metal door. A cute bleached-blonde haired girl about his age opened it.

Chase said the code words, "Hi, I have your groceries for you."

She replied, "Thanks. Was the traffic bad?"

"No. It was all clear."

"Good, I'm planning on visiting my grandma later today."

Having finished the coded conversation, Chase stepped inside. He noticed she was checking him out.

"Here's your stuff."

"I'll get your money."

"Have you lived here long?"

She shouted from the bedroom, "About a year. How about you?"

"On and off around here for a while."

"Come back here and get your money."

He walked into her bedroom and she held out an envelope. Chase reached and grabbed it, but she didn't let go. When he pulled the envelope toward himself she came right along with it, drawing Chase near.

He looked down at her and she smiled. He reached down and kissed her. Minutes later they heard the front door open and a guy's voice call out.

"Candy, I'm home!"

Chase jumped up off the bed, wide-eyed, not knowing what to do.

"That's my boyfriend, Ax! You gotta get out of here!"

"Ax?! Why do they call him that?"

"You don't want to know! The fire escape. Hurry!"

Chase stepped toward the window, then stopped. He reached back for his envelope, grabbed Candy and kissed her, and then hurried through the window and down the fire escape.

When he got to his car, he jumped in and peeled out! A few minutes later, when he was in the clear and his heart rate had returned to normal, he began to laugh at his close call.

That afternoon, when he was dropping off the money for Lucky and collecting his cut, Misty texted him.

"Cooking dinner 2nite 4 my favorite guy! Burgers & fries! Can't wait to see you, Mr. Cutie-Pie!"

Chase smiled. Although he hated Misty at times, he enjoyed having her around when she was in a good mood. As he drove, he thought about how good life was right now. Things were finally falling into place.

When he entered his new apartment, the aroma of sizzling bacon filled the place.

"Misty, I'm home. Supper smells delicious. Are you making bacon to go on the burgers?"

She came bounding out of the kitchen and excitedly hugged and kissed him.

"Welcome home! I'm so happy to see you! I've missed you like crazy all day!"

"Wow. It's good to see you too. What's this all about?"

"It's about me being madly in love with such a great guy!"

All through the meal Misty uncharacteristically praised Chase and talked about how wonderful he was. After cleaning off the table, Misty walked into the living room and handed Chase a present.

"What's this for?"

"Open it, Mr. Curious!"

Chase studied the gift for a moment. He tore off the wrapping paper and opened the little box. Reaching inside, he pulled out a tiny pair of baby booties.

Misty squealed in delight.

Chase's mind raced, emotions swirling inside of him. Unsure of how to respond, he just stared at the little stockings.

"Looks like the cat's got somebody's tongue. We're going to make the best mommy and daddy in the whole wide world!"

"Yeah. That's great. How long do we have? I mean, how far along are you?"

"About six weeks. We're going to have to get to planning our wedding now!"

"Wedding? Yeah, I don't know about that."

"What do you mean 'you don't know about that'?!"

"Think about it. If we get married, we'll have to pay for everything ourselves. We'll lose a ton of government benefits."

Misty sat quietly contemplating Chase's reasoning. Seeing he had her confused on what to think, he continued.

"I love you with all my heart, and we're going to have a wonderful family. Let's just be smart about this. We'll be able to give our baby a lot more if we wait just a little while longer to get married. I want to give you the very best! We don't need a piece of paper to show we love each other."

Misty was quietly wiping tears from her eyes.

Finally she responded, "I guess you're right. I just wanted my family to be happy we're having a baby...and to not be embarrassed."

"They will be happy. And they will be even happier if we're not having to borrow money to pay for everything."

Chase held Misty as she continued to gently cry.

"Enough of this crying. This is a time to celebrate! I'm going to run and get some champagne! Well, maybe some fancy grape juice for you!"

They laughed. Chase grabbed his keys and told her he would be right back.

On his way to the store, he got a text from Gloria, a girl he had been seeing. She wanted him to come by. It sounded like a bad idea to him right now, but he wanted to get his mind off becoming a father and having to marry Misty.

Gloria met him at the door, excited to see him.

"Hey, Handsome. I'm glad you could come by."

"I'm glad you invited me. It's been a while."

"I know. I've missed you."

Chase felt like she was looking at him funny.

"Are you okay, Gloria?"

"I'm fantastic. I have a surprise for you."

"A surprise? What kind of surprise?"

"One I hope you're going to be super excited about! ...I'm pregnant!"

Chase couldn't believe what she was saying. How could this happen? And why was she excited? This was horrible news.

"Pregnant? I mean...wow. So, are you sure it's mine?"

Gloria exploded, "What do you mean, 'am I sure it's yours?' What kind of girl do you think I am? I haven't been with anyone else! Of course it's yours!"

"Settle down! It's just we haven't seen each other in a while."

Gloria began crying. All Chase wanted to do was get away.

"Look, I shouldn't have said that. It's just such a shock. We'll get through this."

"We'll get through this?! Really? I didn't tell you I have cancer! I told you I'm having your baby. I thought maybe you would be happy. Maybe we could be together. Have a family."

"I really don't know what to say. I should probably just go."

With Gloria still crying, Chase got out of there as quickly as he could. As he drove, his mind raced trying to figure out what to do. He didn't love Gloria; didn't even like her very much. She was just a girl to pass time with, someone to use for his pleasure.

He didn't love Misty either. Anger overwhelmed him. Why was all of this happening? He was only 23 and life had just started getting better.

He couldn't think of worse girls to be the mothers of his children. Deep in his soul, Chase dreaded the thought of being a father.

◀ ◆ ◆ ◆ ▶

Chase's phone buzzed in his pocket as he was cleaning up the weight room. Wiping down the sweaty machines in the gym after a summer morning workout session was one of the glamorous jobs that came with being a graduate assistant coach.

He embraced doing the menial jobs well, knowing this was the cost of becoming the best coach he could be. To inspire his efforts, he repeated a Bible verse he had memorized: *"Whatever you do, do your work heartily, as for the Lord rather than for men. Colossians 3:23."*

With that mindset, Chase had graduated early with a major in kinesiology and a minor in education.

He answered his phone. "Hello?"

"Chase Barkley! How have you been young man?"

"Coach Sanders. It's great to hear from you. I'm doing well."

"That's good to hear. The reason why I'm calling is I heard back from the school board and our principal about your application to teach and coach here. I wanted to call you myself."

"Oh good. I've been wondering when I might hear something. So...good news?"

"Yes, Chase. They want to offer you the job of Silver Springs High School football offensive coordinator and assistant coach for me in baseball! You will also teach science and health classes. I just emailed you the official offer with salary and benefit information. I feel they have made a brilliant decision in offering you the position."

"Great! I'm excited to be coming home to teach those kids."

"I'm happy you decided to follow the high school coaching path instead of college. I realize the salary can be much higher in college, but I believe with your experience and heart, you will thrive in the high school setting. You will have the opportunity to impact a lot of young lives."

"As I prayed about my decision, I felt like that's where God was leading me. I can't wait to tell Heather!"

"Can I give you a word of advice?"

"Of course."

"Instead of just calling or texting Heather with the news, you should do something special. Take her out somewhere nice to eat or cook supper for her and surprise her. Take this opportunity to make a memory."

"That's a great idea. I was just going to call her. This will be fun! Coach Sanders, I look forward to you mentoring me. I'll do my best to make you proud."

"I'm looking forward to our future together as well. Congratulations on your new job. I'll see you in a few weeks!"

Chase hung up and pumped his fist. Smiling from ear-to-ear, he looked around the empty weight room and shouted, "I have to tell someone!"

Andrew met him at a local coffee shop on campus. He was now married to Tonya. He had chosen a career in medical sales, while she was finishing her master's degree in nursing.

Chase excitedly told Andrew of his new job. They laughed and joked about what it would be like being a teacher, instead of a student, at Silver Springs High School.

"So how are you going to tell Heather?"

"I don't know, but I like Coach Sanders' idea of making a memory. We've been praying about this so much, it's awesome to finally have an answer."

"Here's what you do: Go get a pizza and tape a picture of a football and a baseball on the box. Then write a note on it saying, 'Now we can afford extra toppings, because I got a real job!'"

"That is possibly the dumbest idea I've ever heard. How did you get Tonya to marry you?"

Andrew laughed. "I think she felt sorry for me."

"Here's what I think I'll do. Her favorite meal is from Mario's. I'll order pasta from there along with some turtle cheesecake, which she loves. After we eat, I'll give her a present containing a whistle. I'll tape a picture of us in high school to the string, and a note saying 'We're going home.'"

"That's not bad. I still like my pizza idea better."

Both guys laughed as a couple walked up to their table, holding hands.

"Misty Dobbins! Officer Majors. What in the world are you doing here? And together?

"Hey, Chase! Andrew." She rolled her eyes as she said Andrew's name.

Harrison Majors shook the guy's hands.

"I've taken a job here at the university as the security supervisor. Misty and I met at church last year and just got engaged."

"That's fantastic! Congratulations!"

Misty exclaimed, "I can't believe we're all going to be married. I guess we're growing up. Harrison, we better go if we're going to be on time. It's been really good to see you boys."

They said their goodbyes and left.

"I don't know about you Andrew, but I'm happy for her."

"Yeah, I'm happy for her too. It's him I feel sorry for!"

"Seriously man, Nick told me she went through a tough time for a while. She turned her life over to Jesus about a year and a half ago, and is doing much better. I think Harrison will be good for her."

"I'm glad she straightened up. I still feel sorry for him!"

Chase shook his head laughing. He went home to look for a good picture. It didn't take long to find the perfect one of them together at their high school graduation. He hurried back out to get everything else together. About two hours later, he returned home with all of the surprises. When he opened the apartment door, he started to call out to Heather, but she beat him to it.

"Hey, baby! I'm making your favorite! Breakfast for dinner."

Chase stood there in disbelief, with his arms full of food. Heather hurried in to hug him.

"What's all this?"

"I was going to surprise you with Mario's, but I guess you had ideas of your own."

They burst out laughing together.

"Pasta and turtle cheesecake? What's the special occasion?"

"Can I not just pamper my wife?"

"Hand over the cheesecake, and you can tell me the truth later."

They set out all the food and ended up with a buffet of pasta, scrambled eggs, breadsticks, pancakes, Caesar salad, sausage, bacon and turtle cheesecake for dessert.

Chase thought to himself, "*Coach said to make a memory, but I'm not sure this is what he meant!*"

After they ate, Chase said, "Go sit on the couch. I have a surprise for you!"

Heather looked at Chase and made a strange face.

"I have a surprise for you, too."

"A surprise for me? What is it?"

"I'm not telling you, silly. That's why it's called a 'surprise'."

"Ladies first. You tell me, then I'll tell you."

"Nope! Not this time. You first!"

"But my news is bigger than yours."

Heather laughed. "Is everything a competition with you? Don't answer that!"

Chase begrudgingly gave in and handed his gift to Heather.

She unwrapped it and pulled the whistle out of the box. When she saw the picture and note she screamed in delight!

Hugging Chase, she said, "You got the job! I'm so happy we're going home. This is such an answer to our prayers. I'm proud of you, and I know you'll be the best teacher and coach ever."

"I told you my news is bigger than yours. But I still want my surprise!"

Heather smiled and went to get his present. She came back and handed it to him.

He quickly ripped open the package and opened the box. Reaching in, he retrieved a tiny pair of baby booties. It took a minute it to register.

"Heather, are you...are we..."

"Chase, you're going to be a daddy!"

He grabbed Heather and held her, never wanting to let go.

She looked up at him and gently asked, "So, who's news do you think is bigger now?"

They laughed. Heather asked, "Are you going to love me when I get fat?"

"I'll always love you, no matter what."

He couldn't think of a better woman to be the mother of his children.

Deep in his soul, Chase cherished the thought of being a father.

Chapter 21

March 19, 2030

Chase pulled into the Rixey Road Mall parking deck in Bluff City. Lucky had called for a face-to-face meeting with him. Chase parked in the prearranged area and waited.

A shiny black Lexus with tinted windows pulled up and parked. Chase got out and timidly walked over. The passenger side door swung open and a large, bald white man in a dark suit stepped out. He walked up to Chase and frisked him. Afterward, he reached and opened the backdoor of the Lexus.

Chase sat down in the backseat of the car where Lucky was waiting for him.

"Chase, my boy! How have you been?"

"I'm making it."

"Now that is very good news! I hate to jump right into business, but I need to know your head is on straight after the last delivery. I'm sorry you had to endure the beating those guys gave you."

"Like I said, I'm making it."

"Just so you know, I took care of the situation. I made it a priority to even the score after they took the delivery from you without paying and beat you senseless. You won't be seeing any of them again. Louie, the gentleman who opened your door for you, and some of his colleagues ended their selfish existence."

"Those guys were jerks, but I'm fine. I'm ready to get back to work."

"Excellent! That's exactly what I needed to hear. I have a very special delivery that has got to be made by 7 p.m. today.

"There will be a red Dodge Charger sitting under the 9th Street bridge here in Bluff City. Park in front of it and pump your brake lights twice. Take the duffel bag the driver gives you, and deliver it to the building on the corner of fifth and Main over in Rockport.

"That's Warlord territory, Lucky! Are you sure this is safe?"

"Chase, this is a very important assignment. I've always had your back, and I still do."

Chase was tired of this life. He was always stressed and in danger. He knew he was one bad deal away from going back to jail or ending up dead. But he knew he didn't have a choice. He had bills to pay.

"I know you'll take care of me, Lucky. Consider the drop done."

"Good boy, Chase! There will be a little extra in your pay this week! And unless I'm mistaken you have a big birthday coming up in a few months."

"Yeah. I'll be thirty in June. If I'm still around by then."

"You will be! I have faith in you, my boy."

Chase opened the door and climbed out of the luxury car. He lit a cigarette as they pulled away. Still hurting from the beating he took a few weeks ago, he rubbed the ribs he had broken on his right side. They were healing, but still sore. When he checked his phone, he saw it was already 2:00 and noticed a missed call from his mom. He ignored it, knowing he needed to hurry.

As he parked in front of the red Charger under the 9th Street bridge, he pumped his brakes twice. A female stepped out of the car and walked to the trunk of his car, carrying a green duffel bag. She tapped the top of his trunk three times. He popped the trunk, and she placed the bag inside and closed it. Without saying a word, he pulled away.

His phone buzzed and he saw it was his mom calling again. Ignoring it, he headed toward Rockport. Immediately his phone buzzed again. He hesitated, then hit the green accept button.

"Hey, Mom! How are you?"

"Chase, it's your father! He's had a heart attack! We're headed to the hospital now in an ambulance! Chase, it doesn't look good."

"That's terrible, Mom. Are you okay?"

"I don't know, Chase. Can you please meet us at the hospital?"

"Mom, I'm traveling for work. It's going to be several hours before I can make it back to Silver Springs. I'll have to come by when I can."

"Okay. I understand. Chase...is there anything you would like for me to tell your father? You know, just in case."

The phone was dead silent. Finally, Chase answered, "No. I have to get to work, Mom. I'll see you soon."

Chase hung up and was angry: angry at his situation, angry at his dad, angry at God - even though he claimed he didn't believe in God.
He had to focus on making this drop. These guys were dangerous. Just before 7 p.m., he pulled up to his destination on the corner of Fifth and Main. He retrieved the duffel bag from his trunk and walked to the door, focused on taking care of himself.

Over in Silver Springs, Chase's mom sat in the hospital waiting room crying by herself. She felt so alone without her husband or son with her. Truth be told, she had felt alone for several years now. The doctor entered the private waiting room with another man beside him.

"Mrs. Barkley please keep your seat. I met you earlier, I'm Dr. Keene. This is Pastor Tad Allen. He's our chaplain on duty this evening. I'm sorry to have to inform you the heart attack your husband suffered was quite severe. We did all we could. He didn't make it. I'm so sorry."

She broke down crying. The doctor and pastor stayed with her for a long time. Finally, when she regained her composure, Dr. Keene excused himself to go treat other patients. Pastor Tad sat silently with her for a while. He wanted to help her through this tough time.

"Mrs. Barkley, if you don't mind me asking, how did you meet your husband, Mr. Barkley?"

A slight smile crossed her face as she thought back to better times.

"It was the Fourth of July. There was a huge annual picnic over in Boxley. My family always went for the music and fireworks. Douglas was there with a friend of his he was visiting. I was going into my senior year of high school and he had just graduated.

"We hit it off immediately. He was the cutest, kindest, funniest guy I had ever met. He swept me off my feet and we were married the next summer. We wanted kids, but it took a long time before I was able to get pregnant.

211

"We were so excited. Then when we found out we were having a boy, Douglas just glowed. He loved Chase more than life itself. He worked hard to provide everything he could to make our life as good as it could be.

"Chase excelled early in sports. He was a natural, but Douglas wanted him to be the best. I think it was mostly because he saw Chase as the best in his eyes, and he wanted everyone else to see him that way as well.

"When Chase had his mishap his senior year, just before graduation, it killed something inside of Douglas. He couldn't handle it. Douglas numbed his pain with alcohol from then on. He wasn't a bad person, he was just hurting."

Debbie stopped speaking, deep in thought somewhere else.

Pastor Tad said, "It sounds like the two of you had a fantastic life together for the majority of your years. I'm sorry the past few have been difficult."

"Thank you. I know Douglas made some bad decisions, but he was a good man. He provided for us for many years. He had gotten baptized when he was younger. Do you think he's with God now?"

"It's not my place to make that judgement. If he acknowledged Jesus as Lord and followed Him, then he is with God. I certainly hope that he is. Debbie, I want you to know you are not alone."

"I know the Bible says God is always with us. I know He is always there."

"Well, God is with you, but I want you to have some other people with you as well. Could my wife and some women from our church bring you lunch tomorrow?"

Debbie thought about how empty her house would be.

"That would be nice. I'll give you my address. Thank you."

Pastor Tad answered, "It's a blessing from God to have others help us through the storms of life."

◀ ◆ ◆ ◆ ▶

212

"Coach Sanders, we've got the bats, but I'm not sure our pitching is deep enough."

"What else can we do, Chase? With Gibbs hurt, we're just short. I've asked and none of the other guys have shown any interest in pitching."

"I could work with Hunter Simmons. He's great in left field and he's got a strong arm. With some help I think he could pitch a few innings to give us some relief until Gibbs heals up."

"I offered him a chance, but he didn't seem interested. If you can convince him to give it a shot, go ahead and start working with him. Chase, you're going to be a great head coach here next year. I'll be sad to retire, but I'm glad I'm handing it off to you."

"Nobody will ever replace you, Coach."

"Chase, you've turned down a number of higher-paying coaching opportunities the past few years. I'm glad you're sticking around here."

"This is where I'm supposed to be. Heather and the kids are happy. We're close to our parents. We love the school, the students and our church. I can't imagine a better situation."

"You're making a difference in a lot of these student's lives. That First Pitch summer program you started for kids in our community is amazing. Your legacy will be based on much more than your paycheck. I'm proud of you."

"Thanks, Coach. I better get down to my chemistry class before they blow something up! See you at practice."

Red lockers lined both sides of the student-filled hallway Chase was walking down. He saw his left fielder talking to a group of his friends.

"Hey, Hunter. You got a second?"

"Sure, Coach. I'll catch up with you guys later."

Hunter walked over to Chase.

"What's up, Coach Barkley?"

"I need to talk to you about our team. We're short on pitching. Would you be interested in doing some middle relief work when we need you?"

"I don't know. I pitched some when I was younger, and I wasn't great. To be honest the pressure kinda got to me. I didn't love being on the mound with everyone focused on me."

"Hunter, you're a good player and the team needs you. I think with some work, you can be a solid pitcher. I'm not going to force you to do it, but sometimes you have to step up when you're needed."

"You're right, Coach. I guess I could give it a shot. Will you help me?"

"Of course! This will only be situational, until we can get Gibbs healthy. I know this isn't easy, Hunter. I'm proud of you stepping up to help the team."

"I guess it's like you taught us in Sunday school. If God has given me the ability to do something, I should use it when I have the opportunity. Even if it makes me nervous!"

"I'm glad to see you were listening! You're going to do great. And if you don't, I'll just stick you back in left field."

Hunter laughed. "Sounds good! See you at practice!"

Chase headed for his classroom and his phone began vibrating.

"Hey, Heather! How are you, baby?"

"Doing good. Just wanted to remind you to pick up some hamburger buns on your way home. Your parents are coming over to eat tonight."

"I put a reminder on my phone. But it's still good to hear your pretty voice. I'm headed for my 2:00 chemistry class, then practice after school. I should be home by 6:00, no problem!"

"You better be! I miss my man!"

"I'm getting a call from Mom. I better grab this. Love you, bye."

Chase hit the button to switch to his mom's call.

"Hey, Mom. You and Dad still good for sup...?"

"Chase, it's your dad! Something's wrong! He collapsed! I called 911, and they're loading him into an ambulance!"

"Mom, I'm on my way! I'll meet you at the hospital!"

Chase turned and ran for his truck. He called the school office as he drove, informing them of what was going on. Arriving at the hospital, Chase

214

rushed to the emergency room. He found his mom sitting in a chair crying. She jumped up and hugged him.

"Mom! How's Dad?"

"I don't know. They rushed him to the back. Everything happened so fast."

About twenty minutes later a nurse opened the door beside the check-in counter.

"Douglas Barkley family."

Chase and his mom rushed up to her.

"We're here with Douglas Barkley!"

"Please follow me."

The nurse turned and walked down a hallway. She led them into an empty conference room.

"Dr. Keene will be right with you."

"Is there any word on my dad? How's he doing?"

"I'm sorry. Dr. Keene will be right in to answer all of your questions."

The door swung open and a tall, dark-haired man stepped into the conference room.

"Hi. I'm Dr. Keene."

"I'm Chase Barkley and this is my mom, Debbie. How is my dad?"

"Chase, your dad had a massive heart attack. We did everything we could do. I'm sorry, he didn't make it."

Chase felt numb. Wrapping his mom in his arms, they both wept. A short time later, Dr. Keene led them to sit on the couch. He pulled up a chair in front of them.

"I'm sorry for your loss. I want to share something with you. Something that impacted me. There was a point where we resuscitated Mr. Barkley. We were about to intubate him. He was speaking, but most of it was incoherent. All of a sudden, he distinctly said, 'it is well with my soul.' It was so clear and full of conviction it gave me chills. Everyone in that room heard it. I thought you would want to know."

People began to arrive at the hospital. Heather had her parents keep the kids. She hugged Chase and his mom. "I can't believe he's gone."

Chase's mom told her, "He loved you. He always thought of you as the daughter we never had."

A little while later, while Chase was talking to Andrew on the phone, Nick and Robin Cunningham showed up. Andrew and Tonya had two kids now and lived in Bluff City. Several members of Debbie's small group from church also arrived.

Chase's mom was glad to see Pastor Tad and his wife.

"Debbie, I'm so sorry for your loss. Douglas was a great man."

"Thank you for coming. He loved listening to you preach. Of course, we want you to perform the funeral."

"I'd be honored. We'll discuss the arrangements later. Debbie, I know this is a weird request, but would you mind telling everyone about how you and Douglas met?"

"Oh, I doubt anyone would want to hear about that right now."

Nick spoke up, "I'd love to hear the story!"

Everyone in the room encouraged her to tell their story. Her demeanor picked up as she shared the love story of her and her beloved husband.

Slowly, different people shared stories about their time with Chase's dad. They laughed and cried for the next few hours. When she shared Dr. Keene's story about his final words, everyone became silent and very reverent.

Chase said, "He loved that song."

Softly in her beautiful, sweet voice, Heather began singing,

"When peace like a river, attendeth my way,
When sorrows like sea billows roll.
Whatever my lot, thou hast taught me to say:
It is well, it is well, with my soul."

Everyone joined in singing the chorus.

"It is well (it is well)
With my soul (with my soul)

It is well, it is well with my soul."

Silent reverence filled the room. The spirit of the Lord was clearly present. A peace that passes all understanding settled upon the friends and family of Douglas Barkley.

Chase's mom said, "God bless all of you. Thank you for being here tonight."

Pastor Tad answered, "It's a blessing from God to have others help us through the storms of life."

Chapter 22

May 10, 2042

Loud banging on his front door startled Chase, who was fast asleep in his recliner. Upset at being jolted awake, he angrily shouted, "Hold on! I'm coming!"

It wasn't easy for him to climb out of the chair he had passed out in the night before. Beer cans and cigarette butts covered the TV tray beside him and the carpet below. He stumbled over and opened the door, squinting in the bright morning sunlight.

A short, overweight Hispanic man stood facing his apartment door, "Mr. Barkley, you are two months behind on your rent. If you do not catch up by next week, you will be evicted."

"Whatever! Shut up and get out of here! Why are you bothering me this early? This ain't even your country."

"Just get me the money or you are gone!"

Chase slammed the door in his face. Walking toward the bathroom, he mumbled to himself, "Stupid landlord. Why did he have to wake me up so early?" After splashing his face with cold water, he ran his hand through his greasy hair. "Guess I better get cleaned up and go score some cash."

Chase had moved to Bluff City five years ago to take a job at a car repair shop. He performed simple car maintenance and cleaned up around the shop for them. Lucky had gotten him the job when Chase told him he was done being a delivery guy. The pay was much less, but so was the stress. He still occasionally did some side jobs when he needed to earn some extra cash.

After getting cleaned up, he walked over to Smitty's Bar. The man behind the counter greeted him. "Hey, Chase. It's a little early for you to be here, isn't it?"

"Yep. Smitty around?"

"Yeah. He's in his office. You can go on back."

Chase walked down the narrow hallway and knocked on a door at the end of it.

"Come in."

Chase opened the door, "Hey, Smitty. You got a minute?"

A black man with a mustache wearing a Hawaiian shirt was sitting behind a desk counting money. A 9mm pistol laid on the desk to his right. "Sure, Chase. Have a seat. What brings you by so early?"

"I need to earn some extra cash. Quick."

"How much are we talking?"

"A grand."

"A thousand, huh. That's a chunk of change. I only know of one job available for a grand right now. But it's not an easy one."

"What is it?"

"It's a repo job. A 1964 ½ original fastback Mustang. Fully restored with that sweet V-8 engine."

"They're paying a thousand to repo a car. What's the catch?"

"The catch is the Warlords have her. She's at their place over on Fourth and Victory. If you can get her delivered to Diamonds Car Center they'll pay you a G, straight cash."

"Sounds like my day just got a lot more interesting."

Smitty laughed a deep belly laugh. "You are one cool cat. You don't even bat an eye at danger. Lord knows you'll regret it if you get caught. Hey, if you survive this one, come by and have a drink with me on the house."

Chase left and headed toward Fourth and Victory. He knew he was taking his life into his hands with this decision, but there wasn't any other way he could make this much money in enough time to keep his place. And he didn't feel like moving again.

On his way over, he noticed someone had left their garage door open. Slipping in and stealing a screwdriver seemed completely natural to him. A little while later he saw the shiny, candy apple red Mustang sitting on the street in front of a trashy two-story house.

Chase studied the house, watching for any lookouts or gang members roaming around. Once he felt it was safe, he made his move. Adrenaline pumped through his veins, but he remained calm as he eased over to the car and popped open the driver's side door lock. Quickly tearing the steering column apart with his screwdriver, he got the starter cables free. Realizing once he started the car the loud engine would probably draw unwanted attention from inside, he prepared to make a quick getaway. He stopped just before touching the wires together, a thought forming in his mind.

The car was sitting on a slight hill. Chase slid up into the seat and pushed the clutch in with his left foot, while moving the gear shift into neutral. The mustang began to slowly roll down the incline. He silently guided it down the hill, about two blocks away, until it came to a stop. Quickly hot-wiring it, the engine fired up and he calmly drove away.

After dropping off the car at Diamonds and collecting his cash, Chase was ecstatic. He couldn't believe his luck. It was the easiest job he had done in a while. Arriving back at his apartment and grabbing a drink, he settled into his recliner.

Suddenly there was a knock at the door. Chase's heart skipped a beat! Had he been caught? Had the Warlords seen him? Were they here to exact revenge?

Another knock brought him back to the moment. Quietly sneaking over to the window, he peeked through the blinds. Standing at his door was a clean-cut skinny teenager wearing a blue pull-over polo and khaki pants.

Chase reached for the door, forcefully swinging it open while simultaneously asking in an angry tone, "What do you want?"

Startled and nervous, the young man replied, "Hi. I'm sorry to bother you. I'm looking for Mr. Chase Barkley."

"Who are you?"

"My name is Paul Davis. My mom was Gloria Birdsong."

Chase's whole demeanor changed. He hadn't heard the name Gloria Birdsong in nearly twenty years. The last time he had seen her was on the night she had told him she was pregnant. Was this his son?

221

"Come in. Have a seat. Sorry about the mess."

"It's fine. So are you Chase Barkley? I know you probably are, because of the scars on your face. My mom left me letters describing you. She really loved you."

"You keep talking about her in the past tense."

"She overdosed when I was three-years-old. I remember very little about her. About the only thing I can remember is her singing to me every night at bedtime. I really only know who she was from the letters she left for me."

"I'm sorry to hear she's gone. We knew each other a long time ago. She was a sweet girl."

"She wrote in her letters how much she loved you. How she wanted to have a family with you, but she knew you weren't interested. Raising a child alone turned out to be too much for her."

"Hey, I didn't ask to be a father! I'm sorry she couldn't handle things, but it's not my fault. What do you want? Money?"

"No, I didn't come here for any of your money. When Mom died, I was placed in foster care. Fortunately a great Christian couple adopted me. My family doesn't know I'm here today, but I had to come. The reason why I'm here is to tell you this: I forgive you."

Something deep inside of Chase stirred. It was a weird feeling he hadn't felt in a long time.

"Mr. Barkley, you may be my physical father, but you have done nothing in this life except abandon me. In the same way, I didn't deserve the forgiveness of Jesus, but He still offered it to me. Because of the grace He extended to me, I can now extend it to you."

The mention of God reminded Chase of when he had felt the weird stirring inside of him before. It was when people had talked to him about Jesus. It made him angry to think back to those times.

He roared, "I didn't ask for your forgiveness! I don't want it. I couldn't care less about you."

Although obviously frightened, Paul found his voice. "I can see life has been hard on you. I've prayed for years that I would be able to meet you and tell you in person what I've told you today. And I also want you to know Jesus still loves you. You can repent of your ways and follow Him. It's not too late."

Paul stood up and walked to the door.

"I've got to get home. Thank you for allowing me a few minutes of your time."

He turned and walked out the door. As the door closed behind Paul, Chase felt the same feeling he had felt so many years ago sitting in Grace Fellowship Church. It was a feeling of being pulled toward something. He knew that something was Jesus. Could he give up his ways and follow the way of the One they call the Christ? Could he acknowledge Jesus as the Lord of his life?

No!

After everything he had been through in this life, there was no way he would put his hope in some invisible God. He wasn't as stupid as all those church people.

Chase decided he needed that free drink waiting for him at Smitty's.

◀ ♦ ♦ ♦ ▶

"I don't know guys. This river is roaring."

"Come on, Chase. We've floated rougher rivers than this before. This will be a great float for our boys' Survivor Man weekend."

Chase and Andrew had taken annual trips like this to help teach their boys how to survive in the wild and intentionally talk to them about manhood. This was an extra-special trip, because Bryce, Chase's oldest son, was turning 18 years old.

Andrew and Tonya had moved back to Silver Springs with their son Tyler and their daughter Savannah when the kids started school. That was right after Chase had lost his father, so he was especially happy to have his best friend back in town.

Their boys grew up going to school and playing sports together. Although Tyler was a year younger than Bryce, they were inseparable best friends. Heather and Tonya would laugh about how much the boys were like their fathers.

"The ranger back at the campground said the river was still open, but the torrential rains up north the past couple of days have raised it to almost flood stage. It's rated expert only. We're going to float 15 miles back down to our campsite. Everyone wears their life jacket. Load up!"

The rest of the group cheered at Chase's approval to float. They had camped, hiked and floated together regularly. When the boys were younger, they had been Boy Scouts.

More recently they focused on sports. They had just won their high school state baseball championship the previous week. It was very special for Chase to coach his son to a title.

Although they were all experienced outdoorsmen and in good shape, Chase was concerned about this trip. He had an uneasy feeling about the river today.

It was a beautiful sunny day, but the temperature was only in the mid-70's which was below average for this time of year. The nights dipped into the low 40's, and the water was cold. They had intentionally gotten on the river a little later than normal today to let the air temperature rise.

After floating about an hour, they stopped at a shoal to take a break. All of them grabbed a snack and their fishing poles. Chase knew catching a fish in this roaring river would be tough, but it was still fun to cast the little spinner baits.

They loaded up and floated down the river a few more miles. Stopping for a late lunch, they set up a makeshift camp and ate their sandwiches. Chase and Andrew talked to the boys about some things they had all been reading from the book "Raising a Modern-day Knight" by Robert Lewis. It taught them that a real man rejects passivity, accepts responsibility, leads courageously and invests eternally.

Time got away from them as they talked and laughed. Bryce noticed their canoes were rising with the river against the shore.

"Hey! Our canoes are about to float away!"

They rushed down and grabbed them.

"The river has risen a lot since we stopped. We pulled them almost all the way out of the water when got out. I bet it's risen over a foot. We better get moving."

"I think you're right, Chase. You and Bryce lead the way. Tyler and I will follow."

"Okay, Andrew. Echo Falls will be tricky. Be careful. We won't stop again until we get back to camp."

The guys pushed off in their canoes. As the water briskly carried them, there was no need to paddle except to keep the boat straight.

Chase could hear Echo Fall's rapids roaring around the next bend. He knew if they could make it through there, they would be able to get back to camp before dark. The river got louder and louder as they approached the bend.

As they turned the corner on the river the current got faster. Chase and Bryce kept the canoe in position to hit the rapids. Chase had never seen Echo Falls at flood stage. White water was churning. They went over the first rapids and dug their paddles in to keep the canoe straight. Ramping a boulder, their canoe dropped several feet. They landed, taking in a large amount of water. Seconds later, Chase felt the canoe flipping! He yelled, "Swim, Bryce!"

Freezing, powerful water submerged Chase. The icy cold water caused all of his muscles to constrict. Gasping for air he fought against the undercurrent as the river carried him downstream. As the rapids spit him out, he forced his arms to move and swam for the shoreline. Quickly assessing the situation, he began looking for Bryce. He was relieved to spot his son about 20 yards on down from him, swimming for the shore as well.

Chase saw Andrew and his overturned canoe go by swiftly. He searched for Tyler, but didn't see him. Sprinting back up the bank of the river, he kept his eyes peeled for Tyler. Chase spotted him pinned to a rock; water rushing over his body. Chase immediately made his way toward Tyler, being careful not to get swept back down the falls. He knew if he lost his footing and was swept away, Tyler would probably drown.

Making it to the boy, he grabbed ahold of the lifejacket Tyler was wearing. Chase pulled with all his might! Tyler sprang free, taking Chase with him back down the rapids. When they finally reached the bottom, Bryce grabbed ahold of his dad, and Andrew snagged Tyler.

They made it to the shore and collapsed. Andrew checked on Tyler.

"You okay, son?"

"Yeah, I think so. When we flipped, I felt myself banging against the rocks as the current pushed me. I expected to pop out any second, but I felt my leg get stuck on something. Next thing I know you're pulling me up here on the bank."

"You got pinned against a rock. Chase got you free. He saved your life."

"Thanks, Mr. Barkley."

"No thanks needed, Tyler. God allowed us all a little while longer here. Now let's get a fire built, it's going to get cold soon. Bryce and Tyler get out of your clothes, and hang them up to dry before the sun sets. Then gather some limbs to burn.

"Andrew, you hike down the river, and see if any of our stuff washed up on shore. Don't go too far. Just around the next bend and back. I'm going to get kindling for a fire. Let's move, guys. Your Survivor Man trip just got real!"

Everyone got to work. Chase gathered dry grass and bark to start the fire. After he had it ready, he removed his waterproof pouch he had strapped to his belt. It contained flint, waterproof matches, a compass and a map of the area. He stopped just before he lit the fire.

"Bryce, this weekend is to help usher you into manhood. You're in charge of starting the fire."

"Are you sure, Dad?"

"Yes. This fire will help us survive the night. It's up to you to start it."

226

Although Bryce had started countless fires growing up, he realized the importance of this one. The group was counting on him. He prepared the stack of tinder and lit it. Carefully adding more fuel as it grew, Bryce soon had a fire going. Sticks, and eventually logs, were added until a blazing campfire was roaring.

As they were building the fire, Andrew came back carrying an ice chest, a folded-up tarp and one fishing pole. Chase walked down to meet him, and helped unload the supplies he had gathered from the river. Fortunately, the ice chest had a thermos filled with potato soup, some protein bars, beef jerky and bottled water in it.

The guys used the tarp to build a roof over a lean-to structure of limbs the boys had built. By the time the sun had set, they had a nice campsite built for the night. Keeping the roaring fire fed with the limbs they had gathered, the chilly night air was kept at bay.

Chase spread out his map. Andrew pulled out a waterproof flashlight he had stored in his jacket pocket.

Chase asked, "Bryce, what's our plan for tomorrow?"

Bryce looked at his dad, realizing he was putting him in charge of their exit strategy. Bryce nodded at his dad and pointed to the map.

"Well, it looks like this is Echo Falls, so we're camped right about here. Our main campsite is...here. It looks like it's about a two-mile hike home if we follow the river, but at flood stage it could be rough traveling. If we cross over this ridge, it will only be about a mile, and we should come out just west of our campsite. The terrain shouldn't be too dense. I say we go over the ridge."

"What if we get over the ridge and run across a flooded creek we can't cross, or the terrain is worse than we expect?"

"Well, Dad, we can always turn back toward the river and follow it. Worst case scenario, we hike a little more, but it's a short enough hike we won't have the possibility of running out of daylight."

"I like it! Good planning, Bryce. Boys, this is life. We make our plans, but situations can quickly change. We should pray like it's up to God, and plan like it's up to us.

"God uses people in this world to accomplish His will. I can't explain why He works the way He does, but I've found if I do my best to follow Him, the outcome is usually pretty good.

"I planned on having a steak dinner tonight, but I'm very happy today worked out the way it did. My old coach once told me to make special occasions memorable. I don't think any of us will forget this trip as long as we live!"

The rest of the night was spent talking and laughing about memories the guys had from past trips. As Chase dozed off, he thought about how proud he was of his son, and thanked Jesus for keeping them safe.

Chapter 23

May 21, 2070

"Why can't I find anything in this place?"

Chase had misplaced his Citizen Identification Card. It was a government-issued card used to pay for everything from groceries to public transportation.

He had chosen carrying the card over having a chip placed in his arm. The government representative encouraged him to get the chip, explaining how he wouldn't have to worry about losing it. He refused, saying he didn't want the government tracking him. The exchange had gotten heated, but eventually he got his way.

"Maybe that woman was right. I can't keep up with anything these days."

Chase was digging through drawers in his dingy, cluttered bedroom. Dirty clothes were piled on the floor all around his unmade bed. As he dug through his bedside drawer, a stack of pictures caught his attention.

He sat down on the side of the bed and flipped through them. He stopped on one taken at a birthday party for Misty, just before she told him she was pregnant. He felt ashamed for running out on her and never paying child support. Last he had heard, she had moved back in with her parents to raise the daughter he never met. That was almost 50 years ago. He flipped through a few other pictures and froze.

He stared intently at the young man in a dirty baseball uniform looking back at him. It was the only picture he had of himself from his days of playing ball as a youngster. He hadn't seen this picture in decades. Memories from those days-gone-by flooded his mind. They filled him with happiness. It was a rare feeling these days.

Looking over at his nightstand, he saw the corner of his Citizen I.D. Card sticking out from underneath an ashtray. He smiled and grabbed it. He was in a good mood and wanted to get out of the apartment today.

Remembering the local minor league baseball team was playing a midday game, he decided to go.

It had been years since he had attended a game in person. Excited about going, he jumped in the shower and got ready. He grabbed his favorite ball cap and walked down to the corner to catch a ride on the public transport. It was a self-driving community bus.

Arriving at the Bluff City Lasers minor league stadium, Chase was enjoying himself. It was a perfect day for baseball; cool and sunny with no humidity. He was able to get upgraded to a great seat behind the mound. It was one of the best days Chase could remember.

Taking his seat, another fan happily greeted him, "Hi, I'm Colt."

"Nice to meet ya, Colt. I'm Chase."

"Great day for a game."

"Yep. How are the Lasers doing this season? I haven't kept up."

"They're doing good, Chase. Second place in their division. This pitcher Will is a big reason why. He's a beast!"

"I love some good pitching. I used to do some pitching myself in high school. I was pretty good back in the day."

"You don't say. Well, you'll appreciate this kid."

Chase did enjoy watching the game. Memories of his playing days rolled through his mind. He thought about Andrew and how much he missed him. They hadn't talked in over 30 years now. Chase thought about his dad. How much they had enjoyed going to ball games together. He hadn't allowed himself to think about his dad in years. He smiled and enjoyed the memories.

During the seventh-inning stretch, he had a coughing fit, so he got up to go have another smoke. Smoking in public was rare these days, but the stadium still had a small smoking area. There was only one other person in there.

As Chase lit up his cigarette, he felt a weird tingling sensation running down his left arm. He reached up to massage it, but suddenly felt dizzy. As the stadium walls around him began to spin, he leaned back against one of the brick walls. He heard someone yelling for help as he slowly slid down to the ground.

Chase heard people asking him questions and felt them lifting him up. He wasn't sure if he was awake or dreaming. Sometime later, his mind cleared up. A doctor was standing over him asking him something.

"Mr. Barkley! Can you hear me?"

Faintly he answered, "Yeah, I can hear you."

"You've had a heart attack. We are monitoring your progress. Do you want us to notify anyone?"

Chase thought, who would they notify? He had no one. His choices had led to a completely empty life. No family or friends who cared about him. Then, in a moment of hope and humility, he asked, "Can I talk to a preacher?"

"You mean our hospital chaplain?"

"Yeah, whatever. Can you just get him?"

A few minutes later, the room cleared out except for one nurse. She exited when a middle-aged, short black man entered Chase Barkley's hospital room.

"Mr. Barkley, I'm Malcolm Turner. I was told you would like to speak with a chaplain."

"No! I said I wanted a preacher, but you'll do."

Malcolm smiled, "I assure you, sir, I am most definitely a preacher. Your records don't list a particular religion for you."

"No, they wouldn't. I'm what guys like you call 'lost.' I swore off religion a long time ago. I've done some horrible things. I never intended to do bad things. They just seemed to happen. Since I was a teenager, my life has been nothing but a path of destruction. Malcolm, can I ask you something?"

"Of course."

"A long, long time ago, I felt like Jesus wanted me to follow His ways. I decided I wasn't ready that night. There have been several other times where I felt like He was offering me that forgiveness again, but every single time I refused. Malcolm, I'm not feeling that calling now. Is it too late for me?"

"I can guarantee you it is NOT too late. Salvation isn't just a feeling or an emotion. Repent of your sins, call on the name of Jesus and believe in your heart that God raised Him from the dead, and you will be saved! He loves you, Chase."

Tears were rolling down Chase's face. It had been years since he last cried. He had finally come to a place where he truly desired Jesus to be His Lord and Savior.

In the quiet hospital room, Chase prayed with Malcolm, submitting his soul to the Lord Jesus Christ. When he was finished praying, he looked up at Malcolm.

"Thank you. When you do my funeral will you tell whoever's there that I'm sorry? I'm truly sorry."

"Do your funeral? ...Yes. Yes, I will."

Chase's breathing had slowed. His life was slipping away.

"Malcolm, I'm glad you're here. I didn't want to go alone. I've been so lonely for so long."

"I'm here. And God is with you. You'll never be alone again."

"I feel something different inside of me now. My anger is gone. It's peaceful."

"That's the Lord, Chase. You'll enjoy getting to know Him, I promise."

"Thanks Malcolm. You know, I can't help but wonder how my life might have been different. What if I had decided to follow Jesus on that night at Grace Fellowship Church all those many years ago? The things I thought I would miss out on didn't turn out as fun as I thought they would be. The embarrassment I was worried about would have been nothing."

"We can't undo the decisions we made in the past, Chase."

"I know. I just wish I would have gotten saved...a long time ago. I think my life...would have been much better. I'm so glad...I finally decided to follow Jesus."

Chase's breathing slowed. Monitors began going off as his heart rate flat-lined. He peacefully moved from this life into life everlasting.

Malcolm held Chase's hand, shedding tears of joy and sadness for this stranger. He silently prayed a prayer of thankfulness to God for saving this man's soul. His prayers turned to those who were still out there who needed a savior. He rededicated his life to sharing the hope of abundant life in Jesus with everyone he could.

◀ ◆ ◆ ◆ ▶

"Heather, are you ready? We need to go."

"Calm down, Chase. It's still early."

"I'm just excited to see all the grandkids!"

"And great-grandchild! She's so cute. It's a beautiful day for a family picnic."

"You look too young to be a great-grandma. The weather turned out perfect. They took the rain totally out of the forecast. I've got everything loaded up in the car, except for the most beautiful grandma in the whole wide world."

"Great-grandma. Okay, Honey, I'm ready. You're more hyper than a kid in a candy store. You take it easy today with those kids, and don't overdo it."

"Oh, I won't. You know me. I don't ever overdo it."

They both laughed as they went to the car. Once they arrived at the park, they unloaded the food and drinks. As kids and grandchildren arrived, Chase and Heather shared hugs and kisses with all of their family. They made a huge circle, holding hands and prayed before lunch. Not long after eating, a game of wiffle ball broke out.

Heather laughed at Chase running around out there with all of their family, while she sat and rocked her sweet little great-grand baby. Their daughter Brooke was snapping pictures of everyone. She made her way over and took a picture of her mom.

"I love it when we can all get together."

"Me too, Brooke. Your father was so happy everyone could be at his induction to the high school hall of fame ceremony last month. He tried to act like it wasn't a big deal, but he was thrilled."

"I could tell. He deserved it. Winning all those state championships, and putting so many guys into college on athletic and academic scholarships. Not to mention everything he's done in our community."

"He got a chance to reconnect with a lot of his former players. We are so blessed to not only have our family, but so many others in our lives."

"Mr. Andrew was hilarious! He really hammered Dad with those old stories of them playing ball together."

"Yes he did! But your daddy held his own during his acceptance speech. Those two are a mess. They always have been."

"Bryce and Tyler are just like them."

"When are you and Tyler leaving to go back to Panama?"

"We're still scheduled to return in July. This has been such a wonderful refreshing trip home, but I miss our friends there. God is doing so much in their lives and in our church, it's hard to be away."

"You and Tyler have been such a blessing in that village. I knew you two would make a great team. I remember your dad and Andrew teasing the two of you when you announced you were getting married. I thought Tonya was going to hurt them both!"

The girls laughed.

Bryce ran over to them. "How's my grand baby?"

"Sweet as sugar, son. This one's a little snuggler like you were."

"I just hope she gets your sweetness and doesn't turn out mean like Brooke!"

Brooke reached over and hit Bryce.

He grabbed his arm, acting hurt. "See Mom! She's got anger issues."

"I'll show you anger issues."

They had always loved to tease each other.

Heather smiled. "Your dad should let those kids hit the ball easier than that."

"You know Dad won't let them win!"

"Well I guess that's what made your daddy so successful in athletics and school. He's competitive, but still a good sport. I remember when they lost state his senior year, because of the missed catch by Trey Lawson. It was good to hear Trey's speech at your daddy's induction giving him credit for encouraging him to continue playing."

Bryce added, "Yeah, and Trey ended up playing professionally for all those years. Matt Tyler's video was great too. I can't believe he became a United States Senator. I loved the story he shared about Dad giving him the laptop in exchange for a Taco Bell gift card."

Heather nostalgically added, "That was such a fun night."

Brooke asked, "Is that Mr. Andrew and Mrs. Tonya pulling up?"

"Yes it is. Your Dad and I didn't want you missing out on being in the family picture. They're going to take our picture. And we'll get some of you and Tyler with them too."

Chase called the family together and they got organized for a family portrait. Afterward, Andrew joined in a game of ultimate frisbee with the whole family. He and Chase teased each other about how slow they had become.

Heather was talking to Tonya when she noticed Chase fall to the ground.

"Why is Chase on the ground?"

Tonya answered, "I don't know, I hope he's okay."

Heather sat up a little straighter. A flash of worry ran through her.

Andrew stood over Chase. Just as Heather began to stand to rush over to Chase, he looked over at her with a smile across his face. A wave of relief washed over Heather. Andrew laughingly helped him up.

"Get up, old man. I remember when you could run through a whole defense untouched for a touchdown."

"Those days are long gone! I think I tripped over my own feet."

A few hours later, Chase and Heather were in the kitchen unloading the cooler.

"What a wonderful day. I'm so proud of all of our kids. God has truly blessed me with more than I could ever imagine. And with such a hot wife."

Heather giggled and stepped into Chase's arms. "Aren't you the charmer? You looked so cute out there with the kids. It reminded me of watching you play in college."

They leaned in and rested their foreheads against one another just like they used to do before Chase would pitch. They shared a kiss.

"Do you still love me, even though I'm not a young scrappy ballplayer anymore?"

Heather smiled. "With all my heart. But you smell like a stinky ballplayer. Now go get cleaned up!"

Chase laughed as he walked back to their bedroom. A few minutes later, Heather walked down the hallway to their bedroom as well. When she stepped in, she saw Chase collapsed on the ground!

Heather screamed and dialed 911. She rolled Chase onto his back and began CPR.

They arrived at the hospital a short time later. All of the family eventually arrived. They were all crying and praying. Many church members and friends were also there.

A nurse called Heather back. They entered the hospital room. Heather rushed to Chase's side and grabbed his hand.

A doctor said, "Mrs. Barkley, your husband has had a massive heart attack. He's coming in and out of consciousness. I'm not sure if he'll make it."

Heather was crying when she heard Chase speak.

"Sweetheart, don't cry. Get the kids in here."

The doctor nodded his head. A nurse rushed out. Moments later Bryce, Brooke, Brody and their spouses were in the room along with Andrew and Tonya.

Softly Chase said, "I'm a very blessed man. To see all my kids following Jesus, and their kids as well. What more could I ask for? I'm rich beyond measure. Kids, as I've told you since you were small, love God and love people. You are each loved abundantly; share that love with others. Tell my grandbabies and great-grandbaby Grandpa loves them. Take care of your momma."

Tears were flowing down every face.

"Tonya, keep Andrew in line. You were always so good for him. He's gonna cry like a big baby, because I beat him to the finish line again."

Everyone laughed through their tears.

"Andrew, you've always been my best friend. I couldn't have become the man I am without you. Jesus really blessed me when he gave me you as a friend. I'll hold off pitching in heaven until you show up to catch for me. Love you, buddy."

"Love you too, Chase. You're the best friend a guy could ever want. But you shook off my pitch selections too much."

"That's probably true. But you should have called more fastballs to begin with."

Andrew smiled through the tears and nodded.

"Heather. My darling. My one true romantic love. They say love rarely runs in a straight line, but I've always loved you. Your beauty made me a tongue-tied teenager. I could barely speak to you when we met. I'm the luckiest man on earth. You've shown me what unconditional love looks like in this life. Keep loving Jesus and don't be sad. Remember our good times. Jesus is leaving you here for a little while longer. People still need you here."

Chase's voice began to soften as his breathing slowed.

"Jesus has been...the difference in my life. I'm happy I got saved when I did. He truly gave me...an abundant life."

The monitor flat lined, and everyone in the room wailed.

Chapter 24

May 24, 2070

Rev. Malcolm Turner entered Faith Assembly Church in Bluff City on this overcast Saturday morning. The past few days had filled his soul with mixed emotions. The great joy of praying with Chase Barkley for salvation on his deathbed was tempered by the remorse he had clearly heard in Chase's words about his wasted life.

Malcolm reflected on the past few days, as he prepared the church sanctuary for the arrival of Chase's body. He had used every available resource he could think of to learn more about the stranger he would be performing the funeral for today.

No friends or family could be located. The lack of anyone in his life helped Malcolm understood the pain and loneliness he had heard in Chase's voice on the night he passed away. The best he could piece together was Chase Barkley had been a local high school star athlete over in Silver Springs, who had ended up in and out of prison. Beyond that, nothing was discovered. The scars on Chase's body told a story of a hard life filled with pain.

In a last ditch effort to announce the passing of Chase Barkley to anyone who might be concerned, he placed an ad in the regional community online forum. Malcolm took it upon himself to prepare the funeral and choose a grave site.

His heart hurt for this man he barely knew. A life of emptiness isn't easy to celebrate, but Malcolm would do his best to honor him today.

Chase's body was delivered to the church a short time later. Malcolm had them place the casket in front of the pulpit and arrange some flowers on top of it. Putting on some quiet worship music, he spent time in deep prayer. He thanked Jesus for saving this man's soul, and prayed for the lost who were still in need of a Savior. He asked for wisdom in delivering his eulogy.

At 11 o'clock, the pastor stepped to the pulpit. His wife and three children were sitting on the front pew. Some members of the church choir sat behind him on the stage. Seven other members of his church sat in the audience. The large sanctuary felt empty with so few people in attendance. Malcolm noticed a stranger slip into the back of the room as he began.

"Chase Douglas Barkley was born on the 21st day of June in the year 2000. His parents were Douglas and Debbie Barkley. He passed away earlier this week on May 21st, 2070. Let us pray."

Malcolm led a heartfelt prayer. When he finished, a lady moved to the front of the choir and led them in singing "The Lord's Prayer."

At the conclusion of the song, Malcolm moved back to the pulpit.

"As we walk through this life, we encounter a variety of people. Some we build very close relationships with during our time here. Our mothers and fathers. Sisters and brothers. Aunts, uncles and cousins. Our best friends and coworkers who we spend lots of time with.

"Other people we get to know, but aren't what we would call close relationships. A person you sat by in a class, a waiter or waitress who serves you regularly or a bank teller who you see routinely.

"Then there are those we just cross paths with, but never really get to know at all. The gas station attendant when you're on vacation. The concierge who checks you into your hotel. The airplane stewardess who brings you pretzels and a drink.

"Today, I have the honor of celebrating the life of someone I barely got to know. But God ordained our meeting. He placed this man in my path and we became brothers.

"Chase Barkley is virtually a stranger to me. I searched for information on him, but found very few details about his life. What I did discover was a life which started out full of potential. Chase Barkley received many awards in a variety of sports and in academics until his senior year of high school. I'm not sure what happened at that point, but his life changed dramatically.

"By his own admission, Chase made some bad choices. Along Chase's journey through this life, God allowed other people to plant seeds of hope.

In his final moments, God's amazing grace was poured out upon Chase Barkley. He was saved by God's grace through faith, repenting of his sins, confessing Jesus is Lord and believing in his heart God raised Jesus from the dead.

"A peace came over Chase Barkley that only those who have experienced the weight of a heavy burden of the soul lifted can understand. Chase shared how the anger inside of him was replaced with peace.

"His last request was one of forgiveness. He wanted me to publicly announce how sorry he was to the people whom he had hurt.

"I've spoken with many men and women who have asked me why they should follow Jesus immediately. Why not have fun now, and on their deathbed ask Jesus for forgiveness?

"These people don't know they have believed a lie. The fun this world has to offer is short-lived and always leads to misery and regret.

"Following Jesus is the way to abundant life, both now and in eternity. Jesus offers us the Kingdom of Heaven immediately. The world tells us we're missing out, but a much better life is available for believers than non-believers. Purpose, fulfillment and love are just a few of the gifts of following Jesus.

"Chase Barkley would tell you he would have followed Jesus much earlier if he could live his life over. Chase would also tell you acknowledging Jesus as Lord was the best decision he ever made! His final words were, 'I'm so glad I finally decided to follow Jesus.'

"The Good Book says, 'Now is the time of salvation.' My friends, don't waste another second. Call upon the mighty name of Jesus and be saved! Just as my brother in Christ Chase Barkley did."

He closed the service announcing the graveside service would follow. When he looked up from closing in prayer he could see the stranger sitting on the back row with his head hung down.

Malcolm walked back to the older man, who looked up at him with tears in his eyes.

"Hello, I'm Malcolm Turner. Did you know Mr. Barkley?"

"Yes. My name is Andrew. We were best friends growing up. I can't believe he's gone."

"I'm sorry for your loss, Andrew."

"Thank you. You know what, pastor? He was my very best friend and we haven't spoken in over 30 years. We had a fight over something so stupid I'm embarrassed to tell you what it was about. I threw away my best friend over nothing. We were both so darn hard-headed it killed our friendship. In your message, you said Chase got saved. Is that true?"

"Yes it is. I only got to speak with him for a short amount of time, but I truly believe Chase came to a point where he realized he needed and accepted Jesus."

"Pastor, I think I need Jesus too. Will you tell me more about Him?"

"I certainly will. Andrew, Chase may be gone from this earth, but I can assure you he is celebrating your decision right now in heaven."

◄ ◆ ◆ ◆ ►

Pastor Hunter Simmons arrived at Grace Fellowship Church on this Saturday morning filled with mixed emotions. He would be performing the funeral service for his old coach, his mentor, his friend, Chase Barkley.

As Hunter sat on the front row of the empty sanctuary, his mind wandered back to the day way back in high school when Coach Barkley had stopped him in the hall to offer him a shot at pitching. Earlier he had avoided the same request from Coach Sanders, but something about the way Coach Barkley approached him was different. Hunter remembered how Coach Barkley inspired him and made him believe he could succeed at anything.

The pitching opportunity worked out better than anyone could have ever imagined. They won state that year using Hunter in some key moments on the mound. He was offered a baseball scholarship, as a pitching prospect. He ended up as a middle reliever pitching at Shelton University. Eventually he was drafted in the 12th round of the Major League Baseball draft, but he declined the opportunity to play pro ball to pursue the call to preach.

After several years on the mission field, Hunter planted successful churches in San Francisco, Boston and Miami. Just over eight years ago, he had accepted pastoring Grace Fellowship Church, where he became his old Coach's pastor. Chase had encouraged and supported Hunter throughout his life. In high school, Chase had taught him the basics of his Christian faith in Sunday school. Later in life, encouraging letters from Chase found their way around the world seemingly when Hunter needed them the most.

Although wildly successful as a pastor, Hunter felt unworthy to perform this great man's funeral. He knew Coach Barkley would tell him that he was right. He was unworthy, save the grace of Jesus which makes him worthy. Hunter smiled at the thought of his coach's words still encouraging him.

People began arriving early for the 11:00 funeral service. A video played with pictures of Chase's life. Moments of him playing ball, coaching teams and enjoying time with his family scrolled across the screen. By 10:00, the church was full and overflow seating was filling up. Local news channels covered the funeral of the city's beloved Coach.

At 11:00, Pastor Hunter stood before the overflowing church.

"Today we gather together to celebrate the life of Chase Douglas Barkley. Born June 21st, 2000. Passed away May 21st, 2070. Chase Barkley is survived by his loving wife, Heather Barkley, his three children, ten grand-children and one great-grand child. Let us pray."

After a powerful prayer, the church choir sang as a different video of Chase's life began playing. Heather smiled through her tears as memories flooded her mind.

Pastor Hunter stepped before the crowd as the song ended.

"Chase Barkley had many roles in this life. Husband, father, grandfather, great-grandfather, quarterback, pitcher, coach, teacher and friend are just a few of the roles he played. And he played them all very well.

"His influence impacted everyone he met. Coach Barkley - he told me to call him Chase, but he'll always be coach to me - won the state baseball title

11 times and was runner-up another four times in his 32 years of coaching at Silver Springs High School. He helped countless students get athletic or academic scholarships. He was recently inducted in the high school hall of fame. He was the MVP in the Division 2 baseball championship game during his abbreviated time playing for the Crossland University Eagles. He was a scout leader, Sunday school teacher and a very bad lip-syncher in a school play just before he retired."

The crowd laughed.

"Coach Chase Barkley began a summer program called First Pitch. This helped keep kids off the streets and gave them a healthy start at learning baseball early in life. He was able to get corporate funding for the program so that all income levels could participate. This program was picked up around the country and many kids attribute their love of baseball and success in life to this program.

"Coach Barkley, along with his beautiful wife Heather, helped spearhead the effort to develop the award-winning Silver Springs Science Center into one of the finest attractions in the state.

"Grace Fellowship Church has also been abundantly blessed by the life of Chase Barkley and his wonderful family. I spoke with Coach Barkley about a year ago sitting right here on the front row. He shared with me about the night God called him to a saving faith in the Lord Jesus Christ. He described how he could still feel the terror of going forward as a teenager and praying for salvation. It's hard to imagine Coach Barkley afraid of anything, but he said making that decision was the toughest yet most wonderful moment of his life.

"He told me the direction of his life changed that night. He believed his success in sports, who he would marry, where he would attend college and everything else in his life was influenced directly by his decision to follow Jesus. It actually scared him to think about how his life might have turned out if he hadn't been saved that very night.

"I don't know what Chase Barkley's life would have looked like without Jesus, but I know he led a beautiful, full life with Him. Today, if you need the forgiveness Jesus offers, accept it right now. Jesus says he loves you and wants you just the way you are. Coach Barkley's life testifies to the abundant life Jesus offers.

"It's not a life without hardships. One of those was when Chase suffered a horrific career-ending injury just as he was gaining national attention. During those days, it was agony for him to watch others play the sports he loved. He overcame the grief and made the best of his situation, becoming a hall of fame coach.

"Let the life of Chase Barkley inspire you to give your best in everything you do, regardless of your circumstances. While he would humbly say he's just another guy, today we celebrate a man who made an incredible difference with his time here on earth. This world is a better place, because of how he lived. Let's pray."

The service ended and people quietly departed the sanctuary.

A long line of cars slowly followed the hearse carrying the body of Chase Barkley. Heather and the rest of his family followed close behind. They were surprised to see crowds of people lined up along both sides of the road all the way to the cemetery. On top of the two bridges they went under were current students from Silver Springs High School standing reverently watching the passing procession.

They arrived at the private graveside service. His family and closest friends moved to a green canopy tent where Chase's casket was placed before them. A freshly dug grave awaited Chase's body.

Chapter 25

May 24, 2070

A gentle breeze blew across the green grass weaving its way between the rows and rows of tombstones in the cemetery. Sunbeams poured down through the gaps in the canopy of clouds overhead. There was a sense of peace in this place as the pastor stepped up beside Chase's casket.

"King Solomon wrote in the 3rd chapter of the book of Ecclesiastes, 'There is an appointed time for everything. And there is a time for every event under heaven:
A time to give birth and a time to die;
A time to plant and a time to uproot what is planted.
A time to kill and a time to heal;
A time to tear down and a time to build up.
A time to weep and a time to laugh;
A time to mourn and a time to dance.'

"It's very possible during our time of weeping and mourning today that Chase is having his own time of laughing and dancing with Jesus in Heaven."

He continued with his voice rising, "We look for that blessed hope when the Lord Himself shall descend from heaven with a shout, the trumpet of God shall sound, and the dead in Christ shall rise first. Then we who remain shall be caught up together with them in the clouds to meet the Lord, and so shall we ever be with the Lord Jesus. Comfort one another with these words.

"We now commit the body of Chase Douglas Barkley back to the ground from which it came: earth to earth, ashes to ashes, dust to dust. Do not look for Chase Barkley here, for he is now with his Savior in paradise. Praise the name of Jesus!

"Mercifully, God in His grace reached down from heaven and adopted Chase as His very own child. Chase Barkley would be the first to tell you that acknowledging Jesus as his Lord was not just another decision in his life; it was The Decision."

The End

A Note to the Reader about your Decision

I hope you enjoyed The Decision. As explained in the story, we all need forgiveness of our sins. The Bible says that every person has sinned (Romans 3:23). It goes on the say, while we don't deserve Salvation, God offers it to us as a free gift (Romans 6:23). In fact, while we were enemies of God and living in sin, God sent His only Son to die for us (Romans 5:8). God did this because He loves us so much and we can receive eternal life with God by believing in His Son Jesus Christ (John 3:16). We show evidence of this faith in Jesus by believing in our hearts and confessing with our mouths that Jesus is Lord (Romans 10:9-10).

The very first thing we're supposed to do to when we are saved is to be baptized (Romans 6:4-5). The next step is fellowship with other believer's and growing spiritually (Colossians 2:6-7).

God loves you no matter how bad you think you are. You are not too far gone for Jesus to reach out and save you. Call out to God, turn from the direction you are going and follow Him.

You can do that right now in your own words if you like. If you need someone to talk with or are interested in learning more about what it means to have a relationship with Jesus Christ, a great resource is 1-888-Need-Him (1-888-633-3446). Or on the web, go to www.needhim.org. You can also chat with someone about what a relationship with Jesus is all about at www.chataboutjesus.com. I pray you acknowledge Jesus as your Lord and receive Salvation today!

45816936R00149

Made in the USA
Middletown, DE
21 May 2019